PENGUIN BOOKS
THE COMPANY OF WOMEN

Khushwant Singh was India's best-known writer and columnist. He was founder-editor of *Yojana* and editor of the *Illustrated Weekly of India*, the *National Herald* and *Hindustan Times*. He authored classics such as *Train to Pakistan*, *I Shall Not Hear the Nightingale* (retitled as *The Lost Victory*) and *Delhi*. His last novel, *The Sunset Club*, written when he was ninety-five, was published by Penguin Books in 2010. His non-fiction includes the classic two-volume *A History of the Sikhs*, a number of translations and works on Sikh religion and culture, Delhi, nature, current affairs and Urdu poetry. His autobiography, *Truth, Love and a Little Malice*, was published by Penguin Books in 2002.

Khushwant Singh was a member of Parliament from 1980 to 1986. He was awarded the Padma Bhushan in 1974 but returned the decoration in 1984 in protest against the storming of the Golden Temple in Amritsar by the Indian Army. In 2007, he was awarded the Padma Vibhushan.

Among the other awards he received were the Punjab Ratan, the Sulabh International award for the most honest Indian of the year, and honorary doctorates from several universities.

Khushwant Singh passed away in 2014 at the age of ninety-nine.

KHUSHWANT SINGH THE COMPANY OF WOMEN

PENGUIN BOOKS

PENGUIN BOOKS

Published by the Penguin Group

Penguin Books India Pvt. Ltd, 7th Floor, Infinity Tower C, DLF Cyber City,
Gurgaon 122 002, Haryana, India

Penguin Group (USA) Inc., 375 Hudson Street, New York, New York 10014, USA

Penguin Group (Canada), 90 Eglinton Avenue East, Suite 700, Toronto,
Ontario, M4P 2Y3, Canada

Penguin Books Ltd, 80 Strand, London WC2R 0RL, England

Penguin Ireland, 25 St Stephen's Green, Dublin 2, Ireland (a division of
Penguin Books Ltd)

Penguin Group (Australia), 707 Collins Street, Melbourne, Victoria 3008, Australia

Penguin Group (NZ), 67 Apollo Drive, Rosedale, Auckland 0632, New Zealand

Penguin Books (South Africa) (Pty) Ltd, Block D, Rosebank Office Park,
181 Jan Smuts Avenue, Parktown North, Johannesburg 2193, South Africa

Penguin Books Ltd, Registered Offices: 80 Strand, London WC2R 0RL, England

First published in Viking by Penguin Books India 1999
Published in Penguin Books 2009
This rejacketed edition published 2016

Copyright © Khushwant Singh 1999

26 25 24

ISBN 9780140290479

Typeset in Perpetua by Mantra Virtual Services, New Delhi
Printed at Replika Press Pvt. Ltd.

A PENGUIN RANDOM HOUSE COMPANY

Contents

Author's Note

As a man gets older, his sex instincts travel from his middle to his head. What he wanted to do in his younger days but did not because of nervousness, lack of response or opportunity, he does in his mind.

I started writing this novel when I was eighty-three. I finished it at eighty-five. An equally apt title for it could be: 'The Fantasies of an Octogenarian.'

No characters in this exposé are real: they are figments of my senile fantasies.

Acknowledgements

I wish to acknowledge my debt to four ladies, all beautiful in their own ways, to whom I turned for advice: Sharda Kaushik, Mrinal Pande, Usha Albuquerque and Sheela Reddy—Sheela, especially, for going over the manuscript.

I also acknowledge my debt to Naina Dayal for her assistance, and to Ravi Singh who edited my text and gave shape to a shapeless mass of events narrated in the novel.

I

The Secret Life of Mohan Kumar

One
A New Beginning

For Mohan Kumar, it should have been a day of rejoicing. It was not.

He had looked forward to it for twelve years. His wife had at long last decided to leave him: despite the months of bitter acrimony that had preceded it, she agreed to give him a divorce provided she had custody of their two children. He was so anxious to get his freedom, that besides the children, he agreed to give her whatever else she wanted in the way of alimony: jewellery that he and his father had given her, furniture, pictures—anything she named. She wanted nothing. She seemed as eager to get rid of him as he was to get rid of her. That afternoon she had packed her things and driven away with the children to her parents' home. She had not bothered to say goodbye. The children sensed that this was not just another visit to their grandparents. They embraced and kissed him before running out to get into their mother's black Mercedes. The car had shot out of the gate with unnecessary speed; she had made sure the children would have no time to turn around and wave goodbye.

Mohan should have been celebrating his newly won freedom from his nagging, ill-tempered wife. But as he sat in the balcony of his double-storied bungalow, his feet resting on the railing, smoking a Havana cigar, he felt empty inside and shrouded in loneliness. There was an all-pervading silence. No screaming of children fighting with each other; his six-year-old daughter rushing to him complaining of her elder brother's bullying and he gruffly ordering them to behave and not disturb him. Their squabbles had often irritated him. Now he missed them. The house suddenly had far too many rooms, and the night too many hours. He was weary.

He thought of his relations with his wife. It was what people described as a love-cum-arranged marriage. But of course it was nothing of the sort. The day after he had returned from the States thirteen years ago with degrees in computers and business management, his proud father, a retired middle-level government servant with middle-class dreams for his only son, had gone round newspaper offices with his photographs and biodata. The next morning some national dailies carried Mohan's picture in their matrimonial pages, with captions extolling his academic achievements. Enquiries from parents of unmarried girls followed. He and his father were invited to tea, introduced to nubile girls, tempted with large dowries and offers of partnerships in business. Even after all these years Mohan was amazed at how easily he had allowed himself to be offered for sale, finally agreeing to marry Sonu.

Her father, Rai Bahadur Lala Achint Ram, had made the highest bid. He owned a couple of sugar mills and considerable real estate in Delhi. Mohan succumbed to the offer more to please his father than out of any wish to settle down with a wife. Sonu was passably fair, high-spirited and convent-educated. Also a virgin eager to opt out of virginity. They had a lavish wedding and moved into a large furnished flat provided by her father. Mohan's father moved in with them. The honeymoon went well, as it usually does with newly married couples who desire little besides the freedom to discover and devour each other's bodies. Their first child, a son, was conceived during those early days of amatory exploration.

Differences in temperament began to surface soon afterwards. Sonu was quick-tempered, possessive and wanted attention all the time. She was jealous, though she herself had no love to give him. And she began to resent his father's presence in their home—her home, for it was, after all, a gift from her father. 'Will your old man live with us all his life?' she once asked in disgust. He did not like her calling his father 'old man' and told her so. 'I married you, not both of you,' she shot back. He realized soon enough that their living arrangements had to change. The garment export business he had started soon after returning from the States was bringing him good money, and he also had enough dollars saved up. Within two months of that unpleasant exchange with Sonu he was able to buy himself a bungalow with a garden in Maharani Bagh, an upper class neighbourhood of Delhi. There was enough space in the new house, and Mohan thought Sonu and his father would be able to keep out of each other's way. But he was wrong. His father, sad and diminished, finally moved to Haridwar. This was not how Mohan had wanted it, but at least there might now be peace. He was relieved to be out of the premises provided by his father-in-law.

In less than two years, Mohan had added semi-precious stones and leather goods to the list of items he exported. His profits more than trebled, and soon he was part of the charmed circle of Delhi's super rich.

None of this improved his relationship with his wife. She was, he realized with some horror, a bitter woman, incapable of happiness and determined to make him unhappy. She had made up her mind to condemn him in everything he did. If he paid the slightest attention to another woman, she would call him a randy bastard. At first he thought they were going through a period of adjustment and hoped that relations would settle down to normal. In the seventh year of their marriage, they had a daughter. But even this child did not bring them any closer. Quarrels became endemic. Hardly an evening passed without their going for each other, leaving them both utterly exhausted. For many days following a spat they would barely exchange a word. Then bodily compulsions would resolve the dispute. They would have sex, usually loveless sex, and resume talking to each other. Only for a few days.

One evening remained etched in his memory. She overheard him talking to one of his women friends on the phone. She accused him of having a liaison with 'that whore'. She called him a lecher. He lost his temper and slapped her across the face. For a while she was stunned into silence, then hissed, 'You dared to hit me. I'll teach you a lesson you'll never forget.' And then she walked out of the house. An hour later she was back with her cousin, an inspector of police, and two constables. Mohan was taken to the police station like a common criminal. His statement was recorded. A couple of hours later the inspector drove him back home. It had cost Mohan Rs 5,000 to get the inspector to record that it was a ghareloo maamla—a domestic affair—and 'rafaa dafaa' the complaint in the police file. That time Sonu had stayed with her parents for over a month.

Mohan thought over the relationships he had had with various women before he married Sonu. Most were with Americans or Europeans—and one Pakistani. They were not meant to be enduring; no strings attached. Great fun while they lasted. He felt they were better than being caught in the vice of one demanding woman who deprived him of the company of others. All said and done, a man or a woman had only one life to live; neither should waste the best years of their lives with someone with whom they had little to share besides occasional, loveless sex. It would be a relief for them both to end their marriage. The only ones to be hurt were the children, but even they would do better in a peaceful home run by a single parent than one where the parents were always bickering with each other. They would grow up and understand why the divorce was good for everyone concerned.

Mohan was not given to introspection. But his stormy marriage had made him an amateur philosopher of marriage and love. Marriages, he concluded, are not made in heaven; they are made on earth by earthlings for earthly reasons. The first priority is money: it may be property, a profitable business or a well-paid job. The couple concerned fall into line without bothering to find out whether or not the person they are committing themselves to will make a good lifelong companion. At the time they are asked to give their consent they are adolescents: their sex urges are of explosive dimensions, and they are eagerly looking forward to exploring each other's bodies. So pass the first few months. In that time the bride of yesterday finds she is pregnant. Then the sex urge begins to abate. Even if they use contraceptives, sex-when-you-want-it begins to lose its urgency. It becomes a routine affair. People they had ignored during their frenetic physical involvement with each other start becoming subjects of sexual fantasies. No matter how close and intimately involved a married couple may be, the possibility of a pleasant diversion in an adulterous relationship is never far from their minds. When an opportunity guaranteeing secrecy presents itself, they succumb to it.

Occasional adultery, Mohan was convinced, did not destroy a marriage; quite often it proved to be a cementing factor, as in cases where the husband could not give his wife as much sex as she needed, or where the wife was frigid. It was silly to condemn adultery as sinful; it often saved marriages from collapsing. It could have saved his.

What bothered Mohan most was the gossip in his large circle of friends. Most of them knew that his marriage was not going smoothly. He had often suffered snide remarks at the club bar when he had gone there alone. 'How's Sonu? Is she not in town?' the bitch Usha Malhotra had said, a little too loud, barely suppressing a leer. He knew what she was driving at, and hit back savagely: 'And how are your husband and your boyfriend getting along?' That would silence her. And her types. He knew that not one of his circle was really happy in his or her marriage. They just got along. And grumbled. Not one of them had the courage to call it off. To hell with the bloody lot! He could feel his temples throb with anger.

Mohan continued sitting in the balcony till well after sunset. His servant switched on the lights in the sitting room and laid out his whisky, glass, soda, and ice bucket. Mohan was reluctant to go into the empty house without the children shouting to each other and his sullen wife pottering about.

He smoked his cigar till there was little left of it and tossed the stub into the garden where the crickets chirped monotonously. He dragged his feet to his silent sitting room and switched on the TV to listen to the news. He poured himself a large Scotch in his favourite cut-glass tumbler and sat facing the screen. His eyes registered the images on the box; his ears did not take in what was being said.

He helped himself to a second and then a third drink. He fiddled with the remote control, tried one channel after another: song and dance, quiz contests, cheetah overtaking a gazelle, politicians lying brazenly and abusing each other, film starlets flirting with fat heroes, and children singing patriotic songs. Nothing held his attention. He poured himself a fourth Scotch—he rarely drank more than three. He felt somewhat drunk. He ordered the bearer to leave his dinner on the table and gave him and the cook leave to go back to their quarters. He drew a chair in front of him and stretched his legs on it. He dozed off in his armchair without switching off the TV or the room lights. In the early hours of the morning a stiffness in his neck woke him up. He switched off the TV and the house lights. He left his dinner untouched and staggered into bed. He fell asleep with his face buried in his pillow.

*

The next morning Mohan resolved to come to terms with his new situation. He had enough going for him in life: his company brought him over twenty lakhs every month; he had the looks and the sophistication to charm women; he was a member of three elite clubs—the Delhi Golf Club, the Gymkhana Club, and the India International Centre. All he lacked was a woman to keep him company and share his bed without being over-possessive or demanding.

He was determined to have as little to do with Sonu as he could and yet be able to keep contact with his children. He knew that he could not do without a woman companion for too long. Having affairs with friends' wives was not what he was looking for. Nor unmarried girls, because they would expect matrimony to follow—which ruled out young widows as well. What he hoped to find was a woman about his own age, early forties or a little younger, sophisticated and willing to stay with him for a few weeks or months. He could afford to provide for her: a chauffeur-driven car, money for shopping, the comforts of his home, clubs, cinemas, and restaurants. What more could any woman want? It was not whoring, it was not concubinage; it was respectable companionship with sex thrown in.

How and where would he find takers for what he was willing to offer? For the next few Sundays he scanned the matrimonial columns of the national dailies: *The Times of India*, *The Indian Express*, *The Hindustan Times*, *The Hindu* and *The Tribune*. He found nothing close to what he was looking for. The matrimonials were caste-obsessed, fair-skin-obsessed, money-obsessed and, with the exception of widows and divorcees, virginity-obsessed. And they were all, of course, matrimony-obsessed. It occurred to him that he should insert an advertisement spelling out his needs. It might not fit the parameters of the matrimonial columns and might be turned down by the advertisement departments, but there was no harm in trying. Some paper might accept it for the money it brought.

One morning, less than a month after his wife left him, Mohan got down to drafting his ad:

Forty-year-old product of an Ivy League College (USA) living separately from his wife and two children. Divorce petition filed. Seeks a live-in companion for a mutually agreed time-duration. Willing to pay air fare to Delhi and back and Rs 10,000 per month for expenses. Free board and lodging in comfortable home with three servants and chauffeur-driven car. Religion no bar. Relationship to be without strings attached on either side. If interested, enclose photograph and biodata.

Correspond box no.———.

He went over the draft a couple of times and counted the number of words to calculate what each insertion might cost. It came to a tidy sum with *The Hindustan Times*, which was the most expensive, but he did not expect any readers of that newspaper to respond. *The Times of India* had a larger circulation with readers spread all over the country and its advertisement rates were lower. So also *The Indian Express*. He ruled out *The Hindu* for the same reasons he ruled out *The Hindustan Times*: rates too high, readership too conservative. He decided to start with the two all-India dailies. He would take the ads himself to the newspaper offices, where no one knew him, rather than entrust his lady secretary with the task.

Mohan went to the office at the usual time: 9 a.m. He was known to be punctual and expected every one of his staff of twelve clerks and accountants to be at their desks when he arrived. He had no doubt that the gossip about his broken marriage would soon reach their ears, if it hadn't already. But no one would dare to bring up his personal affairs in the office. He paid his staff higher wages than other firms. They were happy with him.

He made out a cheque to himself and asked his plump middle-aged secretary, Vimla Sharma, to get it encashed. He looked through the mail-orders received from Germany, USA and Russia and sent his agents to the tailoring firms. He went over the previous day's accounts and examined the goods ready for dispatch. Everything was in order. By 11 a.m. he had cleared his desk of pending business. The canteen bearer brought him his mid-morning cup of coffee. He waved him aside, 'I'm going out for coffee. I will be back in the afternoon.'

He went down to the street where his Mercedes was parked. He told the chauffeur he would drive himself and gave him the afternoon off till office closing time.

It was a long drive from Nehru Place, where he had his office, to Bahadur Shah Zafar Marg, Delhi's Fleet Street, where many newspaper offices were located. It was close to noon but the roads were still congested. It took him over half an hour to reach *The Times of India* building and another ten minutes to find a place to park. He walked in to the reception desk and asked for the advertisement department. The man pointed to a counter. At the counter Mohan handed over the envelope with his draft. 'Matrimonial?' asked the clerk. Mohan nodded his head. The clerk counted the number of words without making any comment on the contents and mentioned the price. Mohan put the required cash on the counter and took the receipt. It went more smoothly than he had anticipated. He walked over to the *The Indian Express* building. Here too the money was accepted without any objection. Mohan felt relieved and triumphant. He gave a five-rupee tip to the parking attendant and drove back to his office.

In his cabin he enjoyed his frugal afternoon meal of cold soup, lettuce and potato mayonnaise, stretched out on the office sofa, switched on the 'Don't disturb' sign and shut his eyes. His siesta was disturbed by the thought of his children. Somehow the decision he had made and acted upon that morning seemed to have put a greater distance between his children and him. He got up and asked his secretary to get them on the line at his father-in-law's residence. They were back from school and asked cheerfully, 'How are you, Daddy? When are you coming to see us?' 'Fine,' he said, reassured by their voices, 'I'll drop by on Sunday and we can go out for some ice-cream.'

He felt lighter. He went through the office routine till it was time to shut shop. He toyed with the idea of going to the club to have a drink. Then decided against it. Somebody was bound to ask about his wife and ruin his evening. He asked his chauffeur to take him home. It no longer looked as inhospitable as it had before. The Scotch tasted mellower and the taped Western classical music was pleasanter to his ears. He had something to look forward to. That night he celebrated his newfound freedom by going down to the garden and urinating noisily into the shrubbery. This was something he had always wanted to do—piss in the open every night in different corners of the garden, like a dog marking its exclusive ownership over a piece of territory. Now that his wife and the children were not around, he could at last do this.

Two
Dhanno

There were still another four days to Sunday, when most papers carried matrimonial ads. And it would be another week or ten days before anyone could respond. Nevertheless, Mohan looked more carefully at the advertisement pages to see if any carried mid-week matrimonials. None did.

As he sat down for his post-breakfast Havana (Romeo & Julieta—Rs 150 each) the sweeper woman came in carrying her broom, a bucket of phenyl water and a mop and asked him if she could do the floors. She had taken orders from Sonu about which room to do first: their bedroom, the children's room and the bathrooms were given priority; the sitting-dining room came last. Without looking up at her Mohan nodded his head.

As she sat on her haunches mopping the floor with a piece of rag soaked in phenyl, Mohan noticed her rounded buttocks separated by a sharp cleavage. He could not take his eyes off her ample behind. He had never bothered to look at her before nor did he know her name. She was just the jamadarni—the sweeper's wife. She often brought her three children with her. He had sometimes seen them playing in the garden while their mother was busy in the house. The sweeperess stood up, turned her face towards him and brushed aside a strand of hair from her forehead. He noticed she was also full-bosomed and had a narrow waist. She was dark but not unattractive. The woman got down on her haunches again to do another part of the room. Mohan turned to his paper.

He recalled his college days in India. One of the boys had told him that sweeper women made the best lovers; they were uninhibited, wild and hot. Apparently there was no better antidote for sore eyes than sex with a sweeperess. Mohan did not suffer from any eye ailment but he had noticed that as a class the so-called untouchable women were in fact the most touchable. What about this one in his own house? It would not be very difficult to persuade her to come to his bedroom when the other servants were in their quarters or out buying provisions. He could double her salary, give her children toys and sweets. Such master-servant liaisons were not uncommon. Poorly paid menials welcomed a second income and their spouses were not very particular about infidelity provided it brought in some money. No messy hassles with women demanding attention and presents and wanting to be taken out to parties. There was also the advantage of convenience: sex on the tap, as it were. Mohan decided to keep the sweeper woman in mind in the event of failure on other fronts. She would provide no companionship but would at least solve his most important problem.

The next morning, when the jamadarni came to do the floors, he spoke to her for the first time. 'What is your name?' he asked as she hitched up her salwar and squatted a few feet ahead of him to mop the floor.

'Dhanno,' she replied, without looking up at him, but clearly expecting to be asked more questions.

'What does your husband do?'

'He is a sweeper with the municipality, sahib.'

'What does he earn?'

'One thousand rupees per month. We have three children. Even with what I earn we barely manage to feed and clothe ourselves. My husband is a sharabi, sahib, wastes a lot of money on liquor.'

Mohan was not sure what he paid her: her salary was paid by his office along with the salaries of other servants and was clubbed together as essential household expenses. He merely signed the cheques every month. If he wanted to give her more, it would have to be in cash. He fished out a hundred-rupee note from his wallet and held it out for her. 'Take this. It is for your children.' The woman took the note, touched it to her forehead and tucked it into her bra. 'Will memsahib not be coming home any more?' she asked directly. 'She has taken her luggage and the children with her.'

Mohan was taken aback by her audacity; working class people did not believe in dropping hints or being tactful: they were direct and blunt. He snubbed her. 'Get on with your work,' he said gruffly.

*

The first few days, weeks and months are the most difficult for people whose marriage or a similar long-term relationship has ended. Not only do they have to come to terms with themselves, their parents, parents-in-law, children, brothers and sisters, they have also to satiate the appetite for detail in their circle of friends. What went wrong? Was your sex life happy? Did she want more than you could give? Was a third party involved? What about those women your wife hated because you made passes at them? And what about that fellow who was always looking lecherously at your wife . . . You could not ignore such people, you could not snub them and tell them to mind their own business. You had to put up with their nastiness till everyone thought they knew everything about your marriage and why it had broken down. Then they lost interest in your personal life.

Mohan toyed with the idea of getting out of Delhi for a few days, then decided against it. It would only sharpen the appetite of gossipmongers and they would be hungry for more when he returned. He would carry on with the routine of office, club and home as if nothing had happened. Perhaps leave out the club for a few days and spend his evenings quietly at home, enjoying his Scotch, listening to music and watching TV.

Mohan soon sensed that his office staff had somehow got to know that his marriage, which they knew to be floundering, had finally collapsed. Vimla Sharma was more solicitous when she brought letters

to be signed or came in to take dictation. In all these years he had
never bothered to take a good look at her. She was a spinster—
technically available—but was not much to look at—a rounded face,
brown hair tied in a bun, a squat figure in which her bosom, belly,
thighs and behind were all a mass of pale white flesh. He now noticed
a little wiggle in her behind as she went out of the room. The rest of
the staff seemed more subdued than usual. And more concerned. He
ignored them as best as he could. He took to working late and was
usually the last to leave the office and hand over the door key to the
sentry on night duty.

*

One day, instead of driving back home, he decided to take a drive
round the city. He had not done this for a long time. He gave his
chauffeur the evening off and drove to India Gate. He got out to take
in the scene. In the east rose the dark-grey walls of Purana Qila, built
by Humayun, the second Mughal Emperor. Blocking the lower half
of the view was the sports stadium built on the orders of a half-crazy
Vicereine, Lady Willingdon, to perpetuate the name of her dynasty.
This was after Lutyens had built his city. The architect could do nothing
about the stadium except gnash his teeth. It ruined his vision of a
broad, tree-lined boulevard running down from the Viceregal Palace
through the War Memorial arch and past the stone canopy under
which had stood a statue of King George VI, right up to the imposing
western entrance of Purana Qila. The rulers of Free India had removed
the statue of the British king, but at least the canopy looked more
beautiful with nothing under it. Mohan recalled that some politicians
had wanted to demolish the whole structure because it was a remnant
of the Raj. Bloody vandals! Fortunately they had been unable to do
anything to the majestic War Memorial arch except change its name to
India Gate. They kept a flame burning under it to honour those who
fell fighting for India.

The rest was much the same as Lutyens had designed it: a boulevard
flanked by a succession of water tanks and flowering largerstroemia

leading to the secretariats and a slight gradient to the black-domed Viceregal Palace, now Rashtrapati Bhavan. There were clouds on the western horizon. The setting sun broke through them and lit up the entire panorama of massive buildings, lawns, water tanks and flowering trees in soft amber hues. A sight for the gods, said Mohan to himself. Delhi was the only city in the world which gave him a sense of belonging. On days like this the city could even make him forget the absence of a woman in his life.

He bought four large coloured balloons and two bricks of vanilla ice-cream from vendors, their carts bright with green and white neon lights, who clustered around India Gate every evening. He had done this before when his children were with him. What was the point of buying balloons and ice-cream when they were no longer around?

When Mohan got home Dhanno was going over the floors once again: in Delhi you had to dust everything at least twice a day. Her children were, as usual, playing in the garden, waiting for their mother to finish. They eyed the balloons but knew they were not for them. Sahib had never brought anything for them. Mohan handed over the balloons and the ice-cream to Dhanno: 'These are for your children,' he said as he switched on the TV.

A minute later Dhanno brought in her children, each holding a balloon. 'Touch the sahib's feet,' she ordered them. 'He has also brought you ice-cream.'

The children touched his feet and ran out as fast as they could. Had Dhanno got the message?

He got his answer the next morning. She was later than usual—after the cook had left for the bazaar to buy the day's groceries and the bearer had gone to his quarter to have his bath. She wore a freshly washed and ironed salwar-kameez and had kajal in her eyes. She said nothing and got down on her haunches to mop the floor. She seemed to sense the sahib's eyes on her. Twice she turned round and caught him staring at her behind. She blushed coyly, turned her face away to get on with her job. Mohan concluded the answer was yes.

He decided not to hurry matters. He must first weigh the pros and cons of taking on his cleaning woman as a mistress. There were fewer hassles than in having an affair with a woman of his own class. There would be less talk. No doubt his two male servants would soon suspect that something was going on between their sahib and the sweeperess. To them she was an untouchable: they never let her enter the kitchen. They avoided physical contact with her, and when she came to get the leftovers, they dropped daal-roti or whatever had not been eaten by their master into utensils she brought with her. If they smelt something, they would tell the neighbours' servants, who in turn would tell their employers. Dhanno was not likely to confide in her husband, but if he had any sense he would begin to suspect his wife's behaviour. Perhaps the extra money she brought in would keep him quiet. Perhaps it would not. But all these anxieties weighed little against the great advantage of being able to have sex whenever he wanted—she would not expect more than a little extra, nor lay any claims to his emotions or his time.

His mind became obsessed with the possibility of taking Dhanno. She hovered before his eyes in the office, at home. He wanted to make sure he did not slip up on any detail. The next morning he asked her when her husband left for work. 'He leaves very early in the morning, sahib. I pack a paratha and some sabzi for his afternoon meal. He returns quite late in the evening. The first few days of the month, after he has got his pay, he drinks with his cronies and doesn't return till midnight.'

'And what about your children? Do you always take them with you wherever you work?'

'No, sahib. Many mornings I ask other servants' wives to keep an eye on them. When I am at home, I look after their children.'

Dhanno sensed what was on the sahib's mind. She let him choose the day and time for their tryst. She did not have to wait long. Two days later she heard him tell the cook to get him fresh fish from INA market. 'Everything in INA market is fresher and cheaper than elsewhere,' he was explaining, 'fish, crabs, prawns, vegetables, fruit, everything. All the people I know shop there for their daily needs.' The INA market was almost an hour by bicycle from Maharani Bagh. Going, coming and shopping would keep the cook away for at least three hours. Then the sahib wrote something on a piece of paper and gave it to the bearer. He had run out of cigars, he said. The kind he smoked were only available at MR Stores in Connaught Circus. He had put the name on the paper. The bearer was to take a bus to Connaught Circus and get a box for the sahib. He handed the bearer several hundred-rupee notes. 'Be sure to get a receipt,' he added. The bearer would also be away for a couple of hours.

Dhanno took good care to leave the house while the other two servants were still there. Back in her quarter she took a second bath, soaping herself vigorously and scrubbing her body. She saw the servants leave on their errands and quietly slipped back into the house.

Mohan was waiting for her. When she came upstairs, he got up from his chair and gently guided her by her shoulders into his bedroom and bolted the door from the inside. He kissed her on her lips and fondled her breasts. She responded vigorously. He slipped his hand inside her kameez to feel her breasts. They were firmer than his wife's and the nipples much harder. Dhanno slipped her shirt off over her shoulders and coyly looked down at her feet. Mohan undid the cord of her salwar and let it fall to the floor. Dhanno was stark naked. 'Not like this, sahib,' she murmured. 'You must be like me.' She unbuckled his belt and pulled his trousers down. She gasped. 'Sahib, I have never seen anything so big!'

'How many have you seen?' asked Mohan with a leer as he took her hand and put it on his penis. Dhanno blushed as she tried to correct herself. 'Only my husband's. His is less than half your size. I haven't seen any other man's—*Saunh Rabb dee* (I swear by God).' Mohan knew she was lying. Dhanno knew that the sahib knew she was lying. But why waste time on trivial details?

Mohan took off his shirt, then pushed her onto his bed. He started making love. When he tried to slip on a condom, she held his hand. 'After my third child I had nasbandi; you will enjoy me more without this thing on you.'

Each time Mohan made love to a new body, it was like exploring a new landscape. Women were much the same in their essentials but enchantingly different in detail. Dhanno's body had a musky odour unlike his wife's which always smelt of French cologne. Mohan could not hold out very long. He lay back defeated. Dhanno was patient with him. She massaged his body gently from head to foot till he was roused once more. This time she came a lot quicker than he.

In the frenzy of orgasm she dug her nails into his scalp, bit his lips before she collapsed with a long gurgle like an animal being slaughtered. Mohan felt triumphant and proud of his manliness.

They washed together in the bathroom. And dressed together in the bedroom. Mohan took two one-hundred- rupee notes from his wallet and pressed them into Dhanno's hands. 'There is no need for this,' she said, tucking the notes into her kameez between her breasts. 'I am your baandee. Whenever you want her, your slave will be at your service.'

Dhanno slipped out of the house unnoticed. Mohan lit his morning Romeo & Julieta and felt all was right with the world. Dhanno was not the sort of companion he had advertised for in the papers. But lust was also an aspect of love—perhaps its most important constituent. When mental and emotional companionship were not available, it was as good a substitute as any that a man could want.

*

Morning sessions with Dhanno became a bi-weekly affair. She was docile, ever willing to cater to his needs. He grew familiar with every contour of her body, down to the large sunburn mark on her right thigh which he always felt with his fingers and kissed before he kissed her eyes and lips. Sex, though still pleasurable, began to lose its novelty. She resisted his attempts to change postures. When he tried to reverse the roles and asked her to get on top, she demurred—'No, sahib! I will never have you beneath me. You are my maalik (lord).' He did not persist. He had made a good bargain and Dhanno was fulfilling her part.

Three
Letter from Rewari

On Sunday Mohan scanned the matrimonial columns of *The Times of India* and *The Indian Express*. Both had four to six pages with headlines to indicate castes and callings. Hindus were the most numerous with different columns for Brahmins, Kshatriyas and Vaishyas. The emphasis was on sub-castes. There were Jains, sub-divided into Digambars, Swetambars and Sthanakvasis. Sikhs into Jats, Khatries, Aroras. Christians into Catholic, Methodist, Syrian Christian, Presbyterian. A few Muslims as well—Sunni, Shia, Bohra, Khoja, Ismaili. The smaller the community, the the more sub-castes it had. On top of the matrimonial ads were NRIs (non-resident Indians) flaunting their sterling, dinar and dollar incomes translated into rupees. They too sought girls of their own community and caste. Preferably virgins.

Where did he fit in these columns? He did not offer marriage, only a concubinage of sorts. But there he was—at the end of the endless columns of both papers was a boxed item entitled 'Miscellaneous'. His was the only entry. It would undoubtedly attract more attention than the others. Many would be scandalized that in a tradition-bound country such advertisements were accepted and published. Indians regarded marriage as a sacrosanct bonding for life. Mohan wondered what his father would have made of it, were he alive. What would Lala Achint Ram say, and his fat Christmas-tree wife? And how would Sonu react to this 'sacrilege'—inviting women for temporary companionship?

Mohan did not have much hope of anyone responding. But he was not disheartened. Dhanno was at his beck and call: a woman in bed is worth ten in one's fantasies, he told himself.

*

The first response came from an unexpected quarter. It was not through the PO Box number indicated in the newspaper advertisement but bore his name and home address. It was a one-word message: 'BASTARD'—all seven letters in capitals. Though the message was in print, Mohan recognized his wife's handwriting in it. He felt anger rising in him. He crumpled up the letter and with a loud oath—'BITCH'—threw it into the waste-paper basket.

He should have known. Gloating over matrimonial columns was Sonu's Sunday pastime. As she read them one after another, she would giggle with delight. 'Do you know what "Good at H H affairs" means?' she would ask, and reply, 'Household affairs. . . And "C&D no bar"?— Caste and Dowry no bar . . . All men want fair-skinned brides. And virgins. All virgins are maidens; not all maidens are virgins,' she would explain. 'No girl seeking a husband asks for a boy who has never slept with a woman.' On more than one occasion she had replied to some ads enclosing her photographs but giving the addresses of her girlfriends. This was her idea of fun. The description Mohan had given of himself in the advertisement would have left her in no doubt that it was her 'goonda' ex-husband shopping for sex.

Four days later, the first genuine response was redirected by *The Times of India* ad department to his home address. It was a two-page letter with a colour photograph of a woman in her mid-thirties. The photograph showed only her face: thick, black hair done up in a bun, thick-lensed glasses, small eyes, bindi on forehead, diamond nose-pin on the left nostril, a severe expression, as in passport photographs. It was not possible to tell whether she was tall or short, buxom or slender. Perhaps the letter might reveal her statistics. He read:

Dear Sir,

This is in response to your ad in the Sunday edition of The Times of India. You are looking for a female companion on a trial basis. I too am looking for a male companion on a trial basis. You are a divorced father of two children. I am a divorced mother of an eleven-year-old boy who is in a boarding school in Mussoorie. I had an arranged marriage with a NRI from Canada. It did not last a month—I discovered he already had a wife in Toronto. Instead of facing charges of fraud and bigamy in India, he simply disappeared.

I have a doctorate in English literature and am teaching undergraduates in a local college. I live in a one-bedroom flat in the professors' quarters. If acceptable, I can take a couple of months leave due to me and share life with you. I am not keen to marry again as my son may not like it. I want to do the best I can for him as a single parent. Whatever you give me will be of help in getting him a better education.

As required, I am enclosing my photograph. It is only fair that if you decide to invite me you should send me your photograph in return. A full-length picture will give me a better idea of your height and build. I am short—five feet one inch—and light-skinned.

Although I have no religious prejudices, I would like you to know that I am a Brahmin by birth and practise Hindu rituals. I am assuming you are also Hindu. If not, please let me know.

I have put my cards on the table. If you are interested please send me your telephone number and address. I will ring you up and make an appointment to meet with you. Perhaps it would be best if we meet in your home so that I could get an idea of your style of living and your environment.

I look forward to hearing from you. Please mark your letter confidential and address it to me at Lady Professors' Hostel, Flat No. 2, Government College for Women, Rewari (Haryana).

Yours,

Sarojini Bharadwaj.

Mohan gazed at the photograph and read the letter a few times before he put it in his pocket. Dhanno though dark was better looking than this bespectacled lady professor. On the other hand he might find a lot in common with an educated woman than he did with his illiterate sweeper woman. He could take her to his clubs, to restaurants and the cinema without being unduly self-conscious of his companion. In any case, it would be another woman and no two women were alike in bed. In variety is spice—and this was exactly what he was looking for.

The next morning he wrote back to the lady professor answering" her queries and enclosing a full-length photograph of himself in an open-collar shirt and flannel trousers, holding a tennis racket in his hand. He looked quite dashing. To make sure the letter reached her as soon as possible he sent it by speed-post, guaranteed to reach its destination within twenty-four hours.

The very next day she rang him up from Rewari. An appointment was made for the evening of the following Saturday. She said she would take the afternoon bus to Delhi and find her way to his house in a taxi or a three wheeler. She could spend a couple of hours with him and return to Rewari by the 9 p.m. bus.

*

Saturday was a half-day at the office. Mohan looked forward to a glass of chilled beer, a light lunch and a long siesta. The beer was ice-cold, the lunch frugal and tasty, but his siesta was disturbed with doubts about his new venture. What bothered him most was how he would square it with Dhanno, who had established certain rights over him. He would have to do some lying. He would tell her and the servants that Sarojini was a distant relative who would stay with him till she found her own accommodation. And of course he would keep paying Dhanno as usual. Money was not a problem. He earned more than enough—a fair proportion of it in unaccounted cash—and he was happy to get rid of it for his pleasures. It was unwise, anyway, to keep too much in his safe, lest those income tax fellows decided to raid his house.

He got up and took a shower. He shaved a second time to erase signs of the day's growth on his chin and upper lip, and doused himself with after-shave lotion. He put on a Lacoste sports shirt and his Levi's jeans. At the end of it all he examined himself in his wife's full-length mirror. He was pleased with what he saw.

He sat in his armchair in the balcony overlooking the small patch of garden and watched an endless line of the tops of buses glide by the boundary walls of his bungalow. He could hear the hooting of cars and the sputtering of scooters. It was a weekend and government offices were closed: clerks, their wives and children were out shopping. He could hear the bearer lay out his Scotch on the table. 'Put out two glasses,' he ordered, 'I am expecting a guest. And tell the cook to fry some paapad to serve with the drinks.'

A three-wheeler pulled up at his gate. He saw a short bespectacled woman dressed very correctly in a white sari examine the number and the name on the gatepost, pay the three-wheeler driver and push open the gate. Mohan got up from his chair and went down to receive his visitor. Before she could ring the bell, he opened the door. 'I am Mohan Kumar,' he smiled, putting out his hand. 'I am Sarojini Bharadwaj,' she replied, unsmiling. She touched both his feet before shaking his hand. The gesture was so incongruous for the occasion and so completely unexpected, that it should have startled Mohan. But it did not. Somehow it seemed to belong to that moment and to the frail, average-looking woman from Rewari. As they stood facing each other, Mohan noticed her head did not come up to his shoulders.

*

Mohan led the diminutive lady professor from small-town Haryana up the stairs to his sitting room with the balcony overlooking the garden. 'Please take a seat,' he said pointing to the chair across the table on which his bearer had laid out his Scotch, two bottles of soda, a bucket of ice and his crystal glass tumblers. Neither knew how to begin.

'Well, here I am,' said the lady professor to break the ice.

'Yes, here you are,' he responded.

The professor took command of the situation. She took off her glasses, wiped the lenses with the hem of her sari and put them on the table. 'You can see what I look like with and without my glasses. I told you something about my past in my letter. If you want to know more, please ask me.'

Mohan had a good look at her. She was petite and reasonably attractive: skin the colour of old ivory, dark brown hair, broad forehead with a bindi, diamonds in her ear lobes, a diamond nosepin, soft, sensuous lips with a dab of fresh lipstick, a pearl necklace which went well with her white sari. No great beauty but quite presentable.

'What happened to your marriage? Why did it break up so quickly?' asked Mohan at last.

'As I explained in my letter, he lived in Canada and had advertised for an Indian wife. My father answered the ad. The man flew over and came to see me at our house in Dehra Dun. A week later we were married. My parents and I knew nothing about him except what he told us. We went for our honeymoon to Mussoorie—all paid for by my father. He took my virginity; he had all the sex he wanted for fifteen days and nights. Then he said he had urgent business to attend to in Toronto and would return in a week to take me back with him. I got a Canadian visa. And waited. He never wrote or came back for me. I discovered I was pregnant. My father was furious and wanted to have him put in jail, especially after he heard from a friend that the fellow had a white woman living with him in Canada. I decided if the man was such a rascal I did not want to have anything to do with him. Some months later I had a son. He's in a boarding school now. And I have a permanent job in a college. Anything more you want to know about me? I know nothing about you.'

'I spelt it out in the ad. Thirteen years of stormy married life which yielded two children but no happiness. So we decided to call it a day.

You will get to know more if you decide to take up my offer. Can I offer you a drink?'

'No, thank you,' she replied firmly. 'I live in Haryana where there is strict prohibition; a woman seen smoking or drinking is looked upon as a whore. So no smoking, no drink. You drink every day?'

'Yes,' he replied. 'I also smoke. I look forward to my couple of Scotches every evening and I enjoy my cigars—four a day. Any objections?'

'None! It's your life. Who am I to object to anything you like.'

'I expect you are vegetarian,' said Mohan.

'I am. But I don't object to others eating what they like.'

'And eggs?'

'No, not even eggs. I hope that doesn't make me a poor companion.'

'Eating habits have nothing to do with companionship,' he replied with a smile.

A silence descended on them. Again it was the lady professor who broke it. 'Can I take a look round your house? It looks quite posh from the outside.'

'Certainly,' he replied, standing up. 'I'll take you round on a conducted tour.' He poured himself a drink and glass in hand took her from one bedroom to another—the master bedroom that he had shared with his wife, the children's room, and the guest room which she would occupy if she accepted his offer. All had air-conditioners. The bathrooms had marble tiles and were spotlessly clean. 'Downstairs I have my study and reception room,' he explained. 'Does my humble abode meet your requirements?' he asked in a tone of mild sarcasm as they returned to the sitting room.

'You live in style,' she replied. 'But I did not see a single book in any room. Don't you read at all?' Her tone was professorial.

'Not since I left college. I do not have the time or the patience to read books. I get a lot of magazines and newspapers, but I only read the captions to pictures and the headlines. I get all my news, information and views from TV. I'm sure as an academic you don't approve of that. Perhaps you will educate me.'

She gave him a wistful smile and took her seat.

'Can I offer you a cold drink?'

'That would be nice.'

Mohan shouted to the bearer to get his guest a Campa-Cola and paapad.

'What next?' she asked in a matter-of-fact way. 'You must have received offers from other women.'

'So far you are the only one. And I am game,' he replied. 'When would it be convenient for you to move in?'

Again there was a long silence before the lady professor, her gaze fixed on her feet, asked, 'I expect you will want to have sex with me?'

Mohan was taken aback by her bluntness. Less than half an hour ago, when she came in, this woman had touched his feet. He took his time to answer. 'It is part of the deal. If you have any reservations, you must tell me right now.'

She continued looking at her feet. 'In that case I should first see a doctor. I don't want to take the risk of getting pregnant again. Children must be born in wedlock, not of a temporary relationship.'

Mohan made no comment.

She paused a long time before she spoke again. 'It's a big gamble for me. My self-esteem might get very bruised. But I'm willing to give it a try. I have to give my college a month's notice to avail of the leave due to me. I also have to spend some time with my son during his school vacations. I'll let you know as soon as I get back to Rewari and have a talk with my principal.'

She got up to leave. 'Will I be able to get a scooter or a taxi to drop me at the bus stand?'

'My chauffeur will drop you there. I would have done it myself but I don't like driving after dark. Car headlights dazzle my eyes and traffic on Delhi roads is very chaotic.'

The Mercedes was parked in the driveway. Mohan opened the rear door to let her in. He was not sure whether plans for the future entitled him to embrace or kiss her. He put his arm round her shoulder as she got into the car. 'It was nice meeting you. Keep in touch. If you have a telephone where I can reach you, send me the number.'

'No telephone,' she replied, 'I'll write. Driver, please take me to the Inter-State Bus Terminal.'

She waved a bangled hand as the car drove out.

While drinking his evening quota of Scotch, Mohan thought about the prospect of having the lady professor share his life for a few weeks or maybe months. His cook and bearer could be expected to accept his explanation— even if they did not believe it—that she was a cousin who had been transferred to Delhi and who would stay with him till she found accommodation of her own. But Dhanno would be more difficult to convince. She had got used to being invited to his bedroom once or twice a week when the other servants were out. With another woman in the house all day, this arrangement would have to be put in abeyance till the lady professor left. Since he himself locked the front and rear entrances to the house before retiring to bed, neither Dhanno nor the other servants would know what went on indoors at night. But women, he knew, had an uncanny sixth sense which warned them of the presence of rivals claiming the attention of their men. Married women could sense their husband's extra-marital affairs without having any tell-tale evidence to substantiate their suspicions. Married men were so absorbed in themselves that their wives could cuckold them for years without being suspected of infidelity.

But then, Dhanno had no moral right, really, to sulk or quibble; she was cheating on her husband. Mohan could be as unfaithful to her as he liked since she was neither his wife nor a concubine—just a pro tem sharer of his bed, for which she was duly compensated. In any case, why brood over it now? He'd see how things developed and deal with problems as they arose.

When he retired for the night, he fantasized about what the lady professor would be like in bed. Would he go to her bedroom or bring her to his own? She appeared somewhat prudish and might insist that the lights be switched off before she lay with him . . . And almost certainly he would have to do a lot of persuading to make her strip and see her as God had made her. What gave him confidence was that she was small and frail and he towered over her. He could impose his will on her. He fell asleep; but when it came to dreaming it was not the lady professor he saw but the sweeper-woman, Dhanno, standing naked before him, arms akimbo, and berating him for being unfaithful to her.

*

Three days later he got a letter from Professor Sarojini Bharadwaj. She addressed him as 'Dear Mohan Ji'. She informed him that the leave she had asked for had been sanctioned. Her son would be with her for a part of his summer vacation; she would then leave him with her parents in Dehra Dun who would take him back to his boarding school in Mussoorie. It was now mid-August; she could join him in mid-September or any time later that suited him. She was retaining her flat in Rewari as she was not sure how long or short her stay in Delhi would be. She ended her letter: 'With love, yours, Saroj.' There was a 'PS' beneath her signature: 'Please reply as soon as you can. Please do not talk about our arrangement to any of your friends.'

Her handwriting was masculine and bold. Mohan wondered whether under the mask of femininity she was a bossy woman in the habit of talking down to people as she undoubtedly did to her students.

Mohan replied to her letter the same afternoon. He wrote that he had some out-of-town business to attend to in September. If it was all right for her, he would expect her on the first of October. He could pick her up at the railway station or the bus terminal if she gave him the exact timings, and assured her of complete secrecy over their arrangement. He also ended his letter with 'Love, ever yours, Mohan.'

In the course of the next week he received more letters from women showing interest in his offer. They were from distant cities—Coimbatore, Goa, Vishakhapatnam, Bombay, Hyderabad, Bhubaneshwar, Calcutta and Guwahati. Five were from Hindu women of different castes, three from Christians, one from a Parsee, one from a Muslim. When he put in the ad he had little hope of receiving any replies, and here within a space of ten days he had eight takers from different parts of the country, belonging to different communities. Most of them were divorced or living separately from their husbands; one was a spinster. All were educated, working women: teachers, nurses, steno-typists. The photographs they enclosed made them look quite attractive. And all of them asked for his photograph in return. He wrote them a standard reply: he was going abroad on business for a few months and would get in touch with them as soon as he returned, and enclosed copies of the same photograph he had sent Sarojini Bharadwaj. He locked up the letters in the desk drawer in his study. He looked forward to the new life he had planned for himself.

*

Mohan resumed his relationship with Dhanno—once a week. Her body had lost its novelty. Sex with her was pleasant enough while it lasted but lacked the frenetic zeal of the first few encounters. In a very matter-of-fact tone he told her that there would have to be a break for some time as a cousin would be coming to stay with him.

'Man or woman?' asked Dhanno bluntly.

'Woman,' he replied tamely. 'She is my aunt's daughter. She has been transferred to Delhi and will stay with me till she has found her own accommodation.'

'How long will she stay?'

'I have no idea. I hope not very long.' He gave her a kiss on her nose to assure her of his affection. 'I will pay you as usual,' he added.

'It's not your money I am after,' snapped Dhanno. 'What does this relation of yours do for a living?'

'She's a professor, you will have no problems with her.'

Dhanno was not convinced. Every time she came to him, she brought up the subject of the not-so-distant relation who would deny her her maalik's affection. Mohan made his irritation clear to her. 'Don't keep asking questions about her,' he said in a sharp voice. Dhanno felt properly snubbed and did not bring up the subject again.

*

Mohan and Sarojini continued exchanging letters. Twice she rang him from Rewari—a day before her son came to stay with her, once again when she took him to her parents in Dehra Dun. She confirmed that she would come by train as she had two heavy suitcases with her, one with her clothes, the other with books which she hoped to read while in Delhi. He was not to come to the railway station as one of her colleagues would be travelling with her. There might be others from Rewari who might recognize her. She would get to his house by taxi. If he was in office, he should leave instructions with his servants to let her in and put her luggage in the guest room. She would ring him up in office to inform him that she had arrived.

*

Mohan made preparations to ensure the privacy of his new relationship. He had an answering machine attached to the telephone to record calls from his children and instructed his servants not to pick up the instrument when it rang. Though there were no dogs in the house, his entrance gate, which he personally locked every evening, had a large signboard saying 'BEWARE OF DOGS'. Now he added another, equally large: 'NO VISITORS WITHOUT PRIOR APPOINTMENT'.

On the morning of the first of October, he checked all the items in his guest room: light switches, air-conditioner, bed lamps, pillow covers and bed sheets. The bathroom had fresh towels, new cakes of soap, tooth brush and paste, comb and brush and a bottle of cologne: everything that a five-star hotel would provide. Before leaving for the office, he switched on the air-conditioner in the room. Though it was October, it could still get uncomfortably warm in the afternoon.

He put twenty five-hundred-rupee notes in a buff envelope with a slip of paper reading: 'Welcome! Make yourself comfortable. The car will be at your disposal. My chauffeur, Jiwan Ram, has been instructed to take you wherever you want to go—shopping, sightseeing or visiting friends. He should pick me up from the office at 6 p.m. The cook has been told to serve you lunch (vegetarian) at the time you ask for it, and afternoon tea if you are at home. Meanwhile unpack and relax. Just let me know all is okay.'

He sealed the envelope and put it on her pillow, then locked the room and gave the keys to Jiwan Ram, his most trustworthy employee, who was to receive the memsahib when she arrived.

Four
Sarojini

Professor Sarojini Bharadwaj arrived at the house a couple of hours after Mohan had left. Jiwan Ram and the bearer took her cases to the guest room.

After the servants had left, she looked round the room. Her eyes fell on the envelope on the pillow. She tore it open. She felt the thick wad of currency notes. For a moment she felt ashamed of herself, then put the money in her handbag. She read the note. It said nothing about the money. He had fulfilled his part of the contract in advance; he was a gentleman, true to his word. She had no option but to fulfil her part of the deal.

Sarojini unpacked; arranged her clothes in the empty wardrobes, laid out her books on the working table. By the time she had finished her bath, it was 10 a.m. She had toast and a cup of coffee for breakfast, then told the bearer she was going out to do some shopping and would be back in time for lunch.

Sarojini was not familiar with New Delhi's shopping areas but had heard that the best saris were to be found in South Extension market. The chauffeur knew exactly where to take her. They made slow progress on the Ring Road choked with overcrowded buses and more cars and two-wheelers than she had ever seen. At the Moolchand traffic light, a fancy steel-grey car stopped next to the Mercedes. Sarojini found herself examining the woman in the back seat. She had her hair permed, had her lips painted a bright red, and rouge on her cheeks. She wore a sleeveless blouse with a plunging neckline. There was a prosperous looking man sitting next to her, with gold rings on his fingers. The man put his arm around her, pulled her to him and said something in her ear. The woman threw her head back and laughed, a manicured hand at her cleavage. 'Slut,' hissed Sarojini under her breath. It was only after the lights had changed and the cars were moving that Sarojini realized what she had done. She had condemned a woman who perhaps was doing nothing worse than what she herself had agreed to do. Only, she, Sarojini Bharadwaj, Professor of English, did not look the type. For the second time that morning she felt ashamed of herself. But the feeling soon died. Only a vague apprehension remained.

The market was crowded, but the chauffeur took her to a shop where it did not take her long to find what she wanted. She bought herself a beige coloured cotton sari—beige suited her best—and a pink dressing gown. The two cost her a little over a thousand rupees. While paying for them, she counted the notes. The purchases and what remained amounted to exactly ten thousand rupees.

She was back in time for lunch. The bearer laid out an elaborate meal of cucumber soup, vegetable pilaf, daal and vegetable curry, followed by rice-pudding. She sampled everything but ate very little. She locked herself in her room and tried to get some sleep.

Sleep would not come to her. Her mind was agitated. She dozed off for a few minutes, woke up to check the time. Dozed off again, woke up with a start and again looked at her watch. It seemed as if time had come to a stop. She switched on her bedside lamp and tried to read, but her mind was too disturbed to take in anything. She gave up, closed her eyes and resumed her battle with sleep. So passed the restless afternoon. She heard the servants return from their quarters. By the time she came out to have tea, it was 5 p.m. She found herself looking at her wrist watch every few minutes. As it came closer to 6 p.m., the time when Mohan left office, her nervousness increased. She went back to her room and had yet another bath—her third of the day. She lit sticks of agar and put them in a tumbler that she placed in front of a figurine of Saraswati, her patron goddesss, which she always carried with her. She sat down on the carpet, joined the palms of her hands in prayer and chanted an invocation to Saraswati. Her prayers said, she changed into the beige sari she had bought that morning, put a fresh bindi on her forehead and a light dab of colour on her lips, and splashed cologne on her neck and breasts. She put on her pearl necklace and examined herself in the bathroom mirror. Still nervous, she went out and sat in the balcony to await Mohan's arrival.

The days had begun to shorten; daylight faded away sooner than in the summer months. By half past six the brief twilight had given way to the dark. The evening star twinkled in the darkening sky beside a half moon. Not long afterwards Sarojini heard the car drive up to the gate. The driver got out of the car, opened the iron gate and drove in the sleek black Mercedes with its lights dimmed. Saroj heard Mohan respond to the driver's 'Good night, sir' in English. She heard him come up the stairs. 'What's the smell?' he asked loudly. 'Hello,' said he as he walked out to the balcony and took the chair next to hers. 'Everything okay? Lunch, tea, bedroom?'

'Hello,' she replied, standing up. 'Everything's fine. That's the aroma of the agar I lit for Saraswati. I do Saraswati-puja every evening. Do you mind the smell?'

'Not at all, just not used to it. Please sit down. So what did you do all day?'

'A little shopping. I bought this sari, thanks to you.' She held up the hem of the sari to show him.

'Very nice. And what else?'

'Unpacked, arranged my clothes and books, had lunch, read a little, slept a little, and the day was gone.'

They had nothing more to say to each other. Mohan got up. 'If you'll excuse me for a few minutes, I'll take a quick shower and change. The office is a very sweaty place. Too many hands to shake. Too many dirty files to read.' He loosened his collar and took off his tie.

The first thing he did was to turn on his answering machine. It had recorded no incoming calls. He shaved himself, took a shower and splashed on some after-shave. He got into a sports shirt and slacks and joined Sarojini on the balcony. The bearer brought out his Scotch, soda and the bucket of ice cubes. 'Have you never had a drink?' he asked.

'You mean alcohol? My husband-for-a-month made me try whisky. I didn't like the taste and spat it out. Then he gave me some kind of sweet wine which I did not mind. It didn't do anything to me.'

'It must have been sherry. I have some very good Spanish Oloroso, a ladies drink. You'll like it.'

He got up and pulled out a wine glass and a bottle of Oloroso from his drinks cabinet. He poured out the sherry for her and a stiff Scotch for himself.

'This is not at all bad,' she said, taking a sip. 'I hope it won't make me drunk.'

'A couple of glasses will do you no harm. There's hardly any alcohol in it,' he replied.

Their conversation became stilted.

'So, tell me some more.'

'No, you tell me more about yourself. I have done nothing really interesting today.'

And so on.

Sarojini kept pace with Mohan's drinking and felt she was floating in the air. Mohan felt she was drinking to fortify herself against what was to come. They had dinner (vegetarian for both) without exchanging many words. The servants cleared the table, had their meal in the kitchen and left for their quarters. Mohan got up to lock the doors. Sarojini saw him chain and lock the front gate and then disappear into the house to lock the servants' entrance door. He came out into the front garden, faced a hedge and unbuttoned his flies. She heard the splash of his jet of urine on the leaves. 'Curious fellow!' she said to herself. She went into her bedroom, took off her sari, petticoat and blouse and slipped on the new silk dressing gown. She was a little unsteady on her feet and slumped down in her chair. Mohan latched the rear door and came up to join her. He took her hand in his and asked, 'Are you okay?'

'Yes. Only a little tired. I should not have drunk all that sherry. I'm not used to alcohol. I'll sleep it off,' she said standing up.

'Let me see you to your bedroom,' he said putting his arm round her shoulder and directing her towards her bed. She put her head against his broad chest and murmured, 'Be gentle with me. I have not been near a man for eleven years. I'm scared.'

He took her in a gentle bear hug to reassure her: 'There's nothing to be scared of; I'm not a sex maniac. If you don't want it, we won't do it. Just let me lie with you for a while and I'll go back to my room.'

Sarojini felt reassured but clung to him. Mohan laid her on the bed and stretched himself beside her. She dug her face in his chest, clasped him by the waist and lay still. He slipped his hand under her dressing gown and gently rubbed her shoulders and the back of her neck. Then her spine and her little buttocks. The tension went out of her body and she faced him. 'Switch off the table lamp,' she said.

'You don't want me to see your body?' he asked as he switched off the lamp.

'There is not much to see,' she replied. 'I'm like any other woman of my age. Only plainer. And not as well endowed.'

'Let's have a dekho,' he said as he undid the belt of her gown and cupped one of her breasts in his hand. Indeed, she was not as well endowed as his wife or Dhanno or any of the other women he had bedded. The difference made her more desirable. He kissed her nipples and took one breast in his mouth. She began to gurgle with pleasure. 'Don't neglect the other one,' she murmured. He did the same to the other breast. He unbuttoned his trousers and she felt his stiff penis throb against her belly.

'My God you are big!' she exclaimed in alarm. 'This thing will tear me to pieces.' She clasped it between her thighs to prevent it piercing her. 'Promise you won't hurt me. Remember I'm very small and have had no sex for a very, very long time.'

He felt elated, powerfully macho and grandly overpowering. And more patient than he had been with other women. He sensed she was ready to receive him. She spread out her thighs and he entered her very slowly. 'Oh God, you will split me into two,' she said clasping him by the neck. She was fully aroused. In a hoarse voice she whispered urgently, 'Ram it in.' He did as he was told.

She screamed, not in agony but in the ecstasy of a multiple orgasm. She had never experienced it before nor believed it was possible. Her body quivered, relaxed . . . Then a fit of hysteria overtook her. She clawed Mohan's face and arms and chest and began to sob. 'I'm a whore, a common tart! I'm a bitch,' she cried. Mohan held her closer and reassured her, 'You are none of those; you are a nice gentle woman who has not known love.'

She knew his words meant nothing but they were strangely soothing. She rested her head on his arm and was soon snoring softly. Neither of them felt the need to wash and fell asleep in each other's arms. Many hours later it was Sarojini who shook Mohan awake. 'Better go to your own room and make your bed look as if it has been slept in.'

Mohan staggered out of her room. He did not know what time it was. He undid the latch of the servants' entrance door and lay down on his bed. He was fast asleep within minutes.

*

Mohan was an hour later than his usual waking up time. He quickly brushed his teeth, got into his dressing gown (he had slept in his sports shirt and slacks) and came out for his morning tea. Sarojini was already there, calmly sipping from her cup and turning the pages of the morning paper. She looked neat and relaxed. He had expected to see her hair dishevelled and her lips bruised. She beamed a smile at him; she looked radiantly happy. Mohan was reminded of what some psychologists had said—that when it came to sex, women were much stronger than men. She was her bossy professorial self. 'Bearer, get the sahib a fresh cup of coffee,' she ordered. She put aside the paper and asked him, 'How do you feel after last night?'

'Grand! Top of the world. And you?'

'Transported to seventh heaven. Back to earth with a thud. Do you come home for lunch?'

'Only on weekends and holidays,' he replied. 'On working days I get something from the office canteen and doze on my sofa for half an hour. Often I have to entertain my business partners, I take them to the Gymkhana Club or the India International Centre. You can get reasonably good food at modest prices. It all goes as business expenses. The only meal I normally have at home is dinner.'

'What would you like for dinner? You don't have to suffer eating vegetarian stuff because of me. I can tell the cook to make you fish or chicken or whatever you fancy. I can eat what the servants cook for themselves,' she said.

Mohan did not like her taking over the household. He administered a slight snub. 'The cook knows what I like and from where to get it. I give him money every morning to buy provisions. He renders accounts to me. You don't have to worry about the servants or my food. Just order whatever you like for yourself.'

Sarojini felt she had been put in her place.

They had breakfast together. He left for his office. The car came back and was at her disposal for the day. She decided to stay at home in the morning to do some reading and get to know the servants. She went to the kitchen to chat with the cook. She stood at the entrance to the kitchen for a while, watching him clean up. She felt like an intruder. For all the discord, Mohan's marriage had lasted thirteen years. There had been a mistress of the house who had managed his life—ordered the servants about, supervised the cooking and bought things for the house. Sarojini felt a sense of loss and regret taking hold of her. Mohan was right to snub her. She was a pro tem mistress, not mistress of the house. The cook saw her and asked if she needed anything. 'No, I was just looking around, khansamaji,' she replied. 'What are you giving the sahib for dinner?'

'Fish, memsahib. He likes fish and chicken on alternate days.' The cook thought she looked a little nervous, and to make her feel at home, he spoke a little longer. 'The sahib also likes king prawns and crab. I get them from INA market. It's a long way from here but I like to keep the sahib happy. He's a very kind master.'

The bearer was less communicative. He was gruff in his replies to her questions about his duties and made it clear that he resented her as an outsider. The jamadarni proved more difficult than the male servants. As she came in with her broom, pail of phenyl and a mop, she greeted Sarojini: 'Namaste, bhainji.'

Sarojini responded and asked her name. 'Dhanno,' she replied, without looking at her. 'I do the floors and the bathrooms. Memsahibji, how are you related to the sahib?'

'I am his cousin,' she replied, keeping up the lie Mohan had told her about.

'And what do you do?'

'I teach in a college. I've been transferred to Delhi. I'm here till I find a place of my own.'

The two women sized each other up. Sarojini noticed that the untouchable woman was a lot more desirable than herself: large protruding breasts, narrow waist and large hips. She was dark, poorly clad, but sexy. Dhanno saw the college teacher as a rival: sexless but brainy. She had everything Dhanno had but in smaller measure. Men were not discriminating, they took whatever was available. This woman he called his cousin was available to the sahib round the clock. Men set little store by fidelity. They soon tired of having one woman and went looking for another. Bastards, all of them.

Sarojini spent the morning reading. She had her lunch and a long siesta; sex had soothed her, relaxed her body, and now induced sleep. In the afternoon she had the driver take her out. 'Show me the sahib's office. I don't want to go in but just see what it looks like. Then take me to a bookstore.'

'Sahib's office is in Nehru Place. The offices are in high rise buildings with many lifts. He has the two top storeys of a block, what will you see from the ground? And I don't know of any bookstore. Sahib does not buy books. You give me the address and I'll take you there.'

Sarojini did not know the names of any of Delhi's bookstores but knew that there were a few in some place called Khan Market. 'Take me to Khan Market,' she ordered curtly, irritated with the chauffeur's indifferent manners. She may be his master's paid companion, but how was he to know that? She was determined to have them all respect her.

Khan Market was closer than she had thought. And crammed

with cars. The driver dropped her in front of a bookstore, Bahri &
Sons. This time he got out and opened the car door for her. Her curt
tone had obviously made a difference. 'I will find a place for parking,
memsahib, and come back for you here after you have seen this and
other bookstores.'

Sarojini looked at the books on display in the windows. Instead of
going in she decided to take a look round the market to see what else
there was she could buy. She went from one shop to the other looking
at what they had to offer. There was just about everything anyone
could want: six book stores, eight magazine stalls, shops selling saris
and suit lengths and children's garments. Shoe stores, chemists, green-
grocer's, butchers, halwais, paanwalas, a florist, an ice-cream parlour
and a couple of restaurants. From a green-grocer's she bought half a
kilo of baby corn which she had never seen before. At the florist's she
picked up a dozen bright red gladioli—Mohan had no flowers in his
house or garden. Her final purchase was from The Bookshop—an
illustrated edition of Fitzgerald's translation of Omar Khayyam's rubais.
It was as good a primer as any to introduce a man to English poetry.

Her arms full of flowers, two plastic bags in one hand, her handbag slung over her shoulder, Sarojini waited outside Bahri & Sons for
her car. She was startled by a girl's enthusiastic cry: 'Aunty Saroj?!
What are you doing here? Remember me? Sheetal?' It was one of her
old students now married and settled in Delhi. 'Oh . . . Hi. I'm here
for a few days to do some shopping and sightseeing,' replied Sarojini,
trying hard to keep the panic out of her voice.

'You *must* come home, Aunty. My husband would *love* to meet
you. Have lunch or dinner with us. Give me your address and
telephone number.'

Sarojini felt cornered. 'I'm not sure if I can make it this time,
Sheetal. I don't know the address or the telephone number of the
people I'm staying with. You give me yours and I will ring you up.'

The girl quickly scribbled her telephone number on a slip of
paper. 'Please, *please* don't forget to get in touch with me. Can I drop
you somewhere?'

'No, thanks, my host has lent me his car for the afternoon.'

Just then Mohan's Mercedes pulled up. A line of cars lined up behind it and began to honk impatiently. Sarojini got into the car, waved the girl goodbye and was driven away. She sank into the seat and sighed with relief.

*

Sarojini reached home, and asked the bearer to put the gladioli in a vase. She took a shower, got into her nightie, and went through her ritual of lighting agarbatties and invoking the blessings of Saraswati. She folded her hands and began to chant:

> Thou lady clad in celestial white
> A garland of snow-white flowers round Thy neck
> A stringed viol in one hand, royal sceptre in the other,
> Thou Goddess divine seated on a lotus flower!
> To Thee, The Creator, Preserver and Destroyer, I make
>   obeisance
> For Thou art the embodiment of learning;
> With Thy sword of knowledge, slay the ignorance
>   that is within me.
> To Thee I pray and make my offering.

Having propitiated her patron goddess, she drew a chair to the balcony and awaited Mohan's return from office. As on the evening before, she watched the sun go down, the evening star twinkling a little less brightly in the sky lit by the waxing moon. She had not noticed earlier that in the garden were two pine trees. She did not think pines could grow in the plains. But these two looked as lush and healthy as any she had seen in the Shivaliks. She must ask Mohan where he had got them from.

Exactly at 6.30 p.m. the iron front gate opened and the Mercedes slid in noiselessly. Coming up the stairs Mohan got a whiff of agar. As he came up onto the balcony he noticed the vase full of gladioli and an unopened parcel on the dining table.

'I see you've been shopping,' he said by way of greeting.

'I went to Khan Market and got the flowers for you. And some baby corn, it will go nicely with your dinner. I've also bought you a book of poems.'

'A book of poems?' he asked in a tone of surprise. 'I haven't read poetry since I left school. Jack and Jill, Twinkle, twinkle little star, Mary had a little lamb—that kind of kid stuff. I don't understand poetry.'

'Don't worry,' she replied, 'I'll read you some verses. If you don't like them, I'll take the book back to the shop.'

Mohan opened the parcel and was impressed with the binding and illustrations. 'Bookstores don't take back books they've sold. And you've inscribed it to me: "To Mohan—with love", if you please. I'll try to read it.'

He went to his room, had his second shave and shower, got into his sports shirt and slacks and joined her on the balcony. He took out bottles of sherry and Scotch from the drink cabinet.

'Don't give me more than a glass,' pleaded Sarojini. 'I was a bit tipsy last evening. I needed something to fortify myself. One will do me nicely today.'

Mohan handed her a glass of sherry and sat down with his Scotch.

'What was your day like?' she asked.

'Not bad. I received a big order for readymade garments from the United States. Should bring me a lot of dollars. You've proved to be a grihalakshmi—' he said and winked at her, '—the money-bringing goddess of the house.'

'I may have brought you some lolly but can hardly be described as a housewife—that's what griha means, you know.'

They both laughed. Sarojini opened the book of rubais and said, 'Listen to this one. It's my favourite!' Her voice was professional— loud and clear:

Ah love, if thou and I could with fate conspire
To change this sorry scheme of things entire
Would we not shatter it to bits

And remould it nearer
To our hearts' desire?

'How do you like it?'

'Very nice, who wrote it?'

'Omar Khayyam, in Persian, translated by Fitzgerald. He wrote many lovely rubais on the joys of the tavern and the passage of time.'

'One verse is enough for one evening,' Mohan said in a tone of finality. 'I won't be able to digest more.'

They had their drinks. Sarojini was persuaded to take a second glass of sherry. They had dinner together. Then Mohan lit his Havana cigar. The impatience of the evening before had gone. With the cigar in his mouth he went down to lock the main gate and the doors, stood facing the hedge and went through his ritual evening urination. He came up, stubbed out his half-smoked cigar in the ashtray and went to the bathroom to gargle away the smell of tobacco from his mouth. When he returned, Sarojini stretched her hand out to him. He held it for some time; then pulled her up to her feet. 'Time for bed,' he announced.

She followed him to his bedroom. Mohan was pleased about the way in which the equation had changed within twenty-four hours: last evening he was the pursuer and she the frightened little doe dreading the hunter's dart; this evening she was Diana, the huntress, pursuing the boar into its den.

This time she did not plead with him to be gentle nor show any fear of his oversized weapon. She gazed on it with admiration, caressed it lovingly with her fingers and directed it to its goal. Mohan found the second encounter as pleasurable as the first. The first was conquest, the second consolidation of what had been conquered. He slept so soundly that he did not know when Sarojini left his bed to return to her own.

*

The first few days went by pleasantly. However, Mohan sensed growing resentment among the servants. How was it that if the lady professor had been transferred to Delhi she did not go to teach in any college nor go round looking for a place of her own? They learnt from the driver Jiwan Ram that all she did in the afternoons was visit bookstores, museums, art exhibitions and historical monuments. Dhanno turned positively hostile. She said nothing but stopped even looking at Mohan. She swept and mopped the floors in sullen silence and then strode out with her broom, mop and bucket. Even when he gave her an extra two hundred rupees she took it without a gesture of thanks. And once he overheard her say to the cook while having the mug of tea he gave her every morning: 'I don't know what she is to the maalik, she does not behave like his sister.' The cook snubbed her, 'How does it matter to you? You do your work and don't buk buk so much.'

Mohan's ardour for the lady professor lessened. He did not follow her to her bedroom as often as he had done during the first week. Usually it was she who indicated by gestures while they were having their pre-dinner drinks what she had in mind. She would throw back her arms over her head to stretch herself; it was the traditional Indian angdaee, exposing her bosom with languor and wantonness. She developed a liking for sherry: three to four glasses every evening. She had Omar Khayyam to back her up. One evening she said, 'You will like this one; it is in praise of wine.' She read aloud:

> Awake! And in the fire of spring
> The winter garment of repentance fling;
> The bird of time has a little way to go
> And lo! the Bird is on the wing.

'What does it mean?' asked Mohan naively.

'It is very simple. Don't ever regret what you are doing. You have only one life to live. Live it to the full. Time flies as fast as a bird on the wing.'

'Makes good sense to me,' said Mohan. 'That's exactly what we, you and I, are doing.'

'Precisely!' she replied in her didactic manner. 'Follow the dictates of your heart and tell the world to go to hell.'

That night was made for loving. A full moon washed the garden with milky whiteness. Moonbeams filtered through the pine trees. When Mohan went out to urinate against the hedge she could see the stream pour from him. 'Hey Mister!' she shouted to him. 'What do you think you are doing in my garden?' He turned and shouted back, 'You want to see what I'm doing? Have a good look.' He thrust out his pelvis, pointed his member towards her and sent a jet of urine in her direction.

'Shameless creature!' she said flirtatiously as he came up to the balcony.

'Shameless you! You asked me to show you what I have. Here, you can have a closer look.'

He sat down in his chair, legs apart, exposing himself to her. She undid her dressing gown and came over and sat astride him. She put her hands on his shoulder and leaned back, so they could both see and marvel at how a small opening like hers could swallow up his huge organ. All of it, down to its hairy roots. They made love not in the privacy of their bedrooms but in the moonlit balcony. Anyone peering over the boundary wall could have seen her bouncing in his lap. It was more gratifying for both than their previous encounters in bed.

'Have you done this on the balcony before?' she asked him as she got up and tied the cord of her dressing gown.

'Never! You think I'm mad?'

'We are both a little mad,' she said laughing.

That night they slept in the same bed without a stitch of clothing between them. Mohan was woken by the cook banging on the rear door. He quickly slipped into his dressing gown and hurried downstairs. She simply picked up hers and ran stark naked to her bedroom and bolted it from the inside.

*

From almost the time their relationship began, both Mohan and Sarojini had known that it could not last very long; the world outside which they pretended did not exist would eventually catch up with them. But not in the nasty way it did.

Came the first of November. While Sarojini was having her bath, Mohan put an envelope with Rs 10,000 on her pillow. When she joined him for breakfast she just said one word, 'Thanks.' He said nothing.

The crisis came the next morning. Mohan was scanning the pages of *The Hindustan Times*. He had no interest in politics and the paper had little besides politics to fill its pages. The page he usually scanned casually to see if he could recognize the names or faces of the people in it was the one which carried obituaries. That morning there were lots of boxed items with photographs of the people who had died the day before and several 'In Memoriam' messages for people who had died that day some years earlier. He went down the columns and stopped midway. Right in the centre was a picture of his father-in-law. The accompanying text read:

'We deeply regret to announce that our revered father Rai Bahadur Lala Achint Ramji suddenly left for his heavenly abode on the evening of 31 October. Cremation will take place at the Lodhi Road crematorium at 11 a.m. on 1 November. Chautha/Uthala will take place at Mata ka Mandir, Friends Colony East on Sunday, 7 November at 4 p.m.'

Under the line 'Grief Stricken' were the names of the family members, beginning with 'Shobha Achint Ram—wife'. Then the three sons and their wives. His wife was listed singly as 'Sonu—daughter'. At the end were the names of his children, Ranjit and Mohini. The only name missing in the list was his own—Mohan Kumar. Evidently he was no longer regarded a part of his wife's family. The last item in the obituary was a list of the sugar mills and companies that the deceased had owned.

Mohan told Sarojini about it and said, 'I am in two minds about going to the funeral. They obviously don't regard me as a relation any more. But some members of my office staff are bound to go there to condole. What shall I do?'

'It's a very dicey situation,' she replied. 'But I think it is your duty to attend the cremation. Keep your distance from the family and come away as soon as the funeral pyre is lit. You don't have to line up with your mother-in- law, wife and brothers-in-law to thank the people present.'

Mohan thought over the matter for some time and decided to accept her advice. And face the music. He rang up his secretary to give her the news. She had already read it in the paper and offered her condolences. 'Tell the others that the office will remain closed today as a mark of respect for the deceased,' he said. 'Yes, sir, I will,' she replied.

He told the servants that if they wanted to go to the memsahib to condole, they could do so. The professor lady would have her lunch in a restaurant.

At 10.30 a.m. he left for the Lodhi Road cremation ground. 'Was memsahib's father ill?' the driver Jiwan Ram asked to show his concern. 'I don't know,' replied Mohan. 'I only read of his death in the paper this morning.'

There was quite a crowd at the cremation ground. The car park was full. Mohan asked Jiwan Ram to drop him outside the gate and park the car by the road as he would be leaving before the others. Some people came to condole with him; mostly his staff and friends. Mohan saw the hearse come in, followed by a line of cars carrying members of the family. As the corpse was taken out of the van by his wife's brothers, there were emotional scenes: people embracing each other, women clasping the widow and Sonu and sobbing. They noticed Mohan, but no one came to talk to him. Sonu was in a white sari and wore dark glasses to hide her tears. Her brothers turned to look at him and as quickly turned away. Mercifully his children had been kept at home.

Lala Achint Ram's body was placed on the ground and a pandit started chanting mantras. A few feet away some men were piling wood to make a pyre. In the cremation yard some pyres still smouldered; there were others reduced to heaps of ashes.

Mohan stood apart, watching the scene. Suddenly his wife's youngest brother, whom he detested, broke away from the circle surrounding the corpse and came towards him. 'What brings *you* here?' he asked in a voice loaded with sarcasm.

Mohan did not reply.

The brother-in-law persisted. 'You need not have taken the trouble. And who is this cousin you have discovered to keep you company?'

'Mind your own business,' snapped Mohan and turned away. He left the cremation ground before the funeral pyre was lit.

His mind was in turmoil. He had no doubt his cook and bearer had been seeing his wife and had told her of the sahib's 'cousin' staying at the house. She was not the kind to keep things to herself. He could hear her shrill voice screaming, 'She is no cousin-vuzun, she is a randee! A whore who answered his advertisement in the papers for a part-time mistress.'

The servants had anyhow not bought the cousin story. 'There is no rishta-vishta between them,' they'd told Dhanno. 'She's not related to our sahib, she's just a gold-digger exploiting the sahib. He is very bhola bhala, he does not understand the woman's cunning.'

The Mohan-Sarojini honeymoon had been soured. Mohan spent the afternoon reading papers and magazines in the India International Centre library. He took a walk round the Lodhi gardens. The trees and the neat-looking tombs depressed him today. By the time he got home, it was dark. Sarojini was waiting for him—not in her nightie, but properly clad in salwar-kameez. He did not go to his room to take a shower and get into his sports outfit. He sat down beside her.

'Tell me what happened,' she asked taking his hand, 'you look depressed.'

'I have reason to be,' he replied. 'Give me time to collect my thoughts. Fix me a drink.'

Sarojini had never poured out a drink for anyone but knew roughly how much Mohan took. She held up his cut-glass tumbler in her left hand and tilted the bottle of Scotch with her right. 'Tell me when.'

'A Patiala,' he replied, 'quarter of a glass of whiskey, some soda and ice.'

She handed him his glass and poured out a sherry for herself.

'Now tell me all and get it off your chest.'

He told her of his brother-in-law's nastiness and that the servants knew she was no relation of his. 'You don't know my wife. She hates my guts and will do her utmost to hurt me. And you. So far she doesn't know your name, because the servants don't know it. Or in what college you teach. But she will ferret it out. Once she finds out she will persecute you, write to your principal, to your parents. Even to your son in his boarding school; she will stop at nothing.'

For the first time the enormity of the folly she had committed sank in. They sat silently holding hands, each working his or her way out of the predicament. 'Let's sleep over it,' she said at last standing up. 'Tomorrow may bring some ideas.' They spent the night in the same bed. They had no sex nor much sleep.

*

The servants sensed that the sahib and his lady friend were upset. He was reading the paper; she was polishing her nails. They were not talking to each other. Nor to them. Something had transpired at the cremation ground which had put both of them in ill humour. They felt uneasy at their own role in the affair. When Dhanno came in, neither the sahib nor the memsahib as much as looked at her or acknowledged her greeting. After breakfast both left together, telling the servants that they would not be back till after dinner.

Mohan asked the driver to take them to Connaught Place. Sarojini did not want to spend the day at the house. In the car she put her hand on his and without turning towards him, said: 'It was too good to last. We were living in a fool's paradise of our own making. When would you like me to leave?'

'Don't talk like that!' replied Mohan. 'I was hoping you would be with me for at least three months till your college re-opened. Perhaps longer. You have been with me barely one month.'

'One month, two days and two nights,' she corrected him with a smile. 'And you have paid me the second month's wages in advance. I must return your money before I go.' She sounded quite firm in her resolve. 'If you allow me, I will stay another day or two. I'll ring up my parents and ask them if I can spend the remainder of my leave with them. I'll take my son to Mussoorie, come back to them and then return to Rewari. Will that be okay?'

He pressed her hand and replied: 'You stay as long as you like, come back when you like.'

She got the message.

He asked her where she would like to have dinner. 'Your favourite eating place,' she replied. He gave her a list of his favourite haunts for French, Chinese, Italian, Thai and Indian cuisine. 'Depends. What do you fancy this evening?' he asked.

'Somewhere quiet where we can talk undisturbed and unrecognized,' she replied. 'I've heard a lot about Le Meridien. I'm told it is very fancy and very expensive. I'll never be able to go there on my professor's salary.'

'Not a bad idea,' he agreed. 'It has lots of bars with corners where other people cannot see you. Also many restaurants with different kinds of cuisine. We'll decide where to eat when we have our drinks.'

Sarojini got off at the British Council Library, from where Mohan would pick her up for dinner.

Everyone in the office was very solicitous. Everyone also knew that his relations with his wife had been strained for quite some time and had finally broken down. Condoling with him was a formality they were expected to observe before getting down to work.

Before leaving the office, Mohan cashed a personal cheque for Rs 20,300. He put Rs 300 in one envelope and wrote on it: 'Tips for servants'. In a second envelope he put Rs 10,000 and sealed it. He put no name or address on it. The remaining Rs 10,000 he put in his wallet. He asked Jiwan Lal to take him to a well-known jewellers' shop in Connaught Circus, where he bought a gold ring and took a receipt stating it could be exchanged if it did not fit. A few moments after 7 p.m. the car pulled up outside the British Council Library. Saroj was standing there with an armful of books she had bought from Connaught Circus bookstores. 'Haven't you already got enough books to last you a lifetime?' he asked.

'When you have nothing better to do, you read books,' she replied taking the seat beside him. 'I will have nothing to do for some months to come besides eating and sleeping—alone, I may add—so I'll read and read and read.'

'Le Meridien,' said Mohan to Jiwan Ram.

The car went up to Connaught Circus and turned back along Janpath, past Imperial Hotel, round Windsor Circle and went up through the hotel gates to its plate-glassed entrance. Two huge Sikh commissionaires in blue uniforms opened the car doors and greeted them. They escorted the two up four black marble stairs, opened the doors to let them in. Sarojini stopped in the reception hall to take in the grandeur of the glossy black marble floor and the huge chandeliers suspended from the high ceiling. She watched the coming and going of foreign tourists, pretty girls flitting about, and page boys in forage caps, buttoned coats and tight pants which made their buttocks stick out. They went past a row of glass elevators which shot up at rocket speed to the seventeenth floor and dived down to what appeared to be a gurgling pool of water. Mohan led Sarojini past a dark-skinned girl crooning in a husky voice to the strumming of a guitar. They found a cosy little alcove for two and ordered their drinks. 'The lady is vegetarian,' Mohan told the waiter, 'so only vegetarian canapés and potato chips.'

The waiter served him Scotch and placed a glass of sherry before Sarojini. Then he brought a silver salver full of canapés. 'Leave them on the table,' Mohan ordered, 'we'll help ourselves.' The waiter understood they wanted to be left alone.

Mohan fortified himself with a second Scotch before he took out the two envelopes from his pocket and pressed them into her hands. 'Put them in your handbag,' he said.

'What is in them?' she asked.

'Three hundred in one for you to tip the servants, a hundred each. The other has what I still owe you over the deal.'

'You don't owe me anything. It is I who have to return the advance you gave me two days ago,' she replied.

'It is no longer a commercial deal,' he said taking her hand. 'This is to assure you that I value your friendship more than your body.' He took out a small blue velvet box from his pocket and opened it. He took out the gold ring and slipped it on her third finger.

She looked puzzled. 'You seem to be anxious to get rid of me and at the same time you want me to remain with you. I don't understand you.'

'It's not very complicated. Your staying with me will hurt your career and your reputation. I don't want that to happen.' With a meaningful smile he added, 'You still owe me almost two months in services to be rendered. I will avail of them if and when you feel like clearing your debt. I can always put you up in this hotel; I get a hefty rebate as I bring my business partners here. We can spend our holidays together in some unknown place where no one knows us. You will keep in touch with me, won't you?' She nodded her head without committing herself in words.

Mohan finished his third Scotch. She a second sherry. He handed the waiter his credit card and placed two ten-rupee notes on the table for him.

'I have no appetite,' said Sarojini getting up, 'I'll sit with you while you have your dinner.'

'Me neither,' he replied, 'let's go home.'

On his way out he handed ten-rupee notes to the Sikh commissionaires who saluted him again. 'You squander your money without much concern,' she said as they got into the car.

'What else do you do with it?' he said. He half-expected a stern little lecture from her in response, in her best lady professor tone. He wanted to hear it. But she said nothing. He knew he would miss her badly.

The servants were still waiting for them when they got home. It was not yet 9 p.m. Mohan went through his ritual of locking the gate and latching the doors. For some reason he did not go to urinate in the garden.

'May I use your phone to ring up my parents?' she said.

'By all means, go ahead.'

She dialled the code and number. When her mother picked up

the phone, she asked, 'Mama, can I come over for a few weeks before my college re-opens?' Her mother must have replied, 'Of course. When will you come?' 'I'm not sure,' Sarojini said, 'I'll take the first train on which I can get a seat and let you know. How's my Munna?' She listened for a while, then said 'Good night' and put the phone down.

'All is well with everyone. Tomorrow I'll try to book my seat on the Dehra Dun Shatabdi Express. I believe it leaves New Delhi railway station very early in the morning—six or thereabouts.'

'Not to worry,' he replied. 'I'll have the office get your ticket and the reservation. No matter what time it leaves, I'll drive you to the railway station.'

'That will be kind,' she replied, 'but the reservation people will want my name, age and sex. You don't want to divulge all that to your staff, do you?'

'I hadn't thought of that. I'll ask my travel agent to do the booking and have the bill directed to me at my home address. He'll let me know tomorrow when he can get a berth. There should not be much traffic on this sector at this time of the year.'

Sarojini had been careful, yet somehow she had begun to feel that Mohan's house was hers to share as long as she liked. Now the bitter truth confronted her. She felt deserted and forlorn; the tedium of college routine in Rewari was all the reality she would know now. She put both her hands on her face and began to cry. Her mood sparked off a similar emotion in Mohan. He went down on his knees, put his head in her lap and started sobbing. They cried for some time. Sarojini ran her fingers through Mohan's hair and said very gently, 'We don't have to cry like babies; let's behave like grown ups. You know this is going to be much harder for me than for you. The world is more forgiving towards men. You will be envied; I will be condemned as a slut. But never mind that. For me it was a memorable experience.'

They stood up together. He took her in a tight embrace and in a hoarse voice said, 'Saroj, I love you.'

'Mohan, I too love you more than you can imagine.'

It was the first time in their month-long relationship that they had used the word love with each other. All night they lay in each other's arms; neither made any attempt to undress. The word love had made lust profane.

*

The next morning after Mohan left for the office, Sarojini started packing her clothes and books. The bearer and the sweeper woman were anxious to help but she turned down their offers and told them that she had very little to pack and did not want to be disturbed till lunch time. She had a frugal meal and asked Jiwan Ram to take her to Birla Temple. At the entrance she bought several leaf cups of rose petals to make offerings to all the gods and goddesses installed in different parts of the temple complex. She sat a long time, her eyes closed, in front of the idol of her favourite goddess, Saraswati, and chanted hymns in her praise.

She joined the congregation of worshippers at the Krishna temple where a keertan was going on. She fixed her gaze on Lord Krishna's graceful statue. The gentle blue god with both tenderness and mischief in his eyes, holding a flute to his lips. He was the one deity above all others in the pantheon of gods and goddesses who understood the physical compulsions of human beings and forgave them by setting an example. He had a lifelong love affair with his aunt, Radha, and innumerable village girls, married and unmarried. People worshipped him and no one dared to call him a womanizer or the women in his life harlots. And here was she, abandoned by her husband for no fault of hers, who had briefly found physical fulfilment with another man— what great sin had she committed?

Sarojini left the temple light of heart. She knew this chapter of her life was over. She would forge her future destiny with her own hands.

She was back in Mohan's house well before sunset. Jivan Ram went to fetch his boss. The first thing Mohan did as he came up to the balcony where she was sitting in silence watching the sunset was to fish out an envelope from his pocket and place it on the table beside her. 'Your ticket. The travel agent was able to get you a seat on tomorrow morning's Shatabdi. Better ring up your father straightaway and tell him to pick you up at the station. I think it gets to Dehra Dun around eleven.'

Sarojini rang up Dehra Dun and got her son on the line. She sounded happy. 'Hello, beta, I'll be with you tomorrow morning. Come with your nana to pick me up at the station. He knows the time the Delhi Shatabdi gets in.'

She put the phone down and came and sat next to Mohan. He thought he should say something but then saw that she was content. The sound of her son's voice had comforted her. And then he thought of his own loss. Sonu would now make sure he got to see as little of the children as possible. And she would turn them against him. When the bearer came to lay out the drinks, Sarojini gave him a hundred-rupee note. 'This is for you; I'll be leaving very early tomorrow morning. Send the cook and the jamadarni.' The bearer took the note and touched her feet. 'If I have erred in any way, please forgive me,' he said humbly. Sarojini knew he did not refer to any error on his part; it was the standard formula used by servants to express thanks. The cook and the jamadarni accepted their tips with both hands without saying anything. Sarojini examined her railway ticket. The computer print described her as Dr S. Bharadwaj, 37, F. It was as nondescript as could be. She put the ticket in her handbag.

They had their drinks and dinner without much conversation. The servants bade her goodbye and left for their quarters. Mohan went down to lock the gate and latch the doors. He marked another corner of the garden with his urine and came up to join her. 'I think we should go to bed early. I've set the alarm for four. It will give us plenty of time to wash up and get ready.'

They got up together. 'Can I spend this last night with you?' he asked.

'As you wish, I have a lot owing to you,' she replied.

'Don't make it sound so businesslike.'

She took his hand and led him to her bed. 'I'll do whatever you want me to do,' she said, taking off her clothes.

'I want you to do nothing except lie with me till the alarm clock wakes us up.'

They got into a tight embrace. She noticed that Mohan had no desire for sex; he only wanted the warmth of her body against his. They dozed off into a light sleep, turning away from each other, then turned round to encircle each other in their arms. The shrill ringing of the alarm clock roused Mohan in more ways than one. He found Sarojini awake and receptive. They rocked and buffetted against each other as if it was the last time in their lives they would savour each other's bodies. For both of them it was a farewell celebration.

They showered together. Sarojini changed, put the old clothes into her suitcase and declared that she was ready to leave. She did this firmly, determined not to give herself any chance to dawdle; there was still a temptation to delay the departure, but she should not succumb to it. The heavier case containing her books had been put in the boot of the car the night before. Mohan picked up the other suitcase and put it on the rear seat. He unlocked the front gate. They drove out into a deserted street with the street lights glowing eerily in the early dawn. The headlights caught an occasional newspaper vendor on his bicycle, tossing papers into peoples' houses and balconies, or a milk-seller, weaving his bicycle through non-existent traffic, cans dangling from the handle bars and the pillion seat. They drove past India Gate into Connaught Circus, past early morning walkers doing their rounds, wearing sweaters or shawls as the mornings had become quite chilly.

Despite the early hour, around the railway station there was bedlam—an unruly jumble of buses, cars, scooters, cyclists and pedestrians. They were assaulted by the ceaseless blowing of horns, the harsh glare of neon lights and people yelling at each other. It took Mohan some time to find a place in the parking lot and a coolie to carry Sarojini's two cases. They wove their way through the jostling crowd, up an overbridge and down to the designated platform. Mohan found Sarojini her coach and seat. The coolie placed both cases on the rack, took the ten-rupee note Mohan gave him. There were only a handful of passengers in the coach. Sarojini took her seat by the window.

He sat beside her. While he held her hand, he kept an eye on his wrist-watch—these Shatabdis were notoriously punctual and picked up speed very quickly. Tears welled up in Sarojini's eyes. Mohan held her face in his hands and wiped the tears off with his thumbs. 'This is not the end,' he assured her. 'We will keep in touch and meet whenever we can.' His assurance sounded hollow to him. And to her. A minute before the train was due to leave, he stood up. She also stood up. Without bothering about the other passengers they kissed passionately. As he came out of the compartment, he overheard a woman passenger hiss, 'Besharam (shameless)!'

That was the last Mohan saw of Sarojini. She did not call up or write. It took a few days for it to sink in that the Sarojini chapter of his life was over.

Five
After Sarojini

The first few days after Sarojini Bharadwaj left him, Mohan was a little confused by his feelings. He should be missing her: he did a little but not too much. The house looked emptier; curiously, he liked its emptiness—he had it all to himself once again, and that was a pleasant feeling. No one to talk to except himself. Switch on the TV, switch it off. Flip through magazines; toss them aside. Listen to film music on the transistor he kept beside his pillow; switch it off when sleep overtook him. Being absolutely alone had a lot to be said for it.

He ignored his servants. He wanted it to sink into them that they had been disloyal to him by gossiping about Sarojini. Most contrite was Dhanno. Although she had been temporarily deprived of privileges she had enjoyed and had reason to be sore with the intruder, she did not want her maalik to be annoyed with her for too long. He knew she was looking for an opportunity when she would find him alone. She would fall at his feet and crave his forgiveness. He took good care to see that she did not get the opportunity—not for some days to come.

He began to enjoy his evenings alone. A hot shower, a warm camel-hair dressing gown and woollen slippers against the growing autumn chill. Premium Scotch and an enveloping silence. He had much to ruminate over. Every evening he went over the liaisons he had had with women in his college years in the States. Besides him, those women had bedded Americans, Latinos and visiting Scandinavians, but that had never bothered him. In fact that suited him fine; it made them more inventive and uninhibited in bed. It was odd that he could vividly recollect first encounters in detail; how he had courted a particular woman, the first embrace and the love making that followed. Whatever subsequent meetings and beddings there had been had faded from his memory. It only went to prove that sex was really pleasurable only the first time with a new woman; it got less and less exciting when repeated with the same person.

Another conclusion he drew from his many affairs was that women were as eager to have sex with men they liked as men were to fuck them. And given the opportunity they were as willing to try out different men as men were to try out different women. He had no trouble bedding the women he dated. Some were brash and readily stripped themselves for action; others were a little coy to start with. Some were quick comers; others took a long time to climax. He did not much care for the second type because they gave him a feeling of inadequacy. Otherwise they were much the same: big bosomed or small, buxom or skinny, broad-hipped or narrow—when it came to the nitty-gritty, there was very little difference. As Indians would put it, 'Maharani or Mehtarani, same to same.'

Some evenings he brought out the letters and photographs of the women who had responded to his ad. He scrutinized their faces and fantasized about the kind of figures they might have. And how they would respond to his overtures. But he was not ready to take on anyone for some weeks or perhaps months. He put the correspondence back in his drawer lest he change his mind.

*

Dhanno was eager to catch her master alone. Mohan sensed her prowling around and took care not to give her the chance. He left home while the other servants were still around and returned when they were back on duty. After a fortnight, one morning Dhanno found the sahib sitting all by himself; the cook had gone out shopping, the bearer had gone to his quarter. He was smoking his post-breakfast cigar and was engrossed in the morning papers. He was taken unawares. He felt someone grabbing him by both his legs and putting her head between his knees. It was Dhanno. She wailed, 'Maalik, if I have erred, please forgive me; otherwise I will kill myself.' Mohan was familiar with the Indian habit of exaggerating everything. But he was not prepared to take on a sobbing Dhanno threatening suicide. He felt a reprimand was in order. 'You have been gossiping about my guest and me.'

'I had no right to do so,' she conceded. 'After all I have a man at home and yet I serviced you whenever you desired. What right had I to talk? Please, please forgive me this time. I swear by my children, I'll never do it again.'

That was not the end of her protestations. She continued: 'Put your hand on my head and say you have forgiven me. I am your daasi for this life and lives to come.' Mohan was embarrassed and wanted to put a quick end to the melodrama. He put a hand on Dhanno's head and said, 'It's all right, but don't let the servants see you behaving like this. They will make up all sorts of stories and I may be forced to dismiss you.'

Dhanno got up, blew her nose into her dupatta. As she turned away, she added, 'Where will I go if you dismiss me? I and my children will die of hunger.'

Mohan had no intention of dismissing her—only of bringing her to heel. A few days later it was he who told Dhanno that he would be sending both the servants out next morning and expected her to stay after she had finished sweeping the floors.

The following morning Dhanno came in a little later than usual. The sahib was ordering a special meal for the evening as he had invited some friends for dinner. He told the cook what to get from INA market. He gave the bearer a list of items he wanted from M.R. Stores—cheese crackers, savouries and a box of liqueur chocolates. The two servants finished their chores and left on their errands. Mohan latched the two doors from the inside and came up. Dhanno continued mopping the floor, pretending she had not noticed him. Mohan bent down, caught her by the waist and hoisted her to his bed. He stripped

her of her salwar-kameez and mounted her. After such a long gap a
body he had known so well seemed to have regained its newness.
And Dhanno was more than eager to please him. He pounded into
her and she kept begging for more, for that was what he wanted to
hear. It proved to be a successful reunion.

Dhanno got up from the bed. As she slipped on her clothes, she
asked, 'Sahibji, tell me the absolute truth: was your professor memsahib
better than I? I know you liked her only because she could git-pit in
English and I can't.'

*

With Sarojini back in Rewari, and no one to keep him tied to home
and routine, Mohan Kumar found himself frequenting the clubs and
parties that were an essential feature in the lives of Delhi's rich and
able. Delhi had its Young Achievers Club (YAC)—which soon changed
to the Young Millionaires Club (YMC)—of which Mohan was one of
the founder members. It did not have a constitution nor office bearers,
no premises, not even a list of members. Everyone knew everyone
else because only a dozen regarded themselves eligible for
membership. It was understood that if you made your first million
before you were forty, you were welcome to dinner parties arranged
in each other's homes. The inspiration for this club came from the
Yuppies of the United States of America. All YMC members were
products of US colleges. Not one came from a British university.
Americans were money oriented and money was what mattered to
young Oriental millionaires, regardless of how it was made.

Of supreme importance was the style of living. You had to have a
bungalow in one of New Delhi's posh residential localities and,
preferably, a farm house a short distance from the city centre. Three
cars were a must: a Mercedes Benz or a Toyota for the boss; a Maruti,
or a Fiat for the memsahib; and a third one as a spare. Keeping dogs of
high pedigree added to the owners' stature. German shepherds were
fine, but they were regarded as watch dogs. Dalmatians, Red Setters,
Cocker Spaniels, Boxers, Labradors were okay. But a huge Saint

Bernard for the sahib, a tiny Peke or a Chihuahua for the memsahib gave you class.

Membership of the top clubs of the city was of consequence. On top of the list was the Golf Club. Although its membership was restricted, if one paid in foreign currency, it made admission easier, as had happened in Mohan's case. Now Mohan was at the club almost every evening, drinking at the bar, entertaining or being entertained in the restaurant.

Of course, he was spouseless now. Everyone made a point of missing Sonu. She was the perfect wife for a young millionaire—at least outside the home. She had learnt how to adorn herself in a style becoming her husband's wealth. Nothing as flamboyant as heavy south Indian or Benares saris; light silks or chiffons of sober colours showed better taste. The diamonds she wore in her ears or as nose pins had to be small but sparkling. Her perfume or cologne had to be French. Mohan recalled that she never missed her weekly visit to a five-star hotel beauty parlour for a hair wash, hair dressing, facial, waxing of legs and arms, removing hair growth on the upper lip and the chin. The total came to a paltry Rs 1000 a visit. She gave him no peace, not even good sex, but made the most of his money. Spoilt bitch.

After a long time, Mohan got back onto the dinner circuit. He had half-enjoyed it once—all the care and planning. What set the young millionaires apart from other rich people was their style of entertainment. The Scotch had to be premium brand: Blue or Gold label Johnnie Walker, Royal Salute, Chivas Regal or Something Special. The wines had to be vintage French. The vodka had to be Russian, the gin English, the sherry Spanish, the liqueurs English or French. Extra care was taken over preparing menus and outside caterers were briefed on what was to be served and at what time. The crockery had to bear ancient names like Spode or Royal Doulton; the cut-glass, Lalique; the cutlery, Sterling Silver. The waiters had to be in uniforms and wear white gloves. Sonu had enjoyed these parties, chattering with the other memsahibs about the diplomats they had befriended and the troubles they had with their servants.

*

Mohan had two couples for dinner about a fortnight after Sarojini had left. They knew that he had parted company from his wife. So there would be no tension on that score. As they came up he shook hands with the men and kissed their wives on both cheeks. Kissing wives was *de rigueur*: cheeks if the husbands were looking, lips when they were not. 'So, you old bugger, how are you enjoying your bachelorhood?' asked Jas (Jaspal).

'No complaints,' replied Mohan (Mo to fellow YMC members, for they followed the American custom of using nick names for each other). 'It's more peaceful. No nagging, no quarrels. There is much to be said in favour of a broken marriage.'

'Particularly if you find a companion to share your loneliness,' added Jas's wife Satty (Satnam) with a mischievous twinkle in her eyes.

'So you've been listening to gossip,' remarked Mohan.

'Delhi is a small town. Things get round sooner than you think,' added Malik, who had no abbreviation for his name. 'Usually the people concerned are the last to hear what is being said about them.'

'How true,' everyone agreed. They went on to affairs of their other friends and how their businesses were doing. They bitched and gossiped. They drank and ate. They had coffee and liqueurs and lit their cigarettes or cheroots. The bearer removed the plates and glasses. Suddenly Dhanno made her appearance to collect the leftovers of the dinner party. All eyes turned to her. 'And who may this lady be who visits you at this late hour?' asked Satty.

'Oh, she!' answered Mohan tamely, 'she's the jamadarni. She's come to take the leftovers for her husband and children. She has a quarter at the back of the house.'

'Not bad for bad purposes,' remarked Jas.

'O for God's sake!' exploded Mohan. 'She's a sweeperess. I'm not a sex maniac to go after every pussy around.'

It was past midnight when they broke up, yawning and stretching their arms. Mo saw them off to their cars. The party had been a success.

II

The Memoirs of Mohan Kumar

Six
I, Mohan Kumar

I am Mohan Kumar, the man you have been reading about. My friend, Khushwant Singh, who has begun to write a novel based on my life, knows me well, but not well enough. I have persuaded him to let me speak for myself. I had never imagined I would ever need or have the time to record my life. But now that I am unwell and suddenly alone, I seek solace in memory, in thoughts of all the women I have known.

I was the only child of my parents. My mother died giving birth to me. I never knew a mother's love for her son; I have heard that it is a very special love, more so if the son is also the first born. Perhaps. My father sent for a wet nurse from Agra to breastfeed me for six months. My dead mother's unmarried sister looked after me for two years, then she got married and I became a single parent child.

My father was a superintendent in the office of the Northern Railway. We lived in the clerks' quarters close to New Delhi railway station. There was a young maidservant who cooked for us and kept our quarters clean. During the day, when my father was away at work, she kept an eye on me as I played with the neighbours' children. Sometimes, when we were alone and if I pestered her enough, she would lift her kameez to her neck and let me suck her breasts. I was a child then, but I have a good memory—I remember her breasts were smooth and firm and large. In the summer, they glistened with sweat and tasted salty.

When I was five years old, my father got me admitted into a government primary school. My teachers discovered that while I did reasonably well in most subjects, I got every answer to every question in arithmetic right. It was the same in high school; I got full marks in arithmetic, algebra and geometry. That usually put me on top of my class. My father had me take Sanskrit as a special subject. All I was required to do was to mug up original texts and their Hindi translations. I was gifted with a good memory, so I had yet another subject in which I could score full marks. I did well enough in high school to win a state scholarship to DAV college.

Nothing of consequence happened in college, except that I continued to do well academically. Though only sixteen when I entered college, I was already almost six feet tall, a couple of inches taller than my father. It was probably a gift my mother left in my genes. But I was not much interested in sports. The only exercise I did was surya namaskar and some yoga asanas including sheersh asana (head-stand) in the mornings and evenings. That kept me fit without making me muscular. Despite my father being a devout Arya Samaji and the fact that I was studying in an Arya Samaj college, I did not take to religion. Apart from occasionally reciting the Gayatri mantra I said no prayer, nor did I go to the college temple.

I topped the university in the degree examinations. The principal of my college suggested I apply for a scholarship to an American university. He got me the forms from the American embassy and helped me fill them out. I got offers from six universities. My principal advised me to opt for Princeton, where Einstein had taught mathematics and made his home. A senior member of the embassy staff who was an old Princetonian gave me letters of introduction to some professors he knew and showed me pictures of the campus.

In late September, 1975, I took an Air India flight from Delhi to New York. My father was the only one to see me off at Palam Airport. I remember well his parting advice: 'Puttar (son), do whatever you like in America, but don't marry a white woman and never touch bada maas (beef).' I was embarrassed, as at the time the idea of marriage was nowhere in my mind, and I was revolted by the idea of people slaughtering cows for meat.

Seven

Jessica Browne

An hour's bus ride from New York brought me to Princeton. Unlike in Indian colleges where old students make it a point to be nasty to newcomers, I was immediately made welcome. A senior student had been deputed to familiarize me with the campus. He met me at the bus stop, took my suitcase from my hand and showed me to my room in the hostel where I was to stay. He showed me where the loos, the showers and the cafeteria were located, then brought me back to my room and told me where I could find him if I needed further help.

Before I unpacked, I recited the Gayatri mantra. I took a shower and changed my clothes. The student who had taken me round the campus took me with him to the cafeteria. There was a long queue of boys, girls and teachers waiting for their turn to be served. My guide pointed to several distinguished professors, two of them Nobel Laureates, who stood in line behind us. I was not familiar with the kind of food being served but I knew Americans were cow-eaters, and I could not tell beef from other kinds of meat. So I stuck to vegetables, mostly mashed potatoes, carrots and beans, which were all quite tasteless.

We shared our table with other students. Introductions were made. Since they found my name, Mohan Kumar, too much of a mouthful, from the very first evening they began to call me Mo. They assumed that since I had a full scholarship, I must be bright. After dinner a group of them including a couple of girls who were also newcomers were taken round the campus. What beautiful buildings! Some looked as ancient as the Cambridge and Oxford colleges that I had seen pictures of, others seemed to be made of steel and plate glass. There were tennis courts, baseball stadia and football grounds. And everywhere stood huge trees—oaks and beeches. The maple leaves had begun to turn a copper colour. I knew I was going to love the place.

I found Americans very easy to get on with. They were open, frank and aggressively friendly. They were without guile and only lied to avoid hurting people's feelings. I soon discovered that as a nation Americans had more to them in inventiveness than any other people I had known. There was a six-storey building in Princeton, designed by a Japanese architect. When they found it was too close to the road, they simply raised the entire structure from its foundations and placed it in its new site, without disturbing even the furniture and fittings. Near one of the students' hostels there was a lot of vacant land. They thought it would look nicer if it was a forest. No problem. They excavated huge pits and planted half-grown pine and fir trees in them, and in a month they had their forest. A month later birds were nesting in the trees. Which other people could do such things?

*

Princeton offered a lot of courses. Since business management and computers were my main subjects, I was left with many options. I decided on international affairs and comparative religion as additional subjects. I was expected to attend these classes once a week. The rest of the time I could concentrate on my main subjects.

Within a few months of joining the university, I had made some good friends. As I have said, I had no great interest in sports, but my American friends were determined to reform me. They persuaded me to take up games. I gave in, and decided to try my hand at tennis. What followed the first game changed the course of my life.

After sweating it out on the tennis court, I went along with the boys to take a shower. I was shocked to see them strip naked and exchange obscenities about the sizes of their penises as they soaped themselves. I had never exposed myself to anyone before. Very reluctantly I took off my shorts, wrapped a towel around my waist and stood under a shower.

'Hey ho! what are you hiding behind the towel?' yelled one of the boys. 'Or don't you have anything there?' Very gingerly I undid my towel and quickly positioned myself under the shower, hoping for some cover in the spray of water.

'Holy Moses!' cried the boy. 'Look at this one. A real Hindu lingam.'

I became the centre of attention. Indeed my penis was thicker and larger than that of any other boy, white or black.

'You measure this thing with a tape and send it to the Guiness Book of Records. The biggest doodah in the world,' one fellow shouted.

'Ever put that inside a pussy?' asked another.

I knew what he meant but refused to answer what seemed to me a very vulgar question.

Soon my private endowment became public knowledge. 'He's got the biggest dong on the campus,' they said behind my back. One evening a boy asked me the Hindi word for it.

'Lund,' I replied.

'Sounds Swedish,' he remarked.

'Also Laura.'

'Sounds like a girl's name.'

I offered a third choice: 'Lullah.'

'That sounds better than prick or dong: prick makes it the size of a pin; dong something limp and hanging. Lullah is masculine and upright.'

From the boys' tales about the size of my penis travelled to their girl friends. It was hardly the kind of thing I would have liked to be known for in the university. But it paid dividends. Girls were curious to see what their boy friends had seen.

By now I had started going out with girls. It was the done thing, though I felt a little self-conscious in the company of white girls. Then, by sheer luck, I ran into Jessica Browne. She was a sophomore, a year senior to me, and the best woman tennis player in the university. One afternoon after I had finished my game I watched her practising with the coach on the neighbouring court. What a figure the girl had! Tall, slender and chocolate-brown. A big bosom, narrow hips, protruding buttocks and long athletic legs. She sprinted about the court like a panther. I was entranced and gaped at her open-mouthed. When she finished playing with the coach she came up to me and asked, 'Like to knock up with me?'

'I'm a novice; I started to play only a few days ago,' I replied.

'Never mind,' she said taking my hand and hauling me up on my feet, 'I'll teach you.'

I made a fool of myself. She stood in the middle of the court and gently patted the ball from side to side and made me run like a rabbit till I ran out of breath. 'You play with me a few afternoons and you'll pick up the game very fast. There's nothing much to it,' she assured me.

We introduced ourselves, and she promised to meet me at the courts every afternoon. I looked forward to the ten minutes of coaching she gave me every day. We became friends. Jessica became my regular date. Almost every evening after a session on the tennis court, followed by supper, we went for a stroll. We held hands at the pictures. When saying good night, we started with a peck on the cheeks, progressed to kissing on the lips, and then full blooded mouth kissing—she would roll her tongue in my mouth. She sensed that I lacked the confidence to go further and decided to take the initiative. She asked me to have a drink with her in her room. By now I had started drinking a glass or two of beer every now and again. I went to her room. She greeted me with a lusty French kiss. I got worked up. 'Jessica, you have a beautiful figure, the best I have ever seen,' I told her.

'Want to see what I'm really like?' she asked. And without waiting for an answer she slipped off her blouse and skirt. I had never seen a naked woman before. She certainly was beautiful in the African way: jet black fuzzy hair, lustrous eyes and protruding breasts with large black nipples. I was too shy to look below her waist.

'Never seen a naked woman before?' she asked sensing my embarrassment.

'Never,' I replied, 'you are the first.'

'Take them off,' she ordered and strode up to me, her breasts bobbing. I obeyed and stripped myself naked.

'Goodness gracious me!' she chortled. 'Where on earth did you buy that one? Black boys have bigger dicks than the whites but yours is bigger than any I've been. Are all Hindus as well endowed?'

'I have no idea,' I replied.

She clasped it in both her hands and asked, 'Baby, you still a virgin?'

'I'm a man!' I protested. 'Only girls are virgins.'

She laughed, 'If you haven't slept with a girl, son, you're a virgin. We'll soon take care of that.'

She took me to her bed, pulled me above her and directed my thing into her. I felt giddy and breathless with sheer joy as she took me in. She gasped with pleasure as I went right inside her. I could not control myself. This was my first time and I spent myself, moaning helplessly, almost as I entered her. I had never imagined sex could be so thrilling. But I wished it had lasted longer.

'Never mind,' she consoled me. 'The first time it is always like this. As we say, "Wham, bam, thank you ma'am." But it's not over yet.'

'No,' I breathed and dug my face between her breasts. It was not long before I felt my member stiffen and grow against her thigh. I fell on her greedily.

I was determined to do it again and again till it killed me. And so I did.

Boys were not allowed to stay in girls' rooms after 9 p.m. The consequences of being caught after that hour could be serious. But neither of us cared about the consequences. We lay together all night. We made love four times before we dropped off. The next morning I walked out of her room carrying an armful of books to explain away my presence in the girls' dorm. That was how I, Mohan Kumar, aged twenty, lost my virginity.

Those were blissful days. I could not have enough of Jessica; Jessica could not have enough of me. It was like a honeymoon without a wedding. After classes we went out together hand-in-hand for everyone to see that ours was a permanent relationship. On weekends we went to New York by bus and ate in Indian restaurants. On our way back we stopped at Trenton where her parents lived and spent a few hours with them. They were high school teachers and active in the movement for racial equality. They would have preferred Jessica having a black boy friend but were somewhat relieved to see that I was brown and not a white Caucasian.

I learnt a lot about America from Jessica when we went for walks in the woods. She showed me the cottage in which Einstein had lived. She told me the names of trees and birds: the bright red cardinal, different kinds of woodpeckers and squirrels. When we were drinking beer in a bar she told me about Martin Luther King and Malcolm X and the black Muslims; the Ku Klux Klan and the WASPs. She often got very worked up while talking of racial slights she had suffered. Once when she was out with a white boy, a gang of white hoodlums had shouted 'nigger-lover' and roughed up her companion; no one had come to their rescue. 'Your best bet is to stick to a boy who is neither white nor black,' I said to her, patting her hand. She was too angry with the world to respond.

Thus passed my first winter in America. Jessica and I trudged over paths covered with snow; when the snow thawed we saw the tiny green leaves burst on the bare branches of trees. We fed red and grey squirrels peanuts and saw snowdrops and daffodils bloom in campus lawns.

I thought my friendship with Jessica would hold as long as I was in the States. In fact, it did not last much beyond spring. No sooner had the first cherry and magnolia trees come into flower than our relationship soured. I noticed that Jessica got irritated with me over small things. Once when I invited her to come and watch me play a tennis match for freshmen, followed by a dinner dance for which I had bought two tickets, she flatly turned down my invitation. I was hurt. When I told her so, she snapped at me, 'You Orientals are very possessive about your women. I'm not your property. I'm not your wife!'

We began to drift apart. After a few days we stopped dating. Then I saw her go out with another boy, hand-in-hand. I felt a stab of jealousy in my heart. Jealousy is something Americans disdain as a medieval emotion. You break up with one, you take up with another. Then another. There were plenty of girls around Princeton—big beautiful blondes with huge breasts almost bursting through their sweaters; petite Jewish girls with curly black hair and Oriental features; European girls and girls from Mexico and Latin America. Many were eager to date me. So I wrote Jessica off my list of dates and went on the rampage like a stud bull in a herd of cows on heat. I lost count of the girls I bedded the following spring and summer. Now even their names escape me. Only one remains because it was a most bizarre experience.

Eight
Yasmeen

I met Yasmeen attending classes in comparative religion in the department of religion and philosophy.

I had begun to enjoy the lectures on religion by Dr Ashby, our professor. There was a motley group of students in his class from different disciplines— medicine, literature, engineering and others. Among the thirty odd who were regulars, there were two nuns and a woman in salwar-kameez in her late thirties. She wore a lot of gold jewellery and was heavily made up. Since she did not wear a bindi, I presumed she was Muslim. She sat in the front row. I always sat in the last. After each lecture, there were discussions, and some students, the Muslim woman in the front row in particular, had much to say. I took no part in them since I knew very little about any religion.

Dr Ashby took us through the world's major religions: Zoroastrianism, Jainism, Buddhism, Judaism, Hinduism, Christianity and Islam. I was most interested in hearing what he had to say about Hinduism. Despite being a Hindu I knew almost nothing about my religion besides the names of Hindu gods and goddesses and the Gayatri mantra. Three lectures were devoted to Hinduism. Dr Ashby told us of the four Vedas, the Upanishads and the Bhagvad Gita. They made more sense to me than the other religious texts he had dealt with. 'Worship God in any form you like, that essentially is what Hinduism says,' explained Dr Ashby. 'Hindus have no prescribed scriptures: no Zend-Avesta, no Torah, no Bible, no Koran. Read what moves you the most. Seek the Truth within yourself.' And how spiritually elevating was the message of the Gita as the professor explained it—Nish kama karma: do your duty without expectation of reward. When you engage in the battle of life, do so regardless of whether you win or lose, whether it gives you pleasure or pain. There was also the Lord's promise to come again and again to redeem the world from sin and evil-doing. Hinduism had no prophets, no one God, we were told. One could choose any deity one liked and worship him or her. By the end of that lecture I felt elated and wanted to shout: 'I am a Hindu and proud of being one.'

It was that woman in the front row who dampened my spirits. She launched into a furious monologue. 'Professor,' she began as soon as Dr Ashby had finished, 'what you said about Hindu philosophy is all very well. But tell us, why do the Hindus of today worship a monkey as a god, an elephant as a god; they worship trees, snakes, and rivers. They even worship the lingam, which is the phallus, and the yoni, the female genital, as god and goddess,' she screeched, thumping her desk. 'They have obscene sculptures on their temple walls. They have deities for measles, smallpox and plague. Their most popular god, Krishna, started out as a thief and lied when caught thieving; he stole girls' clothes while they were bathing so he could watch them naked; he had over one thousand mistresses; his lifelong companion was not his wife but his aunt Radha. Hinduism is the only religion in the world which declares a section of its followers outcastes by accident of birth. Hindus are the only people in the world who worship living humans as godmen and godwomen. I am told that there are nearly five hundred such men and women who claim to be bhagwans. They believe a dip in the Ganges washes away all their sins, so they can start sinning again! What basis is there for their belief that after death you are reborn in another form depending on your actions in this life? You may be reborn as a rat, mouse, cat, dog or a snake. This is what the Hindus of today believe in, not in the elevated teachings of the Vedas, Upanishads and the Gita! Should we not examine these aspects of Hinduism as it is practised today?'

There was stunned silence. The woman had spoken with such

vehemence that there was little room left for objective dialogue. Dr Ashby restored the atmosphere to an academic level. 'This sort of thing could be said about all religions,' he said gently. 'What their founders taught and what their scriptures stand for are far removed from how they are interpreted and practised today. Our concern is with theory and not practice. Muslims condemn the worship of idols, yet they kiss the meteorite stone in the Kaaba and millions worship the graves of their saints.'

'I can explain Muslim practices,' replied the lady.

Before she could do so, however, the class was over.

'We will resume this discussion next week,' said Professor Ashby as he left the classroom.

I was fuming with rage. As the class began to disperse I quickly walked up to the woman and asked her, 'Madam, why do you hate Hindus so much?'

She was taken aback. 'I don't hate Hindus,' she protested. 'I don't hate anyone.' She looked me up and down as if she was seeing me for the first time. It had not occurred to her that I could be an Indian. She was contrite! 'Are you a Hindu from Bharat?' she asked.

'I am,' I replied as tersely as I could, 'and proud of being both. And I don't worship monkeys, elephants, snakes, phalluses or yonis. My religion is enshrined in one word, Ahimsa—don't hurt anyone.'

She apologized. 'Please forgive me if I hurt your feelings. Perhaps one day you will enlighten me and clear the misgivings I have about Hindus and Bharat.' She put out her hand as a gesture of friendship. I shook it without much enthusiasm.

'My name is Yasmeen Wanchoo,' she said. 'I am from Azad Kashmir on a leadership grant.'

'I'm Mohan Kumar, from Delhi. I'm in business management and computer sciences.'

Like many Kashmiri women Yasmeen was as fair-skinned as Caucasian women. She had nut-brown hair, large gazelle eyes and was fighting a losing battle with fat. She had a double chin, her arms had sagging flesh and there were tyres developing about her waist. She was, as the Punjabis say, goree chittee gole matole—fair, white and roly poly. She was the first Pakistani woman I had ever spoken to, also the first Muslim. I wanted to know if there was any truth in the stories I had heard about Pakistanis hating Indians and the contempt Muslims had for Hindus. I hoped Yasmeen Wanchoo would tell me. It was not very long ago that our two countries had fought a war, their third, but I did not hate Pakistanis. Her outburst had shocked me. I have never understood hatred.

At the next class she came up to me and said, 'No hard feelings. Come and sit next to me.' I declined. 'Madam, I sit in the last row, I hate being in the front.'

'In that case I'll sit with you in the last row. And do not Madam me, it makes me feel old. I am Yasmeen. And if you don't mind I'll call you Mohan.'

At the time I had no steady date so I kept company with Yasmeen. She turned out to be not as aggressive as I had thought, and I began pulling her leg often about her being anti-Hindu and anti-Indian. She told me more about herself. 'My parents lived in Srinagar, now the capital of Indian occupied Kashmir. Our forefathers were Brahmin Pandits till they had the good sense to convert to Islam. It is the best religion in the world. My parents lived in Srinagar till the Indian army occupied it, then they migrated to Muzaffarabad, the capital of Free Kashmir. I was born and educated there. I married another refugee from India, a Kashmiri, also of Brahmin descent—though Muslims, we don't marry below our caste. My husband is a minister in the Azad Kashmir Government. I am also active in politics and a member of the Assembly. We have two children.' I asked her if she did not prefer the freedom she had in America to her life in Pakistan. She would not give me a straight answer. When I persisted, she got a little irritated and said, 'I love my family and my watan. We may not have succeeded yet, but one day we will liberate Kashmir from India's clutches and I will return to Srinagar which I have only seen in pictures.'

'And plant the Pakistani flag on Delhi's Red Fort,' I quipped.

'Inshallah!' she replied, beaming a smile at me.

'One day we will liberate your so-called Azad Kashmir from the clutches of Pakistan and make it a part of Indian Kashmir again.'

'You live in a fool's paradise,' she said warming up. 'One Muslim warrior can take on ten of you Hindus.'

'So it was proved in the last war,' I replied sarcastically. 'The Pakistani army laid down arms after only thirteen days of fighting. Ninety-four thousand five hundred valiant Muslim warriors surrendered tamely to infidel Hindus and Sikhs without putting up a fight. In the history of the world there is no other instance of such abject surrender of an entire army.'

'Now you are being cruel,' she said, almost whined. 'You Indians are cheats. You misled those miserable Bengalis to rise against their Muslim brethren. Now they hate your guts and want to regain our friendship. You see what happens in the next Indo-Pak war.'

Despite our heated arguments Yasmeen and I became friends. She could hardly be described as my date as she was almost twenty years older than me. She sought my company because there were not many men or women of her age on the campus. Though young, I was at least from her part of the world; she could talk to me in Hindustani. We often had coffee together. One day, out of the blue, she gave me a Gold Cross pen as a gift. I did not have much money to spare as I sent much of what I saved from my stipend, and what I earned doing odd jobs in the library or working in the cafeteria, to my father. However, I started looking into shop windows to find something suitable as a return gift for Yasmeen.

After a couple of weeks Professor Ashby went on to Islam. He gave us a long list of books to read—various histories of the Arabs, biographies of Prophet Mohammed, translations of the Koran, essays on Muslim sects and sub-sects. I did not bother to read any of them. What I looked forward to was Yasmeen's comments after the lectures. She did not disappoint me.

She kept her peace during the first two lectures in which Professor Ashby dealt with pre-Muslim Arabia, the life of the Prophet, revelations of the Koran, the Prophet's flight from Makka to Madina, his victorious return to Makka, the traditions (hadith) ascribed to him, the speed at which his message spread to neighbouring countries, the Shia-Sunni schism, and so on. It was factual information but not very inspiring. As soon as he had finished his second lecture, Yasmeen shot up from her seat beside me and delivered an impassioned harangue. 'What you have told us about Islam is historically accurate, Dr Ashby. What you haven't told us is why it is today the most vibrant of religions. This is because it is the most perfect of all religious systems with precise rules of do's and don'ts which everyone can follow. It was only to Prophet Mohammed (peace be upon Him) that God Himself sent down His message for mankind. Mohammed (peace be upon Him) was the most perfect human being that ever trod the face of the earth. There must be some reason behind the spectacular success of His mission. Within a few years of His death, Islam spread like wildfire from the Pacific Coast to the Atlantic Coast of Europe; it spread all over Asia and the African continent. It overcame the opposition of fire worshippers, Jews, Christians, Buddhists and Hindus. Why does Islam gain more converts than any other religion? These are some of the questions that I would like the class to discuss.'

She sat down breathless after her speech. Only one student, a mild-mannered Jew who always wore a skullcap, took up her challenge. 'Perhaps the lady can answer some of my questions before I answer hers,' he said. 'Can she deny that Islam borrowed most of its ideas from Judaism? Their greeting, salam valaikum, is derived from the Hebrew shalom alech; the names of their five daily prayers are taken from Judaism. We turn to Jerusalem to pray; they borrowed the idea from us but instead turn to Makka. Following the Jewish practice they circumcise their male children. They have taken the concept of haraam (unlawful) and halaal (legitimate), what to eat and what not to eat, from the Jewish kosher. We Jews forbid eating pig's meat because we regard it unclean; Muslims do the same. We bleed animals to death before we eat them. Following us, so do they. They revere all the Prophets revered by Jews and Christians. What was there in Islam which was very new? Everything it has is borrowed from Judaism or Christianity.'

Yasmeen was up on her feet again to give battle to the Jew. 'What was new was the advent of Prophet Mohammed (peace be upon Him). He was the greatest of all prophets sent by Allah, and every

Muslim anywhere in the world knows this. We recognize no one after Mohammed (peace be upon Him).'

The Jew did not take that lying down: 'What about the division between Sunnis and Shias? Shias pay greater deference to the Prophet's cousin and son-in-law Ali than they do to the Prophet. And what about Muslim sects founded on sub-prophets of their own? The Aga Khan's, Ismailies, Bohras, Ahmediyas and many others whose names I can't even remember? And while we are at it, I would like the lady to enlighten us on why when Islam talks of giving a fair deal to women, it allows four wives to men, why many Muslim rulers maintained large harems of women and eunuchs. Why are they forever calling for jehad—holy war—with infidels and fighting against each other?'

It was degenerating into a pointless wrangle. Professor Ashby put an end to it. 'I see we are in for another lively debate. Perhaps you can discuss these issues outside the class.'

The lecture period was over. Yasmeen's face was flushed with anger and triumph. 'Don't you think I put that miserable Jew in his place?' she asked me as we walked out. Instead of answering her question, I asked her, 'Yasmeen, why are you so kattar (bigoted)? Muslims are the most bigoted religious community in the world. Their Prophet was the greatest, their religion is the best, Muslims are the most enlightened community, the most God-fearing and righteous of all mankind. If the Jews think they are God's chosen people, Muslims think they are the choicest of the chosen. How can you be so narrow-minded?'

She was taken aback. 'We are not bigoted,' she retorted. 'We follow our religious precepts in letter and in spirit because we know they are the best for humanity. You must give me the opportunity to tell you of the beauty of Islam. You don't know what you are missing in life.'

'I'm happy in my ignorance,' I replied. 'I don't have much patience with any religion. All I say is try not to injure anyone's feelings. The rest is marginal. Gods, prophets, scriptures, rituals, pilgrimages mean very little to me.'

She made no comment.

*

Yasmeen had only a week left in Princeton. Having failed to find anything more suitable to give her, I bought her a university ring made of silver with the Princeton emblem on it. At a coffee session one morning when no one was sharing our table, I took it out of my pocket and slipped it on her finger. 'I see you wear only gold but I could not afford a gold ring. And this being a university ring no one will comment about it. You could have bought it yourself but I'm giving it to you so that it will remind you of your days with a Bharati Hindu boy in Princeton.'

She took my hand and kissed it.

A faint blush came over her face. 'You are a nice boy. I only wish your name was not Mohan Kumar but Mohammed Kareem——or something like that,' she laughed. 'I am not as kattar as you think. I am just concerned about your future.'

During her last week in Princeton we met every day. We spent the afternoons walking around the campus and shopping. She bought lots of things for her husband and children and her household in Muzaffarabad. She seemed to have plenty of cash and dollar traveller's cheques. Came her last day. She invited me for dinner. 'Have you ever tasted Kashmiri food? It is the tastiest in the world, only very rich. I am a good cook. I can make very good goshtaba. Ever tasted goshtaba?'

I admitted that I had not.

'You must tell me what you don't eat,' she said. 'You Hindus have so many food fads. I know you don't eat beef or veal, but believe me, it is the most delicious meat. So many of you are vegetarian; no fish, not even eggs. Some even refuse to eat onions or garlic. How can you make anything tasty without onions or garlic, I ask you?'

'I eat everything except beef. Not that I regard the cow as sacred but because I have been brought up like that. And let me assure you that pig's meat, which you will not touch, can be very clean and tasty: ham, bacon, pork are the staple diet of most Europeans and Americans. One reason why I don't think Islam will spread to the Pacific islands is because their economy is based on the pig. And I know that like the

Jews many Muslims don't eat shrimps, crabs or lobsters. Muslim tribes living along the Arabian and African coast don't eat fish because they think fish are serpents of the sea.'

'You are a very argumentative fellow,' she said patting my cheek. 'Come tomorrow evening as early as you can and sample my Kashmiri cooking. I don't drink but I'll get some beer for you and put it in the fridge.'

I swear I had nothing more on my mind than spending a pleasant evening with Yasmeen. Things did not turn out that way. I took her a bunch of dark red roses. She kissed my hands as I gave them to her and embraced me warmly. While I was casually dressed in a sports shirt and slacks, she wore a silk salwar-kameez with gold borders, a gold necklace with a medallion on which was inscribed a verse from the Koran, gold earrings and gold bangles. She had a lot of make-up on and had doused herself with French perfume. Besides beer in the fridge she had put a half bottle of Scotch, a tumbler and a pitcher of water on the centre table. 'You help yourself to Scotch or beer while I say my evening namaaz.'

She went to her bedroom, put her prayer mat on the floor and stood facing Makka. I poured out a Scotch for myself. While I sipped it, I saw her going through her genuflections. She sat a long time on her knees with the palms of her hands open in front of her face as if reading their lines. I could see her lips moving but could not hear what she was reciting. She looked serene. She turned her face one way, then the other, brushed her face with her hands and stood up. She rolled up her prayer mat and tucked it under her bed.

She went into the kitchen to make sure the goshtaba was cooking nicely and lowered the flame so that it could cook slowly. Then she came and joined me. 'How's the drink?' she asked. 'Very nice,' I replied. 'Would you like one?'

'Tauba! It is haraam. You will make me a sinner, will you? You can fetch me a coke from the fridge.'

I got out a can of coke. Before I could open it, she took it from my hand and put it on the table. Then she held my hands in hers and looked into my eyes till I had to lower my gaze, embarrassed. Suddenly, she put her arms round my neck and said, 'It is our last evening together. Make love to me. Something to remember you by for the rest of my days.'

To say that I was shocked would be an understatement. This was the last thing I had expected of the evening. Besides, Yasmeen had never appeared sexually desirable to me. But she did not give me a chance to protest. She took me by my hand and led me to the bedroom. She took off everything save her jewellery. Her skin was soft but flabby. Her big breasts sagged and she had shaved her pubic hair. None of the girls I had bedded shaved their privates. I was surprised to see that a woman so large who had borne two children, had such a small vagina. It looked vulnerable. While I gazed at her figure, she took off my shirt and pulled down my trousers. She gasped at what she saw. 'Mashallah! What have you got there? Do all Hindus have organs of this size? It must be their reward for worshipping the phallus.' She fondled it for a while with her pudgy hands, her lips glued to mine.

She pulled me over her and stretched her thighs wide to receive me. I entered her. She moaned with pleasure and locked her legs behind my back. She ate up my face with bites and passionate kisses. We came together.

She lay back exhausted. Then she pushed me off her and went into the bathroom to wash. She came back and put on her kameez. 'That goshtaba must be ready by now. It must not get overcooked. You wash yourself and I'll lay the dinner on the table.'

I did as I was told. She was like a political boss in full command of the situation. We sat down to eat. I noticed she had not put on her salwar. Her kameez hung down to her knees, exposing her broad thighs when she stood up or sat down. I understood she had not finished with me and expected another session after dinner. I was not sure if I would be up to it with her. But I let myself in for it by a thoughtless gesture. While she was washing the dishes and I was drying them with a piece of cloth, I put my right hand under her kameez and stroked her huge buttocks. They were like two gourds of a taanpura joined together—massive, rounded, smooth. She beamed a smile and kissed me on the lips. 'You want to do it a second time? So do I. We will make it different this time.' That did it.

For a while we sat holding hands and chatted away. She told me of her daily schedule in Muzaffarabad. 'With both my husband and I being in politics we hardly have a moment to ourselves. It is like a public durbar from sunrise to sunset. Wherever we go we are surrounded by men and women with petitions. For me being here is like being on a holiday. I wish I could extend it but my grant is over and my family will want to know why I am not taking the first flight back to Karachi and home.'

She stood up and stretched her arms above her head and stifled a yawn. 'Time for bed,' she said taking me by the hand and leading me to her bed. She gently pushed me on it. 'This time you relax and I'll do all the work!'

She pulled off my trousers and fondled my limp lingam till it was ready for action. She sat astride my middle, spread her ample frame over me and directed my phallus into her. She was wet and eager and my penis slid in easily. Her breasts smothered my face. She held each in turn and put its nipple in my mouth, urging me to suck it. She kissed me hungrily and noisily on my nose, lips and neck, leaving her saliva on me, while she heaved and thumped me with her huge buttocks. 'I haven't had sex for six months. I am famished,' she said as her movements became more frenzied. 'Fill me up with all you have, you miserable kafir,' she screamed. And with a spectacular shudder and a loud ha, ha, ha she collapsed on me like a lifeless corpse. She did all the fucking. I was simply fucked.

'Wouldn't it be nicer if we settled Pak-India problems this way rather than by abusing each other and fighting?' she asked after a while.

'Sure,' I replied. 'And with Pakistan always on top?'

'Of course! Pakistan must always be on top.'

I was exhausted and wanted to get away.

She clung to me and begged, 'Please stay the night with me. I'll feel very lost if you go away. I promise I won't bother you any more.'

I agreed to spend the night with her and see her off at the bus stand the next morning. I could not resist asking her a few awkward questions. 'You must tell me how you square your belief in Islamic values with what you and I have been doing.'

She paused a long time, fixed me with her large eyes. 'What I did was sinful,' she admitted.

'A sin punishable with death by stoning?'

She was quiet for a long time.

'Doesn't your conscience bother you?' I asked.

'The body has its compulsions,' she said.

'I'm sure it has, but that's the easy way to square your conscience.'

'What would you have me do?'

'I have no idea. But surely there must be something in your religion that allows you to absolve yourself of your sins by going on a pilgrimage?'

'I suppose so,' she said evasively.

'Like the Hindus being forgiven if they take a dip in the Holy Ganga?' I teased.

'O shut up!' she shouted angrily. 'Don't spoil my last night with you.'

She put her head on my right arm and nestled against me. 'You are more curious about things than is good for you.'

'What do you mean?'

'You know, all those questions about my religion and my conscience.'

I laughed and pulled her close and kissed her passionately.

We were soon fast asleep in each other's arms.

I don't know when she slipped out of bed. When I awoke I saw her saying her morning namaaz on the prayer mat by the bed. She had bathed and dressed without my hearing anything. I did not interrupt her prayer and went to her bathroom to take a shower. I had not brought anything with me. I brushed my teeth with her wet tooth brush, and shaved my chin with the razor she had used to shave her pubic hair. When I came out she had finished her prayer and was laying breakfast on the table. The fragrance of fresh coffee filled the apartment.

I took her in my arms and held her in a tight embrace. When I released her I saw her eyes were damp with tears. We had our toast and coffee in silence. She asked me to ring up for a taxi and gave me the key to her apartment to hand over to the caretaker after she left. I offered to accompany her to New York and then to Kennedy Airport. She was quite firm in turning me down. 'The Pakistani Consulate is sending someone to meet me at the Port Authority bus terminal and drive me to the airport. Many Pakistanis know me from my pictures in the papers and appearances on TV. Some of the staff of Pakistan International Airways are sure to recognize me. Being seen off by a Bharati Hindu would not be a very bright idea,' she said.

I took her suitcases down. A taxi pulled up as soon as I had put her three bags on the kerb. The cabby helped me put them in the boot. 'Bus stand for New York bound buses,' I told him as we got into the rear seat. She let me hold her hand. We had no words left to say to each other.

I paid off the taxi. Five minutes later the New York bus pulled up. I put her cases in the back of the bus. I took her in my arms once more without bothering about who was looking and kissed her passionately on her lips. She hurried into the bus, adjusting her hair. She took her seat. She did not turn to look at me or wave goodbye. I saw her bend down and put her face in her hands.

That was the last I saw of Yasmeen Wanchoo.

But I thought of her often. Every time I met a Muslim, man or woman, she came back to my mind. Every time anyone brought up the subject of Indo-Pak relations or the continuing tension over Kashmir, I was reminded of Yasmeen Wanchoo. Although it was not I who had taken the lead but she who had manouvred me into having sex with her, and despite the fact that our copulation was by no means an earth-shattering experience because neither of us was in the slightest way emotionally involved with the other, it had somehow drained out whatever anti-Muslim and anti-Pakistan prejudices I had imbibed during my school and college years in India. Whenever anyone said anything against Muslims, my hackles rose because I had been made love to by a Muslim woman. Whenever anyone said anything against Pakistan, I strongly defended that country because I had been

made love to by a Pakistani woman. It was not love but lust that
proved to be a great healer.

Nine
Homecoming

I finished my final year at Princeton and stayed another year to do an advanced course in finance. The six years I spent at Princeton were the happiest and the most fruitful years of my life. I had done well in my studies. As a sophomore I was the only one in my class to be admitted to Phi Beta Kappa, and in my final exam I was the only Princetonian to earn a summa cum laude, the highest academic distinction anyone could earn in any American university.

During those years I had also bedded scores of women of different races and ages and enjoyed every one of them. While still in university, I was offered highly paid jobs by multinational corporations. But I was not interested; I had earned and saved up a lot of money coaching students and from lectures I was invited to deliver in colleges all over the country. At the end of my course I was offered a lecturer's job in the department of mathematics at Princeton. It should have been easy to get a Green Card and later become an American citizen. However, much as I liked living in the free and easy atmosphere that prevailed in the States, with all the creature comforts it provided, and despite finding Americans the easiest people to befriend, I did not have a sense of belonging to the country or its people. I was Indian, belonged to India, wanted to make my mark in India and nowhere else.

During my sojourn in the States I met scores of my countrymen living in distant parts of the country. There were the old settlers, mostly Sikhs in California, who owned large farms and lived in luxury. There were the late-comers—doctors, engineers, teachers, hoteliers—all doing much better money-wise than they could ever have in India. Even the latest arrivals—mostly factory workers and cab drivers—earned enough in dollars to be able to send decent money back home to ensure that their children went to public schools and their wives lived in comfort in their villages, while the men themselves had women—American, European immigrants and Latinos— to cook, keep house and warm their beds. With everything going for them, they talked of their watan, ate Indian food, listened to Indian film music and often cried in their sleep. Their common theme was, 'Once I have made enough dollars, I will go back to my village.' Hardly any did.

It was different for me. During my vacations I saw almost all that was worth seeing in America: the Niagara Falls, the Rockies, San Francisco, Los Angeles, Las Vegas, the Grand Canyon, Florida—you name it, I had seen it. I loved Americans, loved their cities and the landscape. It was a beautiful country with beautiful people. But it was not my country and they were not my people. What mattered most to me was that I had only one blood relation left in the world, my widowed father. If I did not return to him, it would break his heart.

I wrote to my father almost every week and sent him a couple of hundred dollars every month. He put the money in my bank account. With his provident fund and whatever he had saved he had bought a DDA flat and was living on his pension. He cooked his own food and swept his one-bedroom flat. He had also invested in a room in an ashram in Haridwar where he meant to spend his last days. This much I had gathered from his letters; I had no idea what else he did or how he spent his time.

I had lots of farewell parties at Princeton. I was assured by many friends that if I changed my mind and came back there would be a job waiting for me. I decided not to think about that option until after I had done my duty to my father. I would not abandon him in his old age.

I left America with a heavy heart. At Kennedy Airport over a dozen of my friends came to see me off. I was scarcely able to hold back my tears as I took leave of them. When I boarded the Air India plane, the stewardess took a look at my tourist class boarding pass and asked, 'Are you Mr Mohan Kumar from Princeton?' I nodded, without asking how she knew. 'Sir, you have been upgraded to First Class. Please follow me.' She took my travelling bag from my hand, led me to the front part of the aircraft and showed me to a window seat. I was a little bewildered. I was not a VIP for Air India to show such courtesy to me; only a student who had just finished his studies. The chief steward solved the mystery of my upgrading. 'Sir, the extra fare was paid by one of your friends at the counter. There are also some gifts.' He handed me a big parcel and a bouquet of roses. I unwrapped the parcel. It had boxes of liqueur chocolates, an expensive leather wallet, a Cartier wristwatch, a Mont Blanc gold pen and a large 'come-back-soonest' card with the signatures of my friends. This time I could not contain myself. I buried my face in my hands and wept. As the plane took off, I saw the lights of the city of skyscrapers slowly dissolve into the darkness and wondered, 'What people in the world other than Americans would make such a gesture?'

'Sir, what would you like for a drink before we serve dinner? Scotch? Champagne? Wine?' asked the airhostess as she pulled the trolley of drinks down the aisle. 'And let me put the roses in a vase. You can collect them when you deplane in Delhi.'

I handed her the bouquet of roses and said feebly, 'Scotch-n-Soda, please.'

It was a sumptuous meal of caviar, lobster, lamb curry and varieties of puddings. I glanced through Namaste magazine. Its last pages were devoted to articles on sale in the 'sky shop'. It occurred to me that I had not bought anything for my father. He did not drink, smoke or wear any perfume. I ticked off a woollen scarf and as the stewardess was clearing my table, asked her to get me one. 'What colour?' I thought about it for a moment then said, 'Dark brown or maroon.'

'I'll get it for you before we touch down in London. Anything else: Scotch? Cigarettes?'

'No thanks.'

I put the black eye-mask over my eyes and dozed off into a half-slumber. I was woken up for a snacky breakfast as we began our descent into London.

We had a three-hour stop at Heathrow airport for refuelling, change of crew and partial change of passengers. I took a stroll around the shopping arcades and restaurants. I was surprised to see a number of Indians, Pakistanis and Bangladeshis working as waiters and barmen; women in salwar-kameez scrubbing floors and cleaning toilets. What had they left their countries for? To wash white men's dishes and mop up their urine splattered around urinals?

I bought a cardigan for my father. A woollen scarf and an angora wool cardigan would protect him against Delhi's chill and wet winter months.

I spent most of the eight-and-a-half-hour journey from London to Delhi dozing off or reading Indian newspapers which I had not seen for almost six years. The papers were uniformly dull and had little besides reports of politicians abusing each other. The pictures they used were much the same. So also the strip cartoons, almost all taken from American papers. The only amusing items were obituaries and 'In Memoriams' couched in archaic Indian-English.

We landed in Delhi in the early hours of the morning. Being a first class passenger I was met by an Air India official and escorted through immigration. While I waited for my baggage on the conveyor belt I scanned the faces behind the glass pane on the floor above to see if I could recognize anyone. I noticed an old man frantically waving his arms. It was my father.

I picked up my two cases and took the Green channel to go through customs. I had nothing to declare. Nevertheless a customs officer accosted me. 'Can I see your passport?'

I gave it to him. He scanned its pages and said, 'You have been abroad for six years and have bought nothing dutiable for your relations and friends?'

'I have no relations except a widowed father waiting for me outside. I have a woollen scarf and a cardigan for him. All other items are for personal use.'

The customs man seemed irritated, ready to pick on me because I had denied him an opportunity to appropriate some little gadget or trinket, or at least to throw his weight around and feel important. I was back in India—there was no doubt about that. Then the man noticed the Air India official escorting me and that made him more courteous. He chalked my two cases and my handbag and waved me out of the airport. My father had come alone to receive me. He had a single marigold flower garland in his hand which he put round my neck. I touched his feet with both my hands and let him embrace me. He was too choked with emotion to be able to talk. I pushed my trolley through a throng of people waiting for their relations. We were surrounded by aggressive, pesky cab drivers. My father brushed them aside. 'A friend has lent me his car to pick you up,' he said as he waved to a driver who was waiting for us. A few minutes later a grey Mercedes Benz pulled up. The chauffeur put my cases in the boot and opened the car door. He knew where to take us.

For a while we sat in silence. Then my father took my hand in his and said, 'If your mother had been alive she would have been very proud of you.' He could not say any more. I felt his warm tears dropping on my hand. I did not know what to say.

After another long silence, he asked me, 'Did you say the Gayatri mantra every day?'

'I did, twice a day, morning and evening.'

'Recite it,' he commanded. I knew he was not testing me, only making me thank the gods for bringing me back home to India. I obliged him:

Aum Bhoor Bhuwa Swaha
Tatsavitur Varaniyam
Bhargo Devasya Dheemahi
Dhiyo Yo na Prachodayat.

(O Lord of the Earth and the Heavens! We meditate upon thy supreme splendour. May thy radiant power illuminate our intellects, destroy our sins, and guide us in the right direction!)

'This mantra is in praise of the deities of all the elements in nature. Gayatri is the most powerful mantra in the world, puttar. It wards off all evil.' My father was happy.

'I also did surya namaskar twice a day,' I told him.

'That was very good. It is the best exercise in the world to keep the body fit and free of disease. Gayatri mantra and surya namaskar ensure health and happiness . . . And you did not marry a white woman. You kept your promise to me.'

Obviously I did not tell him of the women I had laid. 'I am what I was when I left Delhi, Papa—a chhara (single).'

'We'll soon fix that. I'll find you a suitable bride. Do you drink or smoke?'

'I don't smoke! But I do drink a glass of beer or wine with meals. I've also tasted Scotch. It's a little too strong for me.'

'And meat? I hope you didn't touch badaa maas?'

'That is hard to say. In the West they put all kinds of meat concoctions in soups and stews and one never knows whether it is beef or pork or mutton.'

'Harey Ram! Harey Ram!' chanted my father. 'You must do pashchataap. We'll go to Haridwar and take a bath in the Ganga to cleanse us of our sins. You can also see the room I have reserved for myself in an ashram. It overlooks Ganga Mata.'

My thoughts went back to Yasmeen. Of all the women I had bedded it was the fat, middle-aged, married Muslim woman, mother of three children, that I thought of the most. She had mocked me about Hindus washing away their sins in the Ganga. She no doubt had cleansed herself of her adulterous intercourse with a Bharati Hindu kafir by going on a pilgrimage to Makka and Madina.

*

By the time we reached my father's DDA flat, the eastern horizon had begun to turn a light grey. My father had put a charpoy for himself in his little sitting-dining room and vacated his bedroom for me. He refused to alter the arrangement. 'Puttar, you must be very tired after travelling round half the globe. You need rest. The bedroom is more comfortable. Anyway, it's nearing my waking time. I take an early morning walk and then go to the temple. I'll wake you up when I come back and we'll have breakfast together. You can tell me all you did in America and about your future plans.'

He lay down on his charpoy without changing his clothes. I got into my night clothes, stretched myself on the charpoy in the bedroom and closed my eyes. It was not very comfortable. I had got used to sleeping on soft mattresses with feather pillows. The coarse durrie hurt my back; the pillow stuffed with cotton was like a block of wood. The change was too sudden, the surroundings unfamiliar. Sleep would not come to me.

I heard my father get up and go into the bathroom to have his bath. I heard him leave the flat and bolt the door from the outside. I got up to take a look at my surroundings. It was a dismal scene I saw through the window—multi-storeyed sickly-grey apartments, all exactly the same, separated by narrow criss-crossing roads lined with dull, thin newly-planted trees. Children loaded with heavy satchels were being escorted by their mothers to the school-bus stand round the corner. Milkmen and newspapermen were going round the block on their bicycles, looking bored. I decided there and then that we could not live in that squalid colony. My father deserved better. I deserved better.

I lay down on the charpoy again and covered my eyes with a handkerchief. Scenes from my time in Princeton and other places I had visited in the States came back to me. There was no scene I recalled that was without a woman I had made love to. Some like Jessica Browne, who had initiated me into sex, and Yasmeen Wanchoo, who had so brazenly forced me into copulating with her, came to mind repeatedly; others appeared briefly and I barely recognized them. Come to think of it, none of my liaisons had lasted very long. Jessica was the longest, one whole term. Others were for much shorter durations because by then I had discovered that safety lay in numbers. This was before AIDS had made casual sex too risky. At times I was dating two or three girls at the same time. And there was no date I did not take to bed. As soon as I sensed a girl was getting emotionally involved with me, I dropped her. Which left me with the uncomplicated memories that were now coming back to me. Images of all those women—one with breasts like melons; another with buttocks that I adored, so she walked around bare-arsed whenever we were alone in her room or mine; the Mexican girl who was never satisfied till I took her from behind, while she grunted with pleasure, her bottom raised high and her face buried in the pillow . . .

I must have dozed off re-enacting this blue-film montage in my head when I heard my father come in. 'Puttar, it is time to wake up. I will make you an omelette and tea while you bathe and change.'

Ten
Getting Married

I went along with whatever my father wanted me to do. He had missed me a great deal and wanted to smother me with affection. He was proud of my achievements and wanted to show me off to his cronies. He was old; I had been away for six years enjoying life while he had slogged here, alone. So I indulged him. The day after I arrived he invited a dozen of his friends and relatives to the tiny apartment and plied them with tea, coffee, cakes and biscuits. They were a bunch of old fogies, Hindus and Sikhs, who began their day by listening to shabad-keertan at the nearest gurudwara, met in Lodhi Gardens in the afternoon to mourn over the ways of Indian politicians, and ended the day with a visit to the Sai Baba temple near by. Once a month, usually on a Thursday, they also went to the dargah of Hazrat Nizamuddin Auliya to listen to qawwalis. That Father had turned to religious ritual during my stay abroad did not surprise me. He had aged quite a bit, and like most other ageing Indians had taken to temple-going and prayer. I knew he would not insist on my accompanying him to these prayer sessions, but Haridwar and a dip in the Ganga were unavoidable. This I could endure, because I needed to see where Father wanted to take sanyas—retirement from the world.

What did surprise me—only because I had not anticipated it—was my father's anxiety to see me married. For him it was the top priority. Without consulting me he put in an advertisement, with my photograph, in the matrimonial columns of *The Hindustan Times* and *The Times of India*. There was little finesse in what he had to say: the advertisement mentioned my Phi Beta Kappa and summa cum laude, and, for good measure, added that I held a Green Card. He included details of the salary I had been offered by a multinational corporation. In rupees the figure came to several lakhs a month. He did not bother to conceal his own identity behind a box number: he gave his name, address and telephone number and asked interested parties to get in touch with him. I only got to know when the first family arrived with father, mother, bride-to-be, her uncles and brothers. Father interviewed them like the chairman of the Public Service Commission: How far had the girl studied? Was she working? What salary was she drawing? What was the family worth? Who were their references? And so on. In turn they interrogated Father. I sat silently watching the girl and wondering what she would be like in bed. After a few weeks of abstinence, sex had again reared its ugly head in my mind. I had got used to bedding women almost on a daily basis; sometimes two in one day. What a woman looked like no longer mattered very much to me; more important was her bed-worthiness. I caught the girl, decked up in a Kanjeevaram sari and gold jewellery, stealing a coy glance at me. We did not exchange a word.

It was after the family had left that I spoke angrily to my father: 'Papa, what is all this? You should at least have asked me about it.'

'Why?' he replied truculently. 'It is a father's duty to see his son married in his lifetime. I am only fulfilling my dharma. If your mother had been alive, she would have been helping me. Now I have to do it alone.'

I would not let him get away with that excuse. 'Papa, if you had a daughter whom strangers came to inspect and then rejected, how would you have felt? It is very humiliating for girls of marriageable age to be treated like this. I don't like it one bit.'

He did not relent. 'You leave this business to me,' he said in a tone of finality. 'If I like a girl and her family, I will ask for your approval. I will leave the final choice to you.'

Thereafter not a day passed without a family being invited over for tea or soft drinks and an interview session. I remained a mute spectator, eyeing one girl after another, my eyes stripping them of their saris or salwar-kameez. I found all of them beddable in different ways and fantasized about them at night. My father recorded his opinions on paper and filed them. He could not get over the habit acquired in a lifetime of government service of noting down everything and methodically filing it for future reference.

I began to tire of these daily sessions and felt sorry for the girls and their parents who were told that we would get back to them. At the end of every meeting Father would ask me, 'What did you think of the girl?' I would give him the standard reply: 'Okay, you decide.'

'So far all the parties we have met were lower middle class,' he said once. 'You deserve the richest and the best-looking girl in Delhi.'

'What about that visit to Haridwar?' I asked to change the subject. 'I still have to atone for my sins.'

'I haven't forgotten that,' he replied, 'I have asked my friend Sardar Mehnga Singh to lend me his Mercedes Benz for a weekend. It was his car I came in to fetch you at the airport. He's as generous as he's rich.'

A day before we were to leave for Haridwar, a car drew up below our flat and the driver delivered a letter to Father. He was very excited. 'It is from Rai Bahadur Lala Achint Ram. He's one of the wealthiest Punjabis in Delhi: sugar mills, cinema houses, bungalows, farmland. He wants us to come to his house for tea. He has only one daughter— still unmarried!'

Father sent back a note saying he would contact Lala Achint Ram as soon as he and I had returned from Haridwar.

*

I had never seen Haridwar. My father had first visited it over twenty years ago when he had gone there to immerse my mother's ashes in the Ganga. Thereafter he had gone there several times by bus and stayed in the ashram in which he had rented a room for himself. Travelling in a large Mercedes Benz was for him a novel experience. We left early in the morning. All the way from Ghaziabad through Meerut, Aligarh and Roorkee, he talked of nothing else except the

Achint Ram family. 'If it comes through, it will be a very good alliance—brains from our side, money from theirs,' he pronounced. 'He will set you up in a good business or help you in whatever you choose to do.' And so on.

We reached Haridwar before noon and drove straight to his ashram. He had his room opened. The only furniture it boasted was a charpoy, a chair and a table. The ceiling fan hung precariously in the the middle of the room, and some distance from it dangled a naked bulb. The lavatory was Indian style. A bucket under a tap and a lota on a stool were the only items in the bathroom. 'What more do I need?' Father said when I remarked that the arrangement was a little too basic. 'I bring my own bedding roll and soap. I use keekar twigs to brush my teeth.'

'They serve good vegetarian food,' he went on. 'There is katha and keertan every evening. Scholars and pundits expound the teachings of our holy books and people from all parts of the country come to listen to them. And there is Mother Ganga herself, descending from the tresses of Lord Shiva in Gangotri high up in the Himalayas.'

We had our afternoon meal with many other ashram regulars, sitting cross-legged on the ground, served by men wearing nothing besides their sacred threads and flimsy dhotis. I had lost the art of eating with my hands and spilt quite a bit of the daal and vegetables on my shirt. My father retired for his afternoon siesta. I went out to take a look at the city and find something that would make me feel less out of place.

All the streets in Haridwar ran off from the main road and led to the river bank. I had to dodge a succession of paandas wanting to tell me vital facts about my ancestors or armed with receipt books asking for donations for gaushalas (cow pens) orphanages and temples. I came to the Ganga. A bridge took one across to an island with an ugly white clock tower standing in the middle of it. I stood on the bridge to take in the scene. To the north was a range of hills covered with thick forests. To the east, low hillocks. To the south, the plains through which the river ran. To the west was a mountain wall overlooking the city. And under the bridge flowed a very fast-moving river. Along the banks was an endless stretch of nondescript temples of no architectural merit. Well-fed, good-looking cows roamed along the ghats looking for pilgrims offering them bananas. Every few yards there were conclaves of ash-smeared sadhus sitting around smouldering fires and smoking chillums. There was nothing very sacred about the river front except the clear blue water of the Ganga sparkling in the sunshine.

I returned to the ashram to fetch my father. He was waiting for me. We walked back to the ghat. A large crowd had gathered at the ghat called Har Ki Pauri, Steps of the Lord. 'We will get a better view from the clock tower,' said my father. We crossed the bridge to the island and took our places on the tower facing Har Ki Pauri. The sun went over the western range. A deep shadow spread over the ghat. The scene changed dramatically. From temples along the banks emerged priests bearing huge candelabras of lamps. They came down the steps of Har Ki Pauri, as if in a majestic procession. The huge wicks soaked in ghee produced fierce, tall flames. The heat must have been intense, for some priests had what looked like white gloves covering their hands and forearms. As they waved their candelabras over the river, touching the bases to the water, tracing the sacred 'Om' with the bright flames in the night air, they intoned a hymn in praise of Mother Ganga. All at once the temple bells started clanging. Pilgrims placed leaf-boats with flowers and lit oil lamps in them on the stream. They floated away bobbing up and down. The dark river reflected a myriad quivering lights. I stood entranced by the magical scene spread before my eyes. My father joined the palms of his hands above his head and loudly sang the hymn of praise to the holy river:

> Om! Victory to thee, holy Mother Ganga!
> Victory ever be thine.
> Anyone who worships thee
> A true worshipper is he;
> What his heart desires
> You grant without fail.
> Om! Mother Ganga, hail, hail, hail.

The spectacle ended as abruptly as it had begun. The temple bells fell silent. The priests disappeared into their temples, carrying their candelabras with them. The leaf-boats with oil lamps floated away out of sight. I joined a group of Bengali pilgrims and raised a full-throated cry: Jai Ganga Mata—victory to thee, Mother Ganga.

As we were leaving the ghat, a half-moon rose in a clear blue sky. And beside it the evening star, Hesperus, sacred to lovers. The part moon and the star were reflected in the calm river.

The scene haunted me all night. It was to recur in my dreams for the rest of my life.

Early next morning, while it was still dark, Father woke me up and said, 'Get up. We must go to Har Ki Pauri before it gets too crowded. From there we'll drive on to Delhi. Put your things in the car.'

I quickly brushed my teeth, shaved and washed my face with tap water. Though the water came from the Ganga, it was not considered holy. We drove through dimly lit streets past a stream of men and women going towards the ghat. We left the car on the main road and pushed our way through towards the river. Har Ki Pauri was beginning to get crowded. We muscled our way through the crowd, left our clothes in the care of a paanda and went down the steps. The sun was just coming up over the eastern hills when we stepped into the water. It was icy cold. Undaunted, my father went in till the water came up to his chest. I followed him. He scooped some water in his cupped hands and offered it to the rising sun, mumbling some kind of prayer as he did so. He ducked into the river several times and ordered me to do the same. As I dipped myself into the chilly water I thought of Yasmeen humping me and mocking me about the pious Hindu's faith in the cleansing properties of the waters of the Ganga.

We stepped out of the water to dry ourselves. Father reassured me, 'Now we are cleansed of all our sins. Ganga Mata has washed them away and will drown them in the sea.' So he thought. As I rubbed myself with a towel, my eyes fell on other bathers, mainly women with big breasts and bigger buttocks, their wet saris clinging to their bodies and displaying their voluptuous contours. The waters of the

Ganga had done nothing to cleanse my mind of libidinous desires.

On our drive back to Delhi we passed scores of men carrying water-pots slung on either end of poles balanced on their shoulders. My father explained to me that they were carrying water from Har Ki Pauri to their villages to offer as prasad to others. 'These pots must never touch the ground, if they do the holy water loses its purity. Ganga Jal is sacred. Drops are put into the mouths of new born babies as well as the dying. Idols are bathed in it before they are worshipped. Some wealthy Hindus get tanks full for their daily baths . . .' He went on in this fashion till I could not take it anymore. This was as good an opportunity as any I would get to let my father know that not everything he said and did agreed with me. But when I spoke I did so gently. 'Pitaji, this is bharam (superstition). The waters of the Ganga are no more sacred than those of the Yamuna, Ravi, Narmada, Kaveri, Krishna or the Brahmaputra. Or for that matter the Thames, Rhine, Danube, Volga, Seine or the Mississippi. Now most of the rivers in the West are polluted with industrial effluents as ours are with garbage, human excreta and half-burnt corpses. At Haridwar the Ganga is clean because it descends from snow-clad mountains. But see it after it has run past Allahabad, Varanasi and Patna and you would hesitate to put your foot in it. By the time it becomes the Hooghly in Bengal, it stinks like a sewer.'

My father snubbed me: 'Don't talk like that! I don't know about other rivers but scientists have analysed the water of the Ganga and found unique healing properties in it. No other river in the world can match it. It is not for nothing that our ancients declared it holy, our sages lived in caves along its course and meditated on its banks. You have been contaminated by Western materialism.'

There was no point arguing with a man so set in his ideas. With the years my father had turned into a religious zealot. He was a good, caring and kindly man who never hurt anyone nor ever said an unkind word against another human being. But he had become a bigot. It was too late to change him. We did not exchange many words during the rest of our journey.

*

Father rang up Rai Bahadur Lala Achint Ram and told him of our return from Haridwar. 'When would it be convenient for us to call on you and pay our respects? Or would you honour us with a visit to our humble abode? We live in a small DDA flat.' His tone was very obsequious. Achint Ram invited us to come for tea the following day.

This time my father did not ask his rich Sikh friend to lend him his Mercedes Benz. 'I don't want to give them a false impression of ourselves. We will go in a taxi.'

My father dressed himself in sherwani and churidars and tied a grey turban round his head. I wore a Princeton T-shirt and blue denims. I knew I looked best in casuals. We hired a taxi and told the driver to take us to the address on Prithvi Raj Road. It was among the most expensive residential areas in New Delhi. Our taxi pulled up under the porch of a large double-storeyed house surrounded by a well-kept garden—an open lawn with a marble fountain in the centre, flower beds with large chrysanthemums. A liveried bearer opened the door and let us into the drawing room. Huge sofas and armchairs, ornate black marble tables, two huge chandeliers hanging from the ceiling, photographs of the President, the Prime Minister and members of the family in silver frames—everything smelt of newly acquired wealth and social status.

The Rai Bahadur came out of his study and embraced my father. They were about the same age and the same height. But Father was a lean man; Rai Bahadur Lala Achint Ram had quite a paunch and wore thick glasses. I bowed my head as I said 'Namaste', and he put his hand on it. He addressed me as 'Beta' and asked us to sit down. He called out to the servant to bring tea and tell the rest of the family that the guests had arrived. His three sons came first and shook hands with me, but there was no warmth in their handshakes. They were followed by their wives—all over-made-up, over-dressed and loaded with jewellery. They folded their hands, said namaste and sat down on the sofa furthest from us. They were not expected to open their mouths. They did not. Then came Achint Ram's wife, a fat woman, also loaded with jewellery. Behind her came her daughter, properly decked up for inspection.

Tea was served and cakes passed round. The Rai Bahadur took my father aside and the two men went into a huddle. The boys got talking to me. They asked me about my school and college in India and my years abroad. In turn I asked them where they had studied. They had gone to the elitist Modern School and then joined their father's business. 'What is the point of getting degrees from colleges?' said the eldest, 'They don't help you in business. For that you need practical experience.' That gave me an opening to talk to the girl. 'Do you agree?' I asked and she snapped back, 'Of course not. I don't want to go into any business or work in any office. I did my BA in English literature from Miranda House. Papa would not let me do an MA.'

Her mother intervened, 'Sonu is our one and only daughter. No one wants to marry girls who are better educated than they. She is the first in our family to have gone to college. We are very proud of her.'

Sonu gave a wan smile. I had a good look at her: fair-skinned, slender but with an alarming resemblance to her obese mother. This was evidently the first time she had been subjected to the indignity of an inspection and she did not relish it. She looked sullen and would undoubtedly take it out on her parents as soon as we left.

When it was time for us to leave, everyone stood up. I towered above all of them. I was certainly a lot more presentable than the girl's brothers. The entire family came to see us off at the porch. The Rai Bahadur saw the waiting taxi and ordered his bearer to pay off the cab driver and send for his car. My father made a mild protest and tried to pay the fare. Rai Bahadur held his hand. 'No, brother, I will not allow it. My driver will take you home in my car.' They embraced again. I touched the Rai Bahadur's and his wife's feet. '*Jeetey raho, beta* (May you live long, son),' said the Rai Bahadur. '*Lammee umar hove puttar* (May you have a long life, son),' said his wife. I shook hands with the boys and said namaste to their wives and to Sonu, who folded her hands in response but said nothing. She looked unsure of herself.

On the way home my father was in an expansive mood. 'The Rai Bahadur told me that his daughter will get an equal share of his property

with her brothers. That could be several crores. He's more than willing
to make you a business partner. The girl is not bad looking. She's
educated. It may take her some time to adjust to our modest lifestyle,
but where would she find a handsomer and better qualified husband
than you? I have told the Rai Bahadur that I cannot make a final
commitment till I have consulted you. Now it is for you to decide. I
have promised to get back to him in two days.'

What did I make of the Achint Ram family? They had everything I
disliked about upstart Punjabi families. Pots of money but no class. I
had seen enough evidence of that in their sitting-room. Black marble
floor, white marble walls, chandeliers more appropriate in the lobby
of a hotel than a private home. Italian marble tables with silver framed
photographs of powerful politicians, but no Gandhi, no Nehru.
Despite the large garden there were plastic flowers in ornate vases
and crystal bowls with plastic bananas, cherries, apples, grapes and
pineapples. I suspected that the chandeliers were not made of cut
glass but of plastic. Achint Ram had dyed his hair and walrus
moustache, but the white at the roots showed they needed a fresh
coat of dye. His black sherwani had gold buttons studded with
diamonds. The walking stick he carried even inside the house was of
black ebony with an ivory handle carved to resemble a snarling lion.
His wife was as fat as him and decorated like a Christmas tree with
heavy gold jewellery: earrings, necklaces, bangles and rings. I had
expected the sons to be more sophisticated than their parents, but
they had turned out to be arrivistes as well. They wore Western clothes
but with shiny bright red ties, and red handkerchiefs sticking out of
their front pockets. All three had used too much perfume, had gold
or platinum rings with precious stones on their fingers, and gold-
chained wrist-watches worn with the dials facing inwards. And they
kept cracking their fingers—*thig, thig, thig*. The youngest was the
most crude; while talking to me in his loud voice he kept jigging his
legs. First he rested one leg on the other which he kept rapidly pushing
up and down. Then he changed his style of shaking them by spreading
out his thighs and bringing them together—endlessly. How could I

have a serious coversation with someone who was fidgeting all the time?

Achint Ram's daughters-in-law sat like dumb painted dolls without any expression on their faces. They kept gaping at me as if envying their sister-in-law for having landed a husband who was more handsome and better educated than their own husbands.

Then there was their Mercedes Benz which brought us home. There was a silver Ganpati on the dashboard and a bottle of perfume beside it. A fluffy gnome dangled on the rear pane.

It was no use telling my father about the lack of class in this rich family; he would not have understood. I also felt it was not fair to club Sonu with the rest of the family. She was beddable enough and I could teach her about the right style of living and behaviour, the difference between crystal, cut glass and plastic.

I weighed the pros and cons of marriage. To me sex was the more pressing need than love or companionship. For too long have we been fooled into believing that the basis of a happy man-woman relationship is love. Love is an elusive concept and means different things to different people. There is nothing elusive about lust because it means the same thing to all people: it is the physical expression of liking a person of the opposite sex. Cuddling, kissing and fondling leading to sexual intercourse. Love cannot last very long without lust. Lust has no time-limit and is the true foundation of love and affection.

In America I had got all the sex I wanted, and without long-term commitments. In India it was not so easy. I did not relish the idea of visiting prostitutes or looking for call girls. Even if I succeeded in persuading a working woman to share my bed, there was no place I could take her to: Indians do not believe in privacy; they are a nosey people and the one thing they will not do is mind their own business. At least marriage would ensure a woman in my bed.

I also thought over the wisdom of marrying a rich man's daughter and bringing her out of a large mansion to a pokey little flat. I would have to find better accommodation and earn enough to keep her in the style she was accustomed to. I did not want to be beholden to her father and be treated as a ghar jamai—the resident son-in-law.

Then there was Sonu herself: passably fair and undoubtedly looking forward to marriage like all Indian girls of her age do, but a little haughty. She was almost certain to be a virgin and looked the kind who might resent my not being one. During the tea session she was sulking, as if preparing herself for a rejection: if you don't like me, go to hell and find another girl. If I said yes, she might think that I was swayed more by her father's wealth and position than her looks.

Father was obviously looking forward to a matrimonial alliance that would raise his status in society. Lala Achint Ram was keen to have an 'America-returned', highly educated boy as his son-in-law to add respectability and sophistication to all the benefits of wealth that he already had. Everything depended on my saying yes.

Ultimately, it was fantasizing about deflowering Sonu, the haughty little memsahib, and having her in bed whenever I wanted to that made me decide in favour of accepting the offer.

The next afternoon my father asked me, 'So, puttar, have you thought over the matter?'

'Yes, Papa,' I replied, 'I'm willing. But I don't think it would be right to bring a girl from that kind of family into a tiny flat like ours. If you agree we can sell this place and get a larger one in a better locality. I think I have enough dollars saved up. We can pool our resources and find something more spacious. At least three bedrooms with bathrooms: one for you, one for ourselves, one for the guests. A sitting-dining room, servant quarters, a garage and perhaps a small garden.'

'I have been thinking about that myself,' he replied, 'but houses like that cost a lot. I'm not sure we'll have enough even with your dollars to buy such a large house in a good neighbourhood. I will get in touch with property dealers straightaway. So can I tell Lalaji that we are agreeable to the match?'

I nodded my head.

I could see my father was bursting with desire to convey the news to Achint Ram but he held himself back. He told me he would first go to Gurudwara Bangla Sahib to seek the blessings of the Sikh Gurus and then to the Sai Baba temple before talking to anyone. He was gone for many hours and come back with prasad from both places and ordered me to eat it. He picked up the phone and got Achint Ram on the line. 'Rai Bahadurji, my son and I are agreed that he and Sonu would make a very happy couple. A hundred thousand felicitations to you and Bhabhiji.'

Rai Bahadur told his wife. She came on the phone. My father repeated the same words to her. 'And Bhabiji we are looking for a nice house for the daughter of a noble family. Our flat is not good enough for her. We hope to find one soon.'

She handed the phone back to her husband. My father told him about looking for a nice house and assured him that we had enough money to buy one. 'But of course, Rai Bahadurji, if we need any help, who else will we turn to? But right now it is all under control, I am contacting property dealers for the best possible deal . . .' He was going on and on. He put his hand on the mouthpiece and said to me, 'He's asking his wife about something.' Achint Ram came back on the line, and father said, 'Oh, shagun! You consult your astrologer and fix a suitable time and date. Give us a week or ten days to get things for Sonu. Perhaps we should have the same astrologer examine both Mohan's and Sonu's horoscopes. I'm sure they will match.'

I was suddenly transported from a world in which men and women bedded each other if they so desired into another where they sought the guidance of palmists, astrologers and soothsayers before taking off their clothes. I decided to go along with everything my father wanted. Perhaps I should not have, but I hate discord and unnecessary complications in life. Father and Rai Bahadur could do what they liked; Sonu was beddable enough, how the marriage was conducted was not important.

Finding a new house proved surprisingly difficult. I had no idea how exorbitant property rates were in Delhi. Father was right; even after selling his flat and using up all the dollars I had saved, we would not have enough money to buy the kind of house I wanted. Besides, every one insisted on more than half the money in cash which would not be shown in the papers. Neither my father nor I had any black money. Lala Achint Ram let us exhaust ourselves and cleverly waited till my father was frustrated and hinted to him that his daughter might have to suffer a small house for a couple of years after marriage till we found a larger one. Then the Lala acted—he bought a three-bedroom flat in Maharani Bagh jointly in his daughter's and my names. Again, I allowed Father to persuade me into accepting the deal. Though to be honest, I too was relieved to be out of our depressing, poky DDA flat.

Once again an astrologer was consulted, prayers offered at Hindu and Sikh temples, and the date and time fixed for a change of residence. We spent the morning of the chosen day helping labourers load our furniture onto trucks. My father oversaw the packing in the old house, I received the furniture at the other end. The new house had been well looked after by the widow who owned it before us and she kindly assisted me in arranging the carpets, sofas, tables and chairs. By the time my father arrived on the last truck carrying odds and ends, the new house looked lived in. He came armed with a Sikh granthi and a Hindu priest. The bearded granthi recited a short ardaas; the pandit chanted shlokas in Sanskrit. We distributed halwa to everyone present, including the truck drivers and labourers.

There were lots of hassles to be overcome before we could settle in comfortably. The telephone number had to be transferred from the old to the new residence; electricity and water bills to be directed to us. And much else. My father knew how to go about such things. He simply paid the linesmen and meter readers more than they expected and they sorted out the details.

A date and time for the shagun was fixed. We, father and son, would go to Rai Bahadur Lala Achint Ram's home at the appointed time with gifts for the family. Sonu and I would exchange rings after which I would be allowed to visit her in her home. The date for the wedding would be fixed by mutual consent, as also details of how many people would come with the bridegroom's party and who would be invited for the wedding reception.

It was a different Sonu I saw when I went with my father for the shagun. She looked radiantly happy; as if she had passed the most important exam in her life with flying colours. Father had brought a suit length for the Rai Bahadur; a sari for his wife; metres of silk for Sonu's salwar-kameez and a gold necklace my mother had worn; suit lengths for the sons. I carried a gold ring in my pocket. After I had touched her parents' feet and shaken hands with her brothers, Sonu asked me saucily, 'Aren't you going to shake hands with me?' I shook her by the hand, put my arm round her shoulders and embraced her. She blushed. Her mother remarked, 'What a lovely couple you make! May both of you live long and have seven sons!'

Sonu went red in the face. 'O shut up, Mummy. No one is allowed to have more than two.'

It was a cordial union. Sonu and I sat on the same sofa. I took out the gold ring I had brought with me and slipped it on her finger. My father put the gold necklace round her neck. Her mother handed her a ring with a diamond. She took my left hand and slipped it on my finger. Presents were exchanged: suit lengths for my father, a suit length and a gold watch for me. Father gave them what he had brought for the family. After another round of embraces, tea was served. Sonu poured out cups for my father and me. She addressed him as Pitaji; me as Mohanji. 'You must tell me about your college days in America,' she said. 'Come out with me this evening,' I replied, 'and I'll tell you all,' to which her mother said, 'Puttar, you come here any time you want to talk to Sonu. We can't allow you to go out together yet; people begin to talk.'

After the ceremony was over, we were driven back in the Rai Bahadur's Toyota. My father was still riding on cloud nine. 'We are very lucky to have made such a good alliance. Your future is assured.' I brought him down to earth. 'Papa, I don't mean to live on Sonu's money. You have already made me accept the house they bought for us. I can't take any further obligations from my father-in-law. I don't intend becoming a ghar jamai. I have to set up my own business and earn my own livelihood.'

The question of my future was in the Rai Bahadur's mind as well. When I visited their house the next day to spend some time with Sonu, he took me out to his garden and asked me, 'Puttar, what are your plans?'

I told him that I meant to buy some running concern which was not doing well or set up one of my own. I was looking for space to set up my office. 'What kind of business?' he asked. 'I have many going concerns, you could pick up one of them with office and staff provided.'

'Pitaji, if you don't mind I would rather have an independent business of my own. Import-export, manufacturing car parts, or machinery. I'm a computer expert; I can handle accounts and staff. I can handle anything.'

He was impressed by my self-confidence. However, eventually it was through him that I got in touch with a couple of society women who were running a garments export outfit on a very modest scale. It brought them more headaches than money, and they readily agreed to sell me their stock which was mostly junk and their goodwill which was worse than junk. They were also willing to give me the list of their clients abroad. I signed a deal with them. Again it was through the Rai Bahadur's influence that I was able to rent two floors of a high-rise building in Nehru Place. I put in advertisements for clerks and accountants and personally interviewed every applicant, offering higher salaries than the going rate in the employment market. I had my firm registered and stationery printed. It was hard work running from one government office to another. I spent a fortune on taxi fares till I bought myself a second-hand Fiat. I was quick to learn the tricks of the trade, the most important being: when you run into an unsolvable problem, use grease liberally; it opens all doors.

I made it a point to drop in at the Achint Ram residence regularly and inform them of the progress I was making. Sonu started nagging me. 'So you found a few minutes to see me as well?' would be her opening remark. I tried to reassure her: 'It is for you, us, that I'm slogging day and night. I want you to have the same comforts you have enjoyed in your parents' home.' She had the last word: 'As if money is everything,' which, considering her lifestyle and the things she expected—cars, servants, jewellery—was a stupid thing to say. But I did not tell her that.

My business picked up very fast. In addition to readymade garments of high quality, I started exporting semi-precious stones, leather goods, spices and basmati rice. I imported nothing, and I earned foreign exchange for my country. The Rai Bahadur made it easy for me to become a member of Delhi's top clubs—the Golf Club, the Gymkhana and the India International Centre. He was keen that I become a member of the Rotary Club of Delhi as well. 'You'll make good business contacts,' he assured me. 'All Rotarians are leaders in their respective fields: top industrialists, doctors, engineers, professors—the cream of Delhi society. You have established yourself as an entrepreneur; you should make it easily. If you like I can speak to the chairman of the South Delhi Rotary. I was chairman twenty years ago.'

I avoided giving a straight answer; 'Let my business pick up a little more,' I said. The fact was that I did not have the slightest wish to join a club like the Rotary or the Lions Club. I had attended a few Rotarian lunches in the States and found them uniformly puerile and boring. They followed a ritual which made no sense. The chairman wearing an insignia round his neck clanged a bell to declare the meeting open. They got down to eating a tasteless meal. The chairman proceeded to welcome new members. A big hand for each. He named members who had celebrated their birthdays that week. Another round of clapping. The hero of the function was the fellow who had not missed a single luncheon meeting. The biggest hand for him. And finally, the guest speaker was asked to deliver a speech. No more than fifteen-twenty minutes, just enough time for the gentlemen of the Rotary to let their gastric juices dissolve what they had consumed or to release gases that had accumulated in their bellies. They were constipated with self-esteem and considered themselves good citizens who performed their civic duties: arranged blood donation camps, and free eye operations, put benches in parks and at roadsides, raised contributions for some charity. I could do all that without lunching every week with the champion bores of the city.

Barely a year after my return from the States, I had acquired, or was well on my way to acquiring, the essentials that a successful businessman should have. The only thing that I did not have was the company of a woman. And sex. I was ready to get married. Father was beginning to get impatient. The Rai Bahadur and his wife were also anxious to fix a date for their daughter's marriage. 'Long engagements are not good,' pronounced Sonu's mother, 'and you have been engaged for over seven months.'

Consultations followed. An auspicious day was found in the Hindu calendar. Fancy wedding cards with an embossed figure of Ganpati were printed by both sides. My father did not have many friends but the news that his son was to marry Rai Bahadur Achint Ram's only daughter revived many old friendships and relations. We were able to muster nearly a hundred people to join the bridegroom's party. For Rai Bahadur it was an occasion to display his wealth and high connections; ministers, governors, judges, senior bureaucrats and over a thousand others of the elite of the city accepted his invitation. I rode from my house to Sonu's on a white horse which had half its body covered with gold cloth. Strings of jasmine buds covered my face. In front of me a brass band played the latest hits from Hindi films, behind me a dozen fat men and women danced the bhangra—amongst them my aged father in a pink turban. He threw handfuls of coins over the crowd. Street urchins dashed in and out from under people's legs to collect them. Dozens of men carrying neon lights on their heads marched along on either side. At another time I would have thrown up on seeing such a garish display of vulgar opulence, but I had to remind myself that I was the central figure of this charade; the bridegroom.

Rai Bahadur's mansion was aglitter with coloured bulbs; red and yellow lights shone on the walls, over the shrubbery in the large garden, even in the trees lining the road leading up to the bungalow. Two shehnai players with tabla accompanists sat on a platform playing wedding melodies. As soon as our party arrived at the gate they stopped. An army band struck up. All around us were offical security guards with guns slung from their shoulders. Clearly the ministers and governors had arrived. I dismounted from my horse and was pushed forward to be received by my in-laws to be. I put a garland of flowers round Sonu's neck; she put one round mine. Rai Bahadur conducted me to the lawn to introduce me to his innumerable guests. I shook hundreds of hands and received hundreds of congratulations. The auspicious hour was near. I was taken to a small square pit in which the sacred fire burnt. Sonu and I were seated side by side. Our respective pandits confronted each other and cross-checked our credentials. Sonu's pandit recited shlokas and every few minutes asked Sonu and me to take a handful of rice, sesame seeds and incense to throw into the fire. Every time we did so he chanted 'Swaha'. This went on for more than half an hour. Then he made us walk round the fire seven times. We sat down again. There were more swahas. He put Sonu's hand in mine and pronounced us husband and wife.

The Rai Bahadur had on display the dowry he was giving his daughter. Stacks of expensive Banaras and Kanjeevaram saris, gold bangles, a diamond necklace, diamond ear studs and a diamond nose pin. Capping them all was a brand new Mercedes Benz decked in flowers in which I was to take away my bride. He asked the most senior Union Minister who was at the wedding—the Finance Minister—to hand me the keys of the car. It was as dazzling a display of wealth as any I had seen.

After everyone had eaten the sumptuous dinner laid out on the lawn, it was time for me to take Sonu to her new home. There was much sobbing and crying. Her parents wept as if they had lost their only child. Even her brothers cried as they bade her farewell. Sonu sat in front with me. My father took the rear seat. We drove in silence to our flat in Maharani Bagh. My father had had it festooned with coloured lights. In the absence of female relations, he had done up my bedroom. Garlands of marigold hung from the ceiling fan. Jasmine petals were strewn on our bed. For some time we sat in the sitting room. We had nothing much to say to each other. At last my father got up and said, 'You must be very tired; I certainly am. I will go to bed. You take your time and retire when you like.' Both of us got up. He put his hands on our heads and said, 'May you be happy for ever and ever.'

Sonu and I sat for a while holding hands. She was bewildered by her new surroundings. And apprehensive of what was to come. She had heard much about the suhaag raat—the first night of marriage.

She later told me that her friends had 'warned' her that being deflowered was painful and bloody. Thereafter, they had said, the same act became something one wanted to be repeated again and again. Sonu dreaded the initiation the way some people dread a doctor's needle.

I escorted her to our bedroom. 'Take off all your jewellery and get into something comfortable,' I told her.

She stood in front of the dressing room mirror and slowly divested herself of the gold teeka dangling on her forehead, the earrings, gold bangles and the necklace. She did not remove the ivory bangles which covered her forearms: a bride has to wear them for at least a fortnight. She went into the bathroom and changed from her sari into a diaphanous dressing gown. I sensed her nervousness and tried to reassure her. 'You are a beautiful girl,' I said. She looked down at her breasts, belly and legs. 'You think so? Nobody has told me that before. Only my mother.'

'I'm telling you, that should be enough.'

I sat down on my bed, still wearing my wedding attire of sherwani and churidars. I took her by the hand, seated her in my lap. 'Are you going to hurt me?' she asked.

I kissed her on the back of her neck and replied, 'It hurts a little the first time.'

'Can't you put it off for a few days? I'm not ready for it.'

'As you wish. There's no hurry. We have a lifetime ahead for it. But you will let me kiss you, won't you? And lie with me for a while?'

She turned her face towards me and pecked me on the nose. 'Not like this,' I told her, as I laid her head on the pillow and pressed my lips on hers. She clenched her mouth. I put my arms round her and held her close to my body. She went stiff. I gently massaged her back till she relaxed. I put my hand on her bosom. She went stiff again and brushed away my hand. 'Enough for the first night,' she said peremptorily. 'Now you sleep in your bed, I will sleep in mine. I have never shared my bed with anyone before.'

She got up and lay down on her bed. I went to the bathroom, brushed my teeth and got into my night clothes. I was aching with lust, desperate to deflower her. That was what the suhaag raat was meant for. It would have to be postponed for a day or two. I switched off the light. And fantasized about Jessica and the other women I had laid, most of all the fat Yasmeen Wanchoo with buttocks like overripe pumpkins pounding away on top of me.

Eleven

The day after our marriage we left for our ten-day honeymoon. The Rai Bahadur had suggested a new hotel, Timber Trail Heights, in the Shivalik Hills on the way to Shimla. He had spent many weekends there and made friends with the proprietor, Ramesh Kumar Garg and his wife, Swaran. Garg was an enterprising man who had built one hotel along the main Kalka-Shimla highway and another on top of a hill across a valley and connected the two by cable car. It started doing well from the day it opened its restaurants and rooms to visitors. The hotel along the highway was always crowded with holiday makers from Chandigarh, Ambala, Patiala and other towns of Punjab, Haryana and Himachal. Timber Trail Heights was quieter. It was near village Bansar across the valley of the Kaushalya, at a height of 5000 feet, and had become the favourite resort of honeymooning couples. After sunset there was no one there besides the hotel staff. The special bridal suite had been reserved for us.

We set out at around ten in the morning. On our way we called on Sonu's parents. In an hour we were out of Delhi on Sher Shah Suri Marg. There was heavy traffic on the highway—trucks, buses, oil tankers, tractors and slow-moving bullock carts. We were in no hurry. Sonu fed the cassette player with tapes of Hindi film songs and crooned along. She was not very musical but sounded very happy.

We passed through Sonepat, Panipat, took the bypass round Karnal and stopped at a lakeside restaurant for a light repast. Seeing the ivory bangles on Sonu's forearms and the gold medallion dangling on her forehead everyone recognized us as a newly married couple. The waiters were over-solicitous. As we left, the manager presented Sonu with a bouquet of flowers. We continued our journey through Ambala, past Pinjore gardens, through Kalka and up the road going to Shimla. Timber Trail Heights was four miles up the road. The car park was packed. A place close to the entrance had been kept free for us. As we stepped out, there was a flurry of activity. The commissionaire ran in to inform the proprietor of our arrival and ran back with a couple of porters to take our luggage. Garg and Swaran were on the porch to welcome us. Mrs Garg had a silver salver with four oil lamps and a small mound of red kumkum powder. She waved the salver in front of our faces and with her thumb put kumkum on our foreheads. A crowd collected to watch the spectacle. Being Rai Bahadur Lala Achint Ram's son-in-law clearly entitled me to many privileges. I felt a little uncomfortable.

The Gargs took us down to their private apartment: a large hall with water cascading down one wall and big chandeliers hanging from the ceiling. In the middle of a circle of armchairs was a bottle of champagne in a bucket of ice. 'You must have a glass with us to celebrate before you go across to your suite on the other side. You should be there before sunset to see the view. I'm sure you will like it,' pronounced Garg.

He opened the champagne bottle himself. The cork blew off with a loud bang. Garg poured the frothing liquid into four wine glasses. I didn't much care for champagne; Sonu had never tasted it. Swaran excused herself, saying she did not touch alcohol. But the occasion demanded politeness. I drank up and after Sonu had taken a sip, emptied her glass as well. Garg finished his glass. His wife stared at her glass of sherbet and kept smiling.

The couple saw us into the cable car. Our suitcases were already in it. They waved to us as the car swung away from its moorings on its voyage to the other side. It was frightening. Also breathtaking. Below us we could see the silver trickle of the Kaushalya. On either side of the valley were terraced corn and rice fields and tiny hamlets. In ten minutes we were across the abyss. On the landing stage the manager welcomed us with a bouquet of flowers and led us to our suite. It was a large bed-sitting room. A table in the centre had a basket of fruits: apples, pears, bananas and mangoes. Also a bottle of Black Label Scotch. The manager opened the fridge: it was packed with miniature bottles of whisky, gin, liqueurs, and packets of potato crispies and dry fruit. 'Sir, everything theek thaak?' he asked. 'If I can be of any service or if you have any complaints please send for me. If you want your dinner served in your room, tell the room bearer. Dinner starts at seven. The bar is open round the clock.' He bowed a couple of times and took his leave.

As the manager shut the door behind him, I took Sonu in my arms and kissed her on the lips. She was taken aback by the suddenness of the gesture but did not go stiff as she had done the evening before. Instead she stepped back, looked me full in the face and said, 'You know what? I think you are a bit of a goonda.'

'That I am,' I replied. 'And you being married to one are a goondee.'

'There is no such word as goondee. Only the males of our species are shameless and debauched,' she insisted childishly and I laughed. 'Let's take a look round the hotel garden and the hills before we unpack,' she suggested.

We went out to take in the scene. The village bazaar had a few shops and farmers' hovels. It commanded a panoramic view of the plains below. We seemed to be perched on top of the world looking down on hills and valleys spread beneath our feet. The monsoon was almost over. It had washed clean the forests of pine, fir, deodar and rhododendrons. The mountains were of different shades of green and blue. Here and there mists nestled in the hollows of hillsides like gossamer caught between branches of trees. The setting sun lit up white clouds on the western horizon in different hues of red, pink and gold. We sat at a look-out point for a while. A young moon wandered into the deep blue sky. The air was clean and fresh. There was a throbbing silence, till the cicadas took over. 'Isn't it beautiful?' I asked Sonu as I put my arm round her shoulder.

'Thanks to Daddy,' she replied, 'this place was his idea.'

We wandered around for a while till the twilight faded into night, leaving the pale moon to light our world. A bewildering crowd of stars twinkled in the vast sky as far as the eye could see. The hotel generator began to sputter phut, phut, phut—phutututut. The lights came on and ruined the after-sunset scene. It also turned chilly. We went back to our room. A small electric radiator glowed red. The room was warm. 'Let's have a drink,' I suggested. I thought it would warm her insides and make her more amenable to what I had in mind.

'I don't drink,' she replied firmly. 'The stuff that Mr Garg gave me tasted like bad lemonade. I could have spat it out.'

'You try Campari and soda. It is bitter-sweet with hardly any alcohol in it. I'm sure you'll like it. If you don't, just pour it down the sink.'

She did not say anything, so I took it to mean that she would try it.

I got out a miniature bottle of Campari from the fridge and a bottle of soda. It was a bit chilly for chilled beer so I poured myself a Scotch. I handed her the glass of bright red liquid. 'Take a sip and see how it tastes.'

She took a sip. 'It's like sherbet,' she replied, 'only somewhat bitter. But I don't want to get drunk. Are you sure this thing has no nashaa?'

'If you feel it has put it aside. People who don't like alcohol drink Campari to keep others company.'

We sat side by side, she sipping Campari, I sipping Scotch-n-soda. With one arm I drew her towards me, put both my hands round her face and kissed her passionately. 'For God's sake open your mouth so that I can feel what's inside it with my tongue.'

She obeyed without enthusiasm. I persisted in kissing her again and again, all over her face and back to her lips. She began to respond to my overtures. I slipped my hand beneath her blouse. For a moment she went stiff; then let me fondle her. I felt her breasts getting warmer under my palm and her nipples hardened like cherry stones. I wasn't sure if it was the right time to take her. The bearer would come in at any moment to take the order for dinner. And we were still in the clothes we had arrived in. I decided I would wait till after we had had our meal. I was pretty certain she would not say no this time.

'Shall we send for dinner here?' I asked.

She pulled out of my embrace and replied, 'Let's go to the dining room and see the raunaq—it will be lively there with all the people. If we eat here, the smell of the food will stay in the room all night.'

In the dining room were almost a hundred people including a few married couples. We eyed each other without exchanging smiles or greetings. Sonu examined the menu. 'Chicken biryani for me,' she said. 'What about you?'

'I'll settle for the same. And some daal.'

The waiter took our order and asked, 'Sahib, anything to drink?' He handed me the list of beverages.

'Another Campari? Or would you like to try some chilled white wine? Grover's is not at all bad, almost as good as the French, better than Californian. Hardly any alcohol in it. Try a glass,' I suggested.

She nodded her head. 'I'll take what you like. If I hate it, you finish it.'

I ordered white wine. The waiter lit the candle on the table. He came back with a bottle of Grover's white and put glasses in front of us. He poured a little into my glass for me to taste. I savoured it and said, 'Theek hai.' He filled our glasses.

'First take the glass in both your hands and inhale the wine's bouquet.' I demonstrated how it was done. She imitated my gestures and took a sip. 'Not bad, you'll soon turn me into a sharaabi. Everyone is looking at us—an Indian bride drinking sharaab. What is India coming to!'

'Let them go to hell.'

It was an excellent meal. And the chilled wine went very well with the biryani. The dining room began to empty. We decided it was time for us to retire to our suite. I told the waiter to keep the remaining half of the bottle for our dinner the next day. Even the two small glasses of wine had made Sonu light-headed. She held my hand as we walked out and went up the flight of stairs to our room. For a while we watched TV. Sonu stood up and said, 'I think I'll take a bath. I feel slightly drunk. There's running hot water in the bathroom.' I assumed she had other, more welcome ideas in her head. She came back in her nightie. I followed her example. I took a hot shower and another shave and changed into my night clothes. When I came out, the TV had been switched off and Sonu was in her bed with a blanket over her head. I slid under the blanket. She made room for me, but said firmly, 'Don't push me too hard. I'm not ready yet.'

'You seemed to be quite ready before dinner; what has happened now?'

'The mood is gone. Give me time.'

I got out of her bed and climbed into mine. 'Don't be cross with me. I'll tell you when I'm ready,' she pleaded.

I was angry, frustrated and impatient. I tried to go to sleep. It had been a long day, I had driven over 200 miles. But sleep would not come to me.

Around midnight I was woken up from my half-slumber by a flash of lightning and a thunderclap which made the hotel building shake. Then more lightning and more thunder. When the monsoon is about to end it does so with a terrifying display of rage. It began to pour till I could hear nothing except the rain battering on the corrugated tin roof.

Sonu got up and stood by my pillow. 'I'm scared. Can I share your bed?' she pleaded.

I made room for her. She clung to me like a frightened child. Every time there was lightning and thunder she dug deeper into my embrace. I soothed her nerves by holding her close to me. We began to kiss; this time she opened her mouth to let me explore its depths. She let me fondle her breasts. I took each in my mouth, sucked them like a hungry babe. She was thoroughly aroused. I slipped my hand between her thighs. I felt the dampness there and gently massaged her. She began to moan. 'O God! don't stop,' she cried. I thought the moment had come. But before I could mount her, she climaxed and became like a corpse.

'That was not fair,' I protested. 'You had all the fun, leaving me high and dry.'

'What do you mean?' she asked. 'Didn't you like it?'

'Take a look at this,' I said taking her hand and putting it on my painfully stiff penis.

She felt it very gingerly. 'It's like an iron rod! A very big iron rod. If you thrust that in me it will kill me!'

'Come, now. Calm down,' I whispered, massaging her back. 'You can take it. You'll like it after the first time.'

An hour later we started kissing again. Again I fondled her breasts and slipped my hand between her thighs. She was damp again. 'This time no cheating,' I warned her. 'No one way traffic.'

'Okay,' she murmured, 'but be very, very gentle.'

I was. I knew she was a virgin. I had never had a virgin before. As I proceeded to enter her, she twitched with every move I made. I could not hold myself any longer and lunged into her. She let out a loud scream of pain and slapped the sides of the bed like a live butterfly flapping its wings when a pin is stuck into it. After months of celibacy I had a tankful of semen stored up. I pumped it into her.

She continued to whimper for some time. 'You brute!' she said, 'see what a mess you have made of me!' She switched on the table lamp. The white bedsheet was splattered with blood. Semen oozed out of her. 'What will the room-bearer think when he comes to do our beds?' she demanded.

'They must be used to it,' I replied. 'This is a honeymoon suite and most virgins bleed when their hymen bursts. Anyway, I'll put it in the tub and wash away the stains.'

We got up, pulled out the bedsheet and put it in a bucket of hot water. I washed myself as I had blood on me as well. She had coagulated blood and sticky semen between her thighs.

'Now we are well and truly married. Our marriage has been consummated.'

'Like bloody hell!' she snapped. 'I'm sore. It hurts.'

We had no choice but to sleep together in her bed. Soon she was fast asleep. By the time we got up the clouds had lifted and a bright sun shone in the rain-washed garden full of chrysanthemums in bloom.

We ordered breakfast in our room. We bathed, dressed and decided to take a stroll along the mountain path which ran from the hotel into the pine forest. 'I'm sore and stiff. I can't take a long walk,' complained Sonu. 'It's all your doing.'

'Put some vaseline or face cream there and you'll be right as rain, ready for more,' I said kissing her on her forehead.

By the afternoon her soreness was gone. So had the memory of what had caused it, and she was looking forward to repeating the pleasure it had given her. She smothered herself liberally with vaseline: no pain, undiluted pleasure. The third day she wanted it in the afternoon as well as at night. On the fourth she wanted it early in the morning to wake her up, after lunch to get a sound siesta, as an appetizer with her sundowner and then at night before going to sleep. She did not seem to tire. She knew how to rouse my interest. She would come out of her bath wearing a see-through half shirt. I could see her breasts through the shirt and half her uncovered bottom. She would brush her hair vigorously in front of the full length mirror: her breasts wobbled. She would bend over to daub her middle with cologne so that her half covered buttocks were fully exposed. She knew that the slow strip-tease yielded dividends. She would walk up to me and look directly at my crotch. 'I can see what you have in mind,' she would say. 'Come along, let's get down to it.'

She was in top form on the fifth evening. A full moon lit the mountains. She switched off the lights. Moonlight flooded into our room. She opened the window which overlooked the Valley of the Kaushalya and leant out to take in the scene. Her gossamer thin chemise exposed her rounded buttocks. 'Come, Mohan, see how beautiful it is.'

I stood behind her with my head resting on her shoulders. She pushed her rear back, into my crotch. I unbuttoned and entered her from behind. It was not very comfortable but very blissful. From experience I knew most women come quicker when entered from the rear. She stayed at the window surveying the scenery. 'It will be better in bed,' I said, barely able to hold out. 'Let the full moon see us making love,' she said, relieving herself of my pinion hold. She removed her chemise and lay on the carpet with the moonlight playing on her body. I lay on top of her. We prolonged our love-making as much as we could. By the time we finished, the moon was no longer shining through the window. A cold breeze blew and chilled our bedroom.

We lay in the same bed to warm ourselves.

The next morning Sonu came down with a heavy cold and a sore throat. She could hardly speak. I rang up to ask Garg if there was a doctor in the hotel. He sent for one from Kalka and came to fetch us. 'I'm going to move you into the lower hotel,' he said.

We stuffed our things into our cases. Sonu wrapped herself in a hotel blanket and we slid down by cable car to the lower hotel. Swaran took Sonu to her guest room. Sonu's eyes were streaming. The doctor took her temperature: she had mild fever. He forced open her mouth with a spoon and examined her throat. 'Streptococcal infection,' he pronounced. 'I will prescribe some antibiotics. You must take complete rest.'

Sonu shook her head vigorously. On a piece of paper she scribbled, 'I want to go home at once.'

I asked the doctor if it was wise to drive her to Delhi in that state. 'I don't advise it,' he replied. 'But if Madam insists, you may undertake the journey. Keep the windows of the car closed and wrap her up in a blanket. I will give her some Aspirin. It will relieve the pain in her throat and make her sleep.'

The porters put our suitcases in the car. Swaran lent us a woollen blanket and pillow. Sonu swallowed a couple of Aspirins with hot water and stretched herself on the rear seat. I went to the counter to settle my bill. 'Don't shame me in this way,' protested Garg holding my hand. 'I will settle it with the Rai Bahadur. Please ask him to ring me up to tell me of your safe arrival in Delhi.'

I drove down to Kalka, had my petrol tank filled up and the speed controller removed. I did the return journey without a stop in a little more than four hours. The Rai Bahadur and his wife who had been informed of our departure by Garg were waiting for us in their garden. There were no smiles of welcome for me. My mother-in-law said very acidly, 'The first time you take our Sonu out you bring her back sick.' The Rai Bahadur said nothing but his manner made me feel as if I had committed a crime. I accompanied Sonu to her bedroom and waited till their family doctor arrived. He took her temperature.

'High fever,' he pronounced giving me a baleful look.

'She has a very sore throat,' I told him. 'The doctor at the hotel said she needed antibiotics.'

He gave me another accusing look, examined her throat and assured her, 'Beta, there is nothing to worry about, I'll get rid of your fever and bad throat in a couple of days. All you need is rest, you are suffering from exhaustion and exposure.' He gave me yet another accusing look.

Sonu's face was flushed. I put my hand on her forehead. It was hot. 'Sonu, you want me to stay here with you for some days?'

She shook her head vigorously and managed to come out with five words: 'Go home to your Papa.'

I sensed I was not wanted. With a heavy heart I drove home. My father was surprised to see me back before I was expected, and without Sonu. I told him what had happened. 'She will be back when she's better,' I assured him. 'She is very delicate,' he replied. 'She has been brought up in a rich home and was probably unable to eat hotel food and bear the cold climate.'

I had brought the half empty bottle of Scotch with me. 'Pitaji, do you mind if I have a drink in your presence? I'm tired and a little upset with the way Sonu's parents spoke to me. They think I'm responsible for her fever and sore throat.'

'Go ahead. Don't mind what they say. They are probably as upset as you are.'

I had a couple of whiskeys—neat, as there was no soda in the house. I asked the cook to make me an omelette, had it with a slice of bread and retired to my bedroom.

My mind was very perturbed. What if Sonu died? Her parents would accuse me of murder: they looked like the kind of people who would. But how could there be any danger of her dying? All she had was fever and a sore throat. Perhaps her period was due in a couple of days: many girls are out of sorts when the curse is about to come over them, I reasoned. I slept fitfully.

My arrival at the office was not expected. In my absence Vimla Sharma had ensured that everyone came on time and cleared the work on their their desks before they left. She was not the seniormost of my staff but they all knew that being my secretary she was closest to me and I trusted her.

I explained to her what had brought me back earlier than planned. 'Nothing serious, I hope?' she asked solicitously.

'Nothing to worry about,' I assured her.

I went through the files for orders received, orders fulfilled and the accounts. Everything was running smoothly. At eleven I drove to Sonu's parents' home to see how she was doing. I went to her room. She was sitting in an armchair wrapped in a blanket. Her fever had abated—perhaps due to the drugs administered to her. Her throat still hurt but she was able to mumble a few words. I had to cheer her up. 'It was great fun being at Timber Trail Heights, wasn't it? The best five days in my life.'

She smiled.

'You must come home as soon as you are well.'

Once again she nodded her head.

Her mother came in. 'How is my beta feeling?' she asked without acknowledging my greeting.

'She's much better,' I replied. 'Fever has come down. She can speak a little.'

My mother-in-law continued to ignore me and kept up a monologue with her daughter. I decided to return to my office. 'I'll drop in again tomorrow, some time,' I said to Sonu. Once again she nodded her head. I did not say goodbye to her mother—the fat bitch.

*

I went to see Sonu every morning. The fever left her, her throat cleared up. She missed her period. She was angry.

'Why didn't you use condoms?' she demanded.

'You didn't ask me to; I didn't take any with me. If you did not want to get pregnant you should have taken precautions. In any case if you don't want a child you can have it aborted. At an early stage it is a very simple operation.'

She turned her face away. I noticed her breasts looked bigger: just five days of hectic sex had filled her up. Her mother came in looking as sour as ever. 'You could have been more patient: she is only a child of twenty-one. There was plenty of time to start a family.'

I didn't answer back. Only noticed how closely her daughter resembled her. A little more fat round the face, bottom and belly and the two would be like twins, though over thirty years apart.

The family now had yet another grouse against me. However, I made it a point to visit them once every day; if not mid-morning then on my way back from the office. My father wanted to see Sonu but I put him off with one excuse or the other to spare him the indignity of being cold-shouldered.

In ten days Sonu was up and about. But every time I suggested she come home she had some excuse to put it off. 'I'm not well,' she would say one day, and on another she would whine, 'I keep throwing up . . .' And each time she would add, 'You are out all day, who will look after me? Not your old man. Mummy says I should stay here till the baby is born.'

I did not like her calling my father 'old man'. I also thought she was behaving badly. 'It's a strange marriage,' I said with some sarcasm. 'A five-day honeymoon and the bride refuses to return to her husband's home. Did I rape you or treat you badly? Don't you want me to make love to you again? You seemed to enjoy it while it lasted.'

She did not have any answers. 'Mummy says pregnant women should not have sex. There is the danger of the child being aborted.'

Frustrated, I did not go to see Sonu for a whole week. Nor did I ring up to find out how she was doing. It was a bad beginning for a marriage meant to last a lifetime. I was determined to call her bluff. If necessary I would move the court for the restitution of conjugal rights. Fortunately better sense prevailed as the Rai Bahadur's family realized they were in the wrong. It was Sonu who rang me up. She complained, 'You haven't come to see me for a week or more; are you angry with me?'

'Yes, I am,' I replied bluntly. 'And with your parents. They have no right to keep you away from your lawfully wedded husband. They make me feel as if I have committed some crime making their daughter pregnant.'

'Don't talk like that!' she pleaded. 'I'll come over whenever you want me to. I'll only spend the day in my parents' home when you are in office.'

'I'll pick you up on my way back from the office. Be ready with your things: six o'clock sharp.' She was waiting for me on the porch that evening with two suitcases beside her. No parents, no brothers. Her servant put the cases in the boot and we drove off without any greetings or farewells.

I took her hand and said, 'Remember, now you belong to me, not to your parents. You go to see them with my permission and come back when I tell you to do so.' I felt it was better to adopt the macho attitude of a Hindu husband.

My father welcomed her home. He had the cook make a special meal for her: he had been told that pregnant women crave spicy food. She ate very little, complained of nausea and rushed to the bathroom. 'Pregnancy sickness,' my father pronounced. 'It will go in a few weeks.'

I was very gentle with Sonu that night. She let me lie with her, her head on my arm. 'I must see my gynaecologist before I let your thing perform more tricks on me,' she said putting her hand on my erection. I did not push her. We spent the night in the same bed without having any sex.

In the morning I dropped her at the entrance gate of her father's home. 'Six,' I repeated.

That became the pattern of our married life for the next six months. Her gynaecologist told her there was no harm in having sex for a few months, but nothing very hectic lest the foetus be disturbed. So we had sex occasionally. It was not the same as it was during the five-day honeymoon. It was a tame affair. I could not enjoy sex that was not full-blooded and where I had to be careful and gentle all the time. And Sonu became bigger and bigger by the day. Her breasts became swollen, her belly protruded as if she had a pitcher tied to it. She became positively unappetizing. I found my eyes wandering towards other women. Somebody had told me that a man's adulterous instincts are at their highest when his wife is pregnant. But I resisted. I refrained from adulterous intercourse during Sonu's first pregnancy.

After the eighth month, with my consent, Sonu moved into her parents' home. There she would be examined every day by her gynaecologist. The nursing home where she was to deliver her child was near their residence. It was her first delivery, probably a difficult one, and they did not want to take any chances.

In the ninth month of Sonu's pregnancy I was woken one night by the persistent ringing of the telephone. Sonu had gone into labour and had been taken to the nursing home. I told my father and left immediately. When I got there Sonu's father was in the waiting room, her mother with her in the labour room. The Rai Bahadur barely acknowledged my greeting and didn't say a word to me for the hour we sat facing each other. There were other families in the room chatting away merrily and asking the nurses coming in and out of operation theatres for news. Over an hour later a nurse came out and asked, 'Mr Mohan Kumar?' I stood up. So did Sonu's father. 'Congratulations,' she said, 'you've became the father of a boy.'

Sonu's father asked her, 'How is she—my daughter?'

'She's fine,' replied the nurse. 'We had to give her a whiff of chloroform, that's all. She had a normal delivery. It's a big boy, eight pounds. He will grow to be a tall man like his father. You can see them after half an hour when the baby has been bathed and cleaned up.'

We waited half an hour. The nurse asked us to follow her into Sonu's private room. Sonu looked exhausted and pale. Nestling against her bosom was a blob of downy hair and puckered flesh frantically searching for its mother's nipple. Sonu put it in its mouth. I put my hand on Sonu's forehead and then kissed the baby. 'Was it difficult?' I asked.

'Not very. The pain was terrible. I'm glad it's over. What does your son look like?'

'Can't say yet. He looks very angry. And hungry.'

I sat with her and her parents for half an hour till the nurse ordered us to leave. By the time I got home it was early morning.

My father was waiting for me. I gave him the news. He was

delighted. 'Our line will go on!' he said. 'Mubarak—congratulations! You must take me along the next time you go to see her. I must have a look at my grandson . . . We must think of a nice name for him.'

In the office I sent for mithai: laddoos, gulab jamuns, rasgullas, to be distributed among the staff.

Twelve

Mary Joseph

During the weeks Sonu was away, I made an important decision. I asked a property dealer close to our house to find me a bigger house with a garden in an upper-class residential area. My firm was making a lot of money and I was determined now to move out of the house gifted by Achint Ram. To put him in his place, I'd buy a much larger house than what he had given his daughter. Of course, it would not match her father's mansion, but I could give Sonu the feeling that she had not done too badly with me. This time buying a house would not be a problem: I still had no real black money, but I could now pay a part in rupees and the rest in dollars, for which there were many takers.

I did not tell anyone about my decision, not even my father. I wanted it to be a big surprise to Sonu and a gift for my newborn son. A week later the realtor came by with a map of New Delhi indicating where the kind of house I wanted would be available and on what terms. I spent a morning travelling with the realtor from one large house to another. I settled for one in Maharani Bagh, not far from where I was living. It was a double-storeyed bungalow with a lawn in front, a modest courtyard at the back, two garages, three big rooms and a terrace on the first floor and a large reception room, two bedrooms, a study and a kitchen on the ground floor. There were servant quarters in the rear. I fell in love with it at once. The owners, an elderly couple shifting out to Chandigarh, were willing to hand over possession as soon as the money was paid to them. I had my company lawyer draw up the agreement for sale and handed the couple a lump sum in cash as part payment.

After the deal had been finalized, I told my father. He was somewhat dismayed. 'Isn't this house good enough for you?' He had spent almost his entire adult life in a government flat and every house looked to him too large for comfort. 'You see it, you will love it,' I assured him. 'You have to give it a name.'

The morning after my son was born, I took my father to see the house. He was very pleased with what he saw. He had chosen a name for my son—Ranjit Kumar; the house was to be named after him—Ranjit Villa.

This is the house I live in today in the style expected of a youngish millionaire. I got pricey interior decorators to do it up. I engaged a Mug cook; the young fellow who cooked for us till then became his assistant, bearer and masalchi. The house had its own cleaning woman who lived in the quarters. I took her on so she could stay where she was. I also engaged a part-time gardener and a chauffeur as I found driving in Delhi somewhat tiresome.

*

I was impatient to bring my wife and child to the new house I had bought for them. 'As far as I'm concerned, you can take them home now,' Sonu's gynaecologist told me. 'I'm always available at all hours. But if Sonu feels nervous, I suggest you hire a night nurse who can keep an eye on the baby so that the mother can sleep undisturbed and only be woken up when the baby wants to be fed.'

The Rai Bahadur did not bother to consult me. 'For a few days she will stay with us,' he told the doctor. 'We will have a day and night nurse for as long as the baby needs breast-feeding.'

So that was that. While I was in the office, Sonu and the baby were shifted to the Rai Bahadur's residence along with two nurses. I only found out when I went to the nursing home to see them. An undeclared tug-of-war restarted between us. I did not go to the Rai Bahadur's house that evening.

The next morning when I met Sonu I complained. 'You did not bother to let me know you had returned home. I looked such a fool when I went to the nursing home. What must the staff have thought about our relationship?'

'You could have rung up before going there. They wanted the room for another expectant mother, so I had to leave.'

'When are you coming home?'

'Give me a few more days here. I have to feed this brat every four hours. He sets up such a howl if his meal is delayed by a few minutes. Here I have these two nurses and my mother to look after us. Mother says we should choose a nice name for the boy.'

'We already have one. Father's chosen it: Ranjit Mohan Kumar. I like it. It was my great-grandfather's name.'

'So you let your father decide his name without consulting me? I am the boy's mother, in case you've forgotten.'

Every time we talked to each other, it became an argument. I was determined not to let her have her way over our son's name. 'Ranjit Mohan Kumar it is going to be. I've named our home after him: Ranjit Villa. You will see it on the door when you decide to come home.' I said nothing about having bought a new house and let her presume I had given our old house a new name.

I let her spend another fortnight in her parents' home. Then my patience ran out. 'You have to come home now,' I told her over the phone one afternoon. 'I have cleared one bedroom for your nurses for as long as you need them. Your parents can come to see you every day if they like while I am in the office. You can spend weekends with them if you like.'

She knew I meant business. She told her parents. Very reluctantly they agreed to let her go. Not on the Saturday following because Saturday was inauspicious, being the day of Shani—Saturn. Sunday would be better. I turned up on the morning of the following Sunday. She had accumulated a lot of baby's things: bed sheets, soft blankets, nappies, talcum powders, gripe-water bottles and a huge teddy bear. There was not enough room for everything in my car, so one nurse got into the Rai Bahadur's car with the baggage. Sonu took the front seat beside me, the senior nurse, with the baby in her lap, took the rear seat. I told the Rai Bahadur's driver, 'You follow me.'

'Sahib, I have been to your house many times.'

'Follow me,' I told him again, 'it's not the same one.'

'Where are we going?' asked Sonu.

'To your new home. I kept it as a surprise for you.'

I pulled up at the gate of my new house and pointed to the brass name plate. 'See! Ranjit Villa.'

I thought she would be happy to see her large new house named after her son. What I saw was sullen resentment written all over her face. 'Without consulting me, without telling me!' she snarled. I knew she would have more to say on the subject when the nurse was not within earshot. The nurse's reaction also quietened her. 'Mr Mohan, what a beautiful house you have! My! My!' she gushed as I took them inside and showed them Sonu's and the baby's bedroom: silk bed covers; large, soft feather pillows imported from Germany; a baby's cot; bathrooms done up like in five star hotels.

My father did his best to welcome them. He applied kum kum powder on Sonu's and the baby's forehead, waved hundred-rupee notes round their heads and pressed them into their hands. The servants came in. I introduced them in turn. They touched her feet. 'Mem-sahib, aap ko bahut bahut mubarak ho,' said the Mug cook, congratulating her in his Bengali-Hindi accent. The bearer she already knew. The jamadarni introduced herself as just the jamadarni, the woman who did the floors and the bathrooms. 'So the staff has also been appointed without consulting the mistress of the house!' remarked Sonu very acidly when we were left alone. 'All I have to do is to eat what is offered to me, sleep with you when I'm expected to and be the wet-nurse for my own child.'

I was exasperated. 'Is there anything I do which pleases you? I've done all this to make you happy. All the thanks I get is a barrage of criticism.'

I stormed out of the room. I hoped this would make her feel she had overdone it. She went round the house inspecting the rooms. She

went to the kitchen and asked the cook what he had made for lunch
and supper; she came down and went round the reception room. I
could hear her open the drinks cabinet and examine the cut glass.
Finally she came into my study where I was pretending to work. 'I'm
sorry to prove such a damper,' she said apologetically. 'Everything is
carefully laid out. You can do very well without me.'

'Well, I'm glad you like the place.'

'What about your nurses?' she asked.

'Ask them their food preferences and tell the cook,' I replied.

She asked the nurses to come down and introduce themselves to
me. 'Saar, my name is Mary Joseph. I am Roman Catholic, from Tamil
Nadu,' said the older one. She was a dark, plump woman in her thirties.
On her ample bosom she had a gold cross dangling. The younger one
introduced herself: 'I am Ittiara Mathews, sir, from Kottayam in Kerala.
I am Syrian Christian.' She was not as dark, nor as plump as the other
nurse. I showed them to their room next to my study. I had two beds
put in it. They would occupy the room in turns, depending on their
hours of duty. 'I am the night nurse,' said the Keralite, 'so Mary will be
here at night; I during the day.' I told them to tell the cook what kind
of food they liked to eat. 'Saar, anything you eat, we eat,' replied Mary.
'Sometimes we like idli-dosa. We can make that ourselves.'

In a couple of days life fell into a pattern. Sonu and the baby slept
in one of the bedrooms upstairs. The nurse from Kerala dozed off in
an armchair in the same room. The baby's bawling every four hours
was her alarm. I had a bed put in my study for myself. The Tamilian
occupied the room next to mine. She was more communicative than
the Keralite. She told me she was married and had a child. 'My husband,
he drink, drink, drink all the time. Like a fish. When I say stop he beat
me. Not enough money in the house and child to bring up. What to
do, saar? So I took course in nursing and after I got my certificate, I
told my husband—Mister, you stay here and drink and look after my
child. I am taking a job in Delhi and send you whatever I save.' She
looked quite cheerful about it. 'Saar, one life to live. Not to waste it on
a drunkard husband. You agree?'

I agreed.

Sonu would not let me come near her. 'The doctor said no sex till I have weaned the baby. After six months I will start giving him milk from a bottle and some solids like Farex. Then we'll see what we can do.'

I had not had proper sex for over six months. Another six months of abstinence would be hard on a lustful man like me.

One evening I had more than my quota of Scotch. Sonu did not touch alcohol as it went into her milk, which was harmful for the baby. My father had taken to eating before sunset and retiring to his room for the night. I waited for the servants to leave and locked the rear entrance which they used. After dinner I took a short stroll in the garden, locked the front gate and came to my study-cum-bedroom. Mary Joseph came to say goodnight to me. I don't know what came over me. I took her in my arms and kissed her passionately. She did not resist. 'Saar, somebody may come in. It is not safe.' I bolted my study from the inside and pushed her on my bed. She was quite willing. She pulled up her white skirt and took off her panties. I tore open her blouse and went hungrily for her large breasts. She stretched her thighs wide apart. As I entered her she exclaimed, 'Aiy Aiy yo! Saar, you are very big. I like it very much.' She responded vigorously to my thrusts. We climaxed together.

'Not safe,' she said as she got up and re-adjusted her dress. 'No good if I become pregnant. I am Catholic; no divorce, no illegitimate child. If Jesus forgives me this time, I will get birth control pills for future. Only one life to live, Saar.'

Did I suffer pangs of guilt? I did not. I justified what I did with Mary Joseph the same way Mary Joseph justified her adultery: only one life to live. Sex is important. When denied it becomes more important. The body's needs come above religious taboos and notions of morality.

Jesus forgave Mary Joseph her transgression. Two days later she had her period. Six days later she was on the pill. Every night it was the same exclamation of surprise and joy—'Aiy Aiy yo! Saar, you are very big.' And every night she thrust her hips up at me, matching my desperate rhythm, leaving me in no doubt that she liked it 'very much'.

Our fun and games did not last long. Apparently I looked more relaxed and cheerful than I had for some time, and Sonu was curious. She had no evidence whatsoever of my infidelity. Of the two nurses, it was the younger Keralite who was more attractive, and she spent the night in Sonu's room. The Tamilian was fat and shapeless. The gold cross dangling between her breasts was proof that she was a devout Christian and would not have sex with anyone besides her husband. But women have a sixth sense which warns them when their security is threatened. Sonu suspected that there was something wrong going on under her own roof. She did not want to take any chances. A fortnight later she announced that she did not need a day nurse any more and had asked her mother to get her an ayah to keep an eye on the child in the day time. Mary Joseph's services were dispensed with. Before she left she gave me her visiting card. It had the name and telephone number of her nursing home. 'Saar, any time you want me, just ring me up and I will come over. Any hotel or friend's house. Anywhere. I don't want any money; just you.'

I put her card in my wallet.

Getting rid of the day nurse did not change Sonu's attitude towards me. I could not understand what had come over her. She found fault with everything I did. Every evening she brought up some topic which ended in an angry exchange of words. I would switch on the TV to avoid her picking a quarrel, and keep it on through the drinks hour and dinner till it was time to go to bed—she to hers and I to mine. In that mood having sex never entered our minds. My thoughts began to stray to Mary Joseph. She was no beauty but she was willing. That made her desirable. I was reluctant to take the initiative. She was not. One afternoon Vimla Sharma buzzed my phone, 'Sir, your baby's nurse wants to talk to you. I hope all is well with the child.'

'Put her on,' I replied.

It was Mary Joseph. 'Saar, excuse me for disturbing you in the office. I wanted to enquire about the baby's health. How is my little baba?'

'He's fine. Look, will you be available on this number if I ring up later in the evening?'

'Yes, saar, for you always available, anytime, anywhere.'

That was what was nice about Mary Joseph. I rang up the Ashoka Hotel to book a room the next day in the name of a business partner in Bombay. The Ashoka had some advantages which other Delhi hotels did not. It was owned by the government and was the largest hotel in the city. It was also very impersonal. Most important of all, it had a third floor with a lift of its own beside the patisserie along the parking lot. Visitors staying on the third floor did not have to go through the large entrance hall with the reception desk, enquiries and the cashier's counters. There were always people sitting or loitering around in the lobby, people who would recognize you and reach all kinds of conclusions—usually the right ones. For the third floor all you had to do was to pretend you had come to pick up fresh bread, cakes or pastries and go round the shop to the elevator. Room waiters on the third floor knew what businessmen from Bombay, Calcutta and Madras wanted in the way of relaxation when they came to Delhi. They went about their jobs silently, asked no questions, only expected to be tipped handsomely.

I got Mary Joseph on my direct line. 'Meet me tomorrow evening at five, Mary. Room number three hundred, third floor, Ashoka Hotel. Not in your nurses' uniform. And don't ask for me, just knock on the door.'

'Sure, sure, saar. Okay.'

The next day I left the office at half past four and told the chauffeur he would not be needed till the next morning. From the patisserie I bought some chicken patties and a chocolate cake. I took the small elevator to the third floor. Room No. 300 was open, with the key in the key hole. I put it in my pocket and went in. It was a comfortable single bedroom. A bottle of Scotch and two glasses sat on the table beside the usual basket of fruits and vase of flowers. There were sodas in the fridge. I helped myself to a Scotch-n-soda. The room bearer came in to take orders. 'I will ring if I want anything,' I replied. 'Put the don't disturb sign on the door and leave it open.'

He had never seen me before, but he knew the drill and departed. A few minutes later there was a gentle knock on the door and in came

Mary Joseph. 'Notice on door says don't disturb,' she said with a broad smile. 'I hope I am not disturbing you, saar.' She was dressed in in a white cotton sari with gold borders. It suited her more than the nurse's uniform. Like modern girls she wore a backless, sleeveless blouse. She had a cute belly button.

'Shut and bolt the door behind you. The notice is not for you but for other people,' I told her.

'I know, saar. I am not stupid.'

She put her arms round my neck and gave me a gentle kiss on the lips. 'Saar, I missed you like anything. I said to myself, Saar will never ring you up. He has his memsahib and big, big business to look after. Who will think of one poor nurse after he has had her, one, two, four, five times?'

We sat down on a sofa. 'Do you like this room?' I asked her.

'Very nice,' she replied. 'There it was always at night and I couldn't see you. And always fear in my mind that someone may suddenly come in. Now it is daylight, we can see what we are doing without bothering about anyone. No?'

I took her in my arms and kissed her hungrily. I slipped my hand under her blouse and fondled her big breasts till her nipples became hard. We got up and moved to the bed. First she took off her gold necklace, kissed the cross and laid it reverently on the table. Then she took off her sari, folded it and put it on a chair. She took off her blouse; her breasts tumbled out. She looked down coyly at them. I untied the knot of her petticoat. It fell to the floor. She put her hands between her thighs to cover herself and giggled. I pushed them aside and saw the mass of healthy curling pubic hair. She had very broad thighs, silken soft. 'You also, saar. Like me. Nothing,' she pleaded.

I stripped myself of my clothing and we lay down side by side on the bed. 'Saar, you have the biggest thing I have ever seen. So big no other man has.'

'How many have you seen?' I asked her, putting it into her caressing hands.

'What seen? My husband not half as big. And so quick to finish. In out, in out. Phut. Once his younger brother had me. Also small and very quick quick. The padre of our village church was much better. But he was sorry for doing it. After he finished he asked me to pardon him and made me pray with him to Jesus to ask his forgiveness. Imagine, no, still naked and sweating and kneeling on the floor and praying to God! He made me feel worse than a prostitute who did it without asking for money. Tell me, saar, is it a sin to do it with somebody you like?'

The only way to stop Mary Joseph from talking was to seal her mouth with mine. This I did again and again while I stroked her thighs and pushed three fingers through the springy pubic hair and into her. She was warm and slick. She began to moan with pleasure, 'Oh! oh! oh! . . . How can such a nice thing be sin? Tell me, saar, tell me.' She pulled my hand away and threw her heavy, smooth legs high and wide. I mounted and entered her and glued my mouth to hers. She was more animated than I expected from a woman of her bulk. And when she came she dug her nails into my neck and bit my lips, then collapsed with her arms and legs stretched wide.

'For me this was heaven,' she said when she had regained her breath, 'and for you, saar?'

'Very nice,' I replied. 'Let's get back into our clothes. Shall I order tea or coffee for us?'

'Coffee for me, saar.'

We washed ourselves together. As I saw her dark, ungainly figure, I could not understand how I could have made love to her. But I had enjoyed every minute of it. I put my clothes on, then sat and watched her dress. First she put her necklace round her neck and again kissed the cross. Then she put on her blouse, then the petticoat and finally— and with surprising swiftness—her sari. I rang for the room bearer and ordered two coffees and a plate of biscuits.

Mary Joseph was in a chatty mood. She wanted to tell me all there was to know about her village, married life, her husband, his brother, her son, the nursing home, the doctors and other nurses. She sensed I was not listening to her. 'I talk too much, saar,' she admitted. 'Everyone calls me chatterbox. I will keep my mouth shut and you do the talking.'

'I don't talk very much,' I told her. She felt she had been

reprimanded. The bearer brought coffee and biscuits. I handed him my credit card. I asked him to give it to the cashier and bring me the receipt. A few minutes later he came back for my signature and with the receipt. It was over a couple of thousand rupees for the two hours with Mary Joesph. I gave the bearer a hundred-rupee note as a tip.

'Let's go,' I said to her. I handed her the two boxes with the cake and patties. 'I bought them for you.'

'O thank you very much, saar. You should not have bother. This is very expensive—room and all in five star hotel!' She put her arms round my neck and looked directly into my eyes. 'Saar, you will see me again, won't you? Soon? I will pay my share of the room charge.'

'Don't be silly. I can afford it, you can't. And I got as much fun out of it as I hope you did.'

There was so much pleading in her eyes that I could not help committing myself to further meetings, if not in the Ashoka, in some other hotel. I asked her to go ahead of me by the small lift, gave her the number of my car and told her to wait for me. A few minutes later, I followed her, opened the car door to let her in. 'How did you come to the hotel?' I asked her.

'In a three-wheeler. I can't afford taxis.'

'You must let me pay for your transport. I can always drop you back home.'

I drove her to the top of the road where her nursing home was and dropped her at the cross roads. 'When will you ring me up, saar?' she asked as she got out of the car. 'Soon,' I replied, 'but don't ring me in the office. They will begin to talk.'

I was back home a little later than usual. Sonu noticed I had driven in myself, and demanded, 'Where were you driving around without the chauffeur?'

'I went to the club to have a drink and told him to go home.'

The smell of the whiskey on my breath spared me further questions. I went to see the baby. He had his tiny feet in his hands and was gurgling away, his large eyes wide open to take in the world. He had begun to recognize me and would show his pleasure by knocking both his legs together and slapping his cot with his hands. I tickled him under the chin; he responded with a toothless smile and a 'gug-gug-gug'. Next to the TV it was the baby who gave me an excuse to avoid getting into an argument with Sonu.

Thirteen
How the Marriage Died

Sonu and I were drifting apart. She never tired of nagging and needling me. We hardly had any sex. I kept out of her way and ignored her when she decided to pick a fight. This infuriated her. So she picked on my father.

Father was a God-fearing and self-effacing man who never raised his voice against anyone. He kept to himself. He went every day to the gurudwara in the mornings and the Sai Baba temple in the evenings. He had his meals in his room where he pored over books on religion—the Upanishads, the writings of Jiddu Krishnamurti—and listened to tapes of the sermons of Sai Baba, Swami Chinmayananda and others. He came only twice a day to the portion of the house we occupied. In the mornings he sat with me for a few minutes and then spent half an hour with baby Ranjit. He stayed a little longer in the evenings, when he did nothing but baby talk with Ranjit. He had become Ranjit's favourite adult. As soon as he heard my father's footsteps, Ranjit would start on a loud 'Dada Dada Dada'. He would stretch out his arms to be picked up. He would smack his grandfather's face with his tiny hands, pull off his glasses, tug at his moustache. My father loved it and gently remonstrated with him, 'Beta, you'll break my glasses. Will you buy me another pair?' When Ranjit learnt to crawl, he would come scuttling on all fours to where my father was sitting and haul himself up. The two would rock in a tight embrace for some time, then Ranjit would resume knocking off Father's glasses and pulling his moustache. He would gather his spit in his mouth and blow bubbles into his grandfather's face. Father loved that too. '*Mera nunha munna,*' he would say. 'What will you be when you grow up?' Ranjit would reply by slapping his face more vigorously and shouting 'Dadadada'.

Sonu did not approve of their closeness. 'Pitaji, you are spoiling him,' she would say. 'He gets too excited when you are around and refuses to go to bed.'

My father kept his peace. Many a time when grandfather and grandchild were deeply involved with each other, Sonu would shout, 'That's enough! Ayah, put the baby to bed. It's very late for him.' As the ayah tried to pick him up from his grandfather's lap Ranjit would fight back and howl. Sonu would storm in, pluck the child roughly from his grandfather's lap and hand him over to the ayah. Ranjit's howling would get louder as he hit the ayah with his fists. You could hear him calling for his 'Dada' between sobs till sleep overcame him. My father would quietly walk away to his room.

It made me angry, very angry. But I did not open my mouth.

'There must be some discipline in the house,' Sonu would say. 'The baby must be taught to eat and go to bed on time. I can't have him spoilt for other people's pleasures.'

I would switch on the TV, pour myself a Scotch. I would continue to watch the screen and drink. Most of our evenings were spent in this manner.

My father sensed that Sonu did not like his living in the house. One day he told me, 'Puttar, I want to go to my ashram for a few days. The weather is nice—not too cold, not too warm. I need to be with myself for a while. Can you book me a seat on a bus?'

'Pitaji, I will drive you to Haridwar. I also want a short break. The sight of the Ganga lifts my spirits.'

I told Sonu of Father's decision to leave for Haridwar. Far from being remorseful, she said, 'That will be good for the baby. He won't be mollycoddled and will learn to be independent of people.'

I decided to take my father to Haridwar on Poornamashi, the day of the full moon. It fell on a Saturday, when the office closed at midday. Father was ready with his luggage when I reached home that afternoon.

Baby Ranjit was asleep. My father gazed at the child's face for a long time. He could not hold back his tears. He murmured a silent prayer as he left. Sonu made a gesture of touching his feet before we drove out of the house. Four hours later we drove into his ashram.

I did not want to miss the sunset aarti at Har Ki Pauri. We put our luggage in the room and walked through the bazaars to the river bank. It was March. The hillsides were ablaze with the crimson red of the flame of the forest in full bloom. As the sun went over the western range, a full moon rose in the sky. It was the same scene of candelabras being waved over the stream to the chanting of shlokas and the loud clanging of temple bells. Leaf boats carrying flickering oil lamps bobbed up and down on the dark water. I realized that if there was one experience which I would get nowhere else in the world it was the worship of the Ganga at Haridwar at sunset.

That night I was strangely at peace with myself. The bickerings with Sonu were out of my mind. All the women who had for short periods become a part of my life were also out of my mind. Even Mary Joseph whom I had been bedding off and on in different hotels ceased to exist for me. Mother Ganga had taken me in her embrace and there was no room for anyone else. I slept soundly all night.

My father woke me up in the morning with a cup of hot tea. We went back to the ghats and bathed in the river. This time my eyes did not stray towards women bathers. Perhaps I was getting the better of my lecherous instincts!

I spent a long time talking to my father. I told him I would visit him every full moon night and any other time he wanted to see me. I pleaded with him to come over at least once a month. I could send my car to fetch him and drop him back. He did not commit himself. 'Let's see,' he replied every time I asked him to make a promise.

I drove back at a leisurely pace through the countryside of wheat fields ready to be harvested, along the cool bank of the broad Ganga canal, through the crowded bazaars of highway towns. I was back home by the afternoon.

Ranjit was having his long siesta. He woke up when I was having tea. He looked very happy to see me, but his eyes looked for someone else. 'Dada?' he asked with a question mark on his face. He went crawling round sofas and chairs calling 'Dada, Dada'. They often played hide and seek. When he failed to find his Dada anywhere Ranjit came back to me and looked me full in the face with his large questioning eyes. 'Dada? Dada?' he asked. I picked him up and put him against my chest. 'Dada's gone to Haridwar. He will be back soon.'

Sonu picked up our dialogue. 'Is he planning to come back soon?' she asked.

'I don't know if he will come back at all. He felt he was unwanted here,' I replied in a huff.

'Why are you always picking on me?' she screamed. 'He went of his own free will. I didn't tell him to go.'

I switched the TV on and asked the bearer to bring out the Scotch.

*

I stuck to my resolve of being in Haridwar on full moon nights with my father. I insisted on his coming back with me so he could spend a few days with his grandson. One had to see them together to understand how elemental and strong are the ties of affection between grandparents and their grandchildren. Sonu accepted the arrangement of having 'the old man' spend four or five days of the month with us. He always brought some prasad from the ashram, a bottle full of Gangajal, and rustic toys for Ranjit.

Sonu had other scores to settle with me. It seemed to be a part of her plan to not let me enjoy even my evening drink. One evening as I poured out one for myself and one for her (having weaned Ranjit some months ago she had started drinking sherry and at times Scotch) she asked me, 'How many women did you take to bed before you married me?'

I knew she was angling for a fight. I tried to be evasive. 'A few, I don't remember how many.'

'And of course you expected your Indian wife to be a virgin. All Indian men are like that; one rule for them, another for their women.'

I did not contradict her. It did not stop her going on with the interrogation: 'Who was the first one?'

I pretended I could not remember. 'I think it was a woman called Jessica Browne, I'm not quite sure.'

'What do you mean you don't remember? No one forgets the person they had sex with the first time. Who was this Jessica woman?'

'Black American. She was captain of the university women's tennis team.'

'Black! You mean a habshi, a nigger?'

'Nigger is regarded as a very rude word by educated Americans. They say coloured or African-American.'

'That's not the point,' she snapped back, 'I know you don't call niggers that to their face. Behind their backs whites still call them niggers. Why did you pick on a black woman?'

'I don't remember. It just happened. I was shy of being seen with white girls. People stared at you. They didn't if you were with a coloured woman because they took me to be coloured—which I was.'

'How many times did you have this Jessica woman?'

'I don't know. A few times. It didn't last long. She started going out with white boys and it ended.'

'Who else?'

'For God's sake stop this cross-examination! It's all in the past and finished. Why go on and on about something that's over and done with?' I said angrily. 'Must you always ruin my evenings by starting arguments?'

I helped myself to another drink, switched on the TV.

She had yet to interrogate me about why I was late from office some evenings and smelt of whisky. I knew she would soon start doing that. And she would do it every evening. I realized I could not go on seeing Mary Joseph for too long. Meeting her in hotel rooms was risky. Someone was sure to recognize me and ask me questions. Or her, as she must have attended to hundreds of patients in her nursing home or as a private nurse. Fortunately for me, it was she who terminated our clandestine meetings. She rang me on my direct number in the office and told me she had to return to her village as her husband was reported to be very sick. 'Cirrhosis of the liver, what else!' she said. 'No one to look after my son. Saar, I will write to you and tell you all about it.'

I did not see Mary Joseph again. She wrote only once to tell me that her husband had died and that she had been appointed senior matron of the village health clinic. She sent me the blessings of Lord Jesus Christ.

*

Sonu and I realized that our marriage was not working out. What concerned us most was what other people would say. Nobody bothers about marriages which hold; everyone is deeply interested if things go wrong. Whenever I dropped in at the Gymkhana or the Golf Club for a drink, my friends and their wives would ask, 'Do you keep Sonu in purdah now? Why don't you bring her with you?' These were loaded questions.

I told Sonu.

'You never ask me to come with you. You go off on your own from the office. We pay subscriptions to three clubs; I haven't been inside one for almost three years,' she said.

We were heading for another unpleasant argument; I cut it short: 'I'll ask the chauffeur to pick you up first and then collect me from the office. I agree that we should be seen together oftener than we are.'

'We've hardly ever been seen together except at home,' she said.

Thereafter, at least twice a week, we began going to the Gymkhana or the Golf Club and spent an hour or more drinking with friends. Occasionally we joined them for dinner on special nights when exotic food was served. It was on our way back that she would pick on me. 'You find that Chopra chap's wife—what's her name— attractive?'

'Mrinal? Passable. She's very vivacious.'

'You didn't notice anyone else at the party. It's not good manners to pay attention to only one person in a party.'

'She happened to be sitting next to me. I didn't have much choice.

On my other side was that fat woman—— what's her name——who has hardly anything to say about anything.'

'Sheila Goel. I find her very interesting. She's very knowledgeable about Hindi movies and light classical music. I'm told she has a lovely voice.'

'You are welcome to her. I'm not interested in Hindi films nor in pakka raag. There is so much happening in the world; one should know something about it and have one's own opinions. That Goel woman has no clue about what's going on in the world around her. When I asked her what she thought of the election results in Delhi, she shut me up by saying she had no interest in politics. She has no interest in sports either. Or for that matter in anything else.'

That was good enough to start a slanging match; I fighting for Mrinal Chopra, she for Sheila Goel. This sort of thing was repeated every time we returned from a party with a little alcohol inside us. With every passing year it got worse. Sometimes she would force me to stop in the middle of the road, get out and walk away shouting that she could not bear to be with a womanizer. The first few times I would park the car by the side of the road and wait for her to return. Then I stopped bothering and left her to find her way back home in a taxi or on her own two feet.

There is a common belief that children cement a marriage. There is little doubt that children need both parents to give them a sense of security which is necessary for their mental stability. However, my experience does not support the belief that this also reduces the tensions in a marriage. On the contrary, the birth of our son had produced more discord than harmony. Admittedly we had not planned to have him; he came because we could not hold ourselves back from exploring each others' bodies and were foolish enough not to use contraceptives. It was not our child who generated any resentment between us. Both of us were devoted to him and made a lot of fuss over him. But even as a baby he reacted to our quarrels by turning to my father for company and comfort. This turned Sonu against my father. She made him feel unwelcome in our home. Being a proud and self-respecting man he decided to move permanently to his ashram in Haridwar. Little Ranjit missed him and turned to his ayah rather than to his mother for company. Sonu did not like that. She fired one ayah after another on the flimsiest of excuses: she steals my things, she is very lazy, she spoils the child, and so on and so forth. Ranjit could not come to terms with the succession of maidservants. He looked forward to my coming home in the evenings and clung to me till it was time for him to have supper and be put to bed. He insisted on my telling him stories till sleep overtook him. Sonu now had something more to hold against me. She began to resent our son's preference for me rather than her. She was convinced I was turning the child against her. 'Will you please leave him alone and let him get proper sleep? He has to get to school in the morning,' she would shout if our story-telling sessions went on longer than she liked.

Sex became a dutiful ritual performed once or twice every month (though even this was irregular) in the hope that Sonu would not suspect that I had found alternatives to the matrimonial bed. Indeed, I had found other outlets, but there was always the apprehension of being found out and so the affairs were not as pleasurable as those I had had in my bachelor days. I could not think of any way out of the impasse except to somehow win back my freedom through separation followed by divorce. The thought often came to my mind after a particularly nasty quarrel, but I never voiced it. It was, in fact, Sonu who suggested it: 'We can't go on like this for much longer,' she said angrily once. 'We make each other unhappy; it would be better if we lived apart.' She awaited my response. I did not react. She said the same thing again some days later, and this time I agreed: 'Yes, we should break up. I have had enough of this matrimonial bliss.' She was taken aback and lapsed into a sullen silence. This sort of exchange happened more than a few times. It was always she who broke the icy silence that followed. It formed a pattern. After some days of not talking to each other, at night she would stretch her hand across to me. I would come over to her and without a word of affection being exchanged she would part her legs and I would mount her. There being no great urgency on my side, I could hold out as long as I liked, switch the woman lying under me from Sonu to one of the many that came to my mind: Jessica one night, Yaasmeen the second, Mary Joseph on the third . . .

Life was becoming a bore. Boredom was written all over my face. Life should be interesting and exciting otherwise what is the point in going on? The clubs or parties we went to were useless. We met the same kind of people, who drank the same kind of liquor, indulged in the same kind of small talk and bitching. All trapped in the meaningless quest for money, creature comforts and hankering for social respectability. We frittered away the best years of our lives in banalities. The world had so much more to offer than we were taking from it: beautiful places, beautiful people. Beautiful paintings and sculptures for the eyes to behold. Beautiful music and songs. The fragrance of flowers; the aroma of the parched earth when the first drops of rain fall on it. Tasty food and wines to tickle the palate; roasted nuts with premium Scotch; avocado pears with chilled Pouille Fusse; wild rice with creamed mushroom sauce and juicy steaks with rich Barolo or Burgundy; trifle followed by sips of Drambuie, Cointreau, orange Curacao, Grand Marniere or Cognac. And after a good meal, a Havana cigar.

But more than sights, sounds, smells and tastes, it was the sense of touch that mattered most to me. More than the feel of silk and velvet, it was the feel of the female body that produced the ultimate thrill. Passionate lips to kiss; firm rounded breasts to caress and suck; well-rounded, smooth buttocks and softer-than-silk thighs to stroke. Most people regard these preoccupations as crude, vulgar, obscene. For me they are the things that make life worth living—all the rest is marginal and of little consequence.

*

I taught myself to hold my temper when Sonu lost hers. When she went on a spree of nagging, I kept my cool. It made her uneasy. She felt I was slipping out of her grasp. She feared that the next time she brought up the subject of separation or divorce, I would call her bluff. She did not bring it up again. Whether it was her own idea or whether it was suggested to her by her mother, she hinted that being the only child Ranjit was getting too much attention. Without more being said we stopped using contraceptives. It did not take long for Sonu to conceive her second child. She reverted to being ratty and quarrelsome. After the sixth month of her pregnancy she moved to her parents home to be nearer her gynaecologist and the nursing home. I made it a point to drop in to see her on my way back from office. Her parents and her brothers made no attempt to be friendlier towards me. For them I was still an educated upstart who assumed fancy airs. They could not accept the fact that I was not dependent on them and was doing well on my own. I was the pillar of the young millionaires' club; neither of Sonu's brothers had made it to the charmed circle.

Our daughter was born six years after Ranjit. Since my father was away in Haridwar, I let Sonu decide on a name for her. She and her parents settled for Mohini: perhaps as a concession to me because my name was Mohan. Ranjit was thrilled with his baby sister. My father was also very happy to get the news. He wrote back saying he would come over after the child came to her own home. Clearly he felt as uncomfortable in Achint Ram's household as I did.

Sonu spent another month with her parents before she came home with Mohini. This time she brought only a night nurse and an ayah. My father came from Haridwar to bless the child; he spent more than a week with us. By now he was fully aware of Sonu's hostility towards him and kept out of her way as much as he could. But Ranjit would not let him alone. He would get home after school and head straight for his Dada's room to play hide and seek and, though already six, sit in his lap and demand to be told stories. Sonu would shout at him to come for his meals. 'I want to eat with Dada,' he would scream. 'You'll do nothing of the sort,' she would shout back. 'Come at once or I will give you a tight slap.' There were scenes every day. My father ate alone in his room; a sobbing, sulking Ranjit kicked up a shindig and had to be force fed by his mother or the servants.

'I can't enforce any discipline in the home when your old man's around,' Sonu complained every evening when I returned from the office. I said nothing. I stuck to my resolve to not let her come between me and my father. After my father left for Haridwar I went to see him every full moon night and spent a couple of days with him each time. I sent my car to fetch him whenever he agreed to come over.

And so it went for another five years without our getting any closer to each other. I loved the children, and for their sake I tried to keep the marriage going. Perhaps Sonu did too. Mohini became a great comfort. I looked forward to getting back home in the evenings when my little daughter would come running to me and insist on being taken for a drive. I would drive her around the neighbourhood myself. But this made Sonu more sullen. How could the children love a man she did not? I knew in my heart that I could not endure this loveless life for ever. I did not anticipate its dramatic end.

One morning in my mail was a post card written in Hindi. It was from Pitaji's ashram and had been posted two days earlier. It read: 'It gives me great sorrow to inform you that your revered father left for Vaikunth this morning. He was in good health and went to Har Ki Pauri for his morning snaan in Ganga Mata. On his return from the snaan he complained of chest pain and asked for a cup of tea. While he was having his tea, the cup slipped out of his hand and he was no more. We could not find your telephone number to inform you immediately. Hence this card. We also could not keep his body too long and cremated it according to Arya Samaj rites. His ashes have been put in an urn for you to come and immerse in the Ganga.'

I was stunned. For many minutes I sat with my head in my hands. There was no one around with whom I could share my sorrow. I asked my secretary to tell Jiwan Ram to fill the petrol tank as I would be leaving for Haridwar. 'My father is not well,' I told her. 'Also ring up home and tell them I will not be back for a couple of days.'

Half an hour later I was on the road to Haridwar—the road on which I had driven many times with my father. After we had got past Ghaziabad Jiwan Ram asked me, 'Sahib, Sharma memsahib told me Pitaji is not in good health. Is it anything serious?'

'No longer, he died two days ago. I'm going to collect his ashes.'

'Harey Ram! Harey Ram! He was such a noble soul! I never heard an angry word escape his lips. He will find an honourable place beside the lotus feet of the Lord.'

Once again I covered my face with both my hands and broke down. Jiwan Ram heard me, 'Sahib, dheeraj dharo (control yourself). No one knows when death comes. One should always be prepared for it and take it as the Lord's will. Be brave, God will comfort you.'

I had heard such words spoken at every death. However hackneyed and meaningless, they gave solace to the afflicted.

As the sun was setting we drove into the ashram. I was conducted to my father's room. In the centre of the charpoy on which he had slept a few days earlier was a brass pot containing his ashes. It had garlands of marigold flowers twined round it. I took it in my arms and again broke down. I heard myself wailing: 'Hai Pitaji! Where have you gone without me? You did not even give me the chance to be with you when the end came!' Ashram inmates gathered round to condole with me and Jiwan Ram let me cry to my heart's content till I ran out of tears. My sorrow slowly ebbed away. I wiped the tears off my face. I took the urn in my arms and asked Jiwan Ram to drive to Har ki Pauri. 'Pitaji will watch the aarti one more time with his son. Tomorrow I will immerse his ashes in the Ganga.'

I reached the clock-tower facing Har ki Pauri a couple of minutes before the aarti. As the priests on the opposite bank started waving their candelabras and chanting hymns and the temple bells began to ring, I stood ankle deep in the stream and waved the brass urn, touching its base to the water. Each time I brought it down I felt at peace with myself and the world. I sat on the ghat till after dark, watching the leaf boats with the oil lamps glide slowly away on the water. If I sat there long enough I would see all the flames die out. That did not depress me. After a long time I walked back to the car, still clutching the urn in my arm. I refused to eat the food offered to me. I held the urn close to me all night and slept fitfully, thinking of my father. I felt he was as close to me in death as he was in life.

*

Early the next morning I returned to the ghat, a furlong or so downstream from Har ki Pauri. Instantly I was surrounded by paandas waiting to help me perform the prayers of immersion and take their fees. They asked me where I came from and whose ashes I was carrying. 'I am the paanda of your family,' said one of them pushing the others aside. 'I knew your father was living in the ashram.' He rattled off names of distant members of my family. He led me to the river bank and had me sit facing him with the urn between us. He began to chant mantras in Sanskrit. Half-way through he stretched out his palm and demanded dakshina.

'How much?' I asked.

'Whatever you think proper. I know you are a rich man and the only son of your father.'

I handed him a hundred-rupee note. It was much more than he had expected. He resumed chanting shlokas with greater vigour. He stretched his hand towards the urn to empty its contents in the river. I grabbed it before he could touch it. 'This I will do myself,' I said in a firm voice. 'No one else will touch my father's remains.'

He let me have my way. I stood knee deep in the stream. As the sun came up over the eastern range of hills, I poured the ashes into the river.

There was more to be done. A barber was summoned. I sat on my haunches while he first cut my hair with a pair of scissors then shaved off the stubble with a razor. I was as bald as an egg. Everyone would know I had lost a parent.

I returned to the ashram to settle my father's account. There was no place for sentiments here. The director of the ashram produced a chit of paper on which he had jotted down the expenses: Rs 50 to get a death certificate; Rs 150 for wood, ghee and incense; Rs 50 to perform puja, Rs 50 for the brass urn. Total: Rs 300. 'If you take away your father's belongings we can rent the room to somebody else,' the director said without any emotion. What kind of human being was he? I remembered the post card he had sent me about Father's death. He could have sent a telegram—but why would he waste any money on a man who was merely a tenant? The ashram had many lonely men like my father.

I gave the ashram director the money and told him I would keep the room for myself at the rate my father had paid. His things were not to be disturbed. The room would remain locked; I would keep the key with me. There were no objections; all that the ashram authorities were interested in was getting the rent. The director came back with a lock and key and handed them to me.

A bald head is not an uncommon sight in Haridwar. Every day scores of men arrive bearing the ashes of their parents to immerse in the Ganga. Besides paandas who recite the appropriate mantras, two other trades have been established in the place. One is the sifting the gold or silver fillings of the teeth of dead persons from their ashes. This is done by urchins who stand waist deep in the river, shining mirrors into the water to catch the glint of precious metal. They then feel the ashes with their toes and dive down to pick any bit of metal they find. They work in partnership with the paandas who make it a point to empty the urns as close to the bank as possible to make the retrieval of gold and silver easier. That was why I had refused to let my paanda touch the urn with Father's ashes and had emptied the contents in the river well out of the reach of probing feet. If my father had any gold or silver in his teeth it was dedicated to Mother Ganga. The other trade that thrives in Haridwar is cap-making. Men don't like what they see in the mirror after their heads have been tonsured. So they buy caps to cover their baldness. I had a healthy crop of jet black hair that curled at its ends. The women I had made love to never tired of running their fingers through my curls and paying me compliments: 'The thing that makes you look so macho and handsome is your hair,' they would say. It would take many months to regain my crowning glory. So I stopped by a cap-maker's shop and after examining different varieties opted for a French style beret. It covered my skull completely and kept my head warm.

I spent another night in my father's room, sleeping on his charpoy. The next morning I set out on my return journey. My sorrow over losing my father turned into sour resentment against Sonu who had treated him so shabbily. I had no forgiveness left in me and resolved to lead my life as I pleased.

The first thing Sonu said to me as I entered the house was, 'Where have you been all these days? Not a word to inform anyone when you would return. As if we matter nothing to you.'

'I went to Haridwar,' I replied. 'I was informed through a post card that my father had died and had been cremated. I went to immerse his ashes in the Ganga.' I took off my beret.

'Oh, I'm sorry to hear that. I truly am.'

'Why should you be? You drove him out of this house,' I said in a burst of rage. 'He will not bother you anymore.'

'That's a nasty and cruel thing to say. You make me out to be a murderess,' she screamed and went sobbing to her room. I collapsed in an armchair and began to cry. Ranjit and Mohini witnessed the scene. They clung to me. 'Papa, what has happened?' asked Ranjit. 'Why is Mummy so angry?'

'My Pitaji, your Dada, is dead. You won't see him again.'

'Why? Where has he gone?' he asked.

'He has gone to Vaikunth.'

'Where is Vaikunth?'

'Far, very far,' I replied. 'No one comes back from Vaikunth.'

'I will go to Vaikunth to see him,' said Ranjit stubbornly. He was still too young to understand that death was for ever. Mohini was barely five and could not make any sense of what I was saying. I gathered the two in my lap. They snuggled against my chest and fell silent.

I could hear Sonu ring up her mother to give her the news. She also told Vimla Sharma to inform the office staff and tell them not to call before tomorrow. The office should be closed as a mark of respect for the deceased, she said.

Later that evening Rai Bahadur Achint Ram, his wife, their sons and their wives, and their domestic servants came to condole. I had just poured myself a Scotch and soda. They embraced me in turn and uttered words of solace. 'Bahut afsos hua (We are very sorry).' Their servants condoled with mine and sat on the floor around us. For a while they talked about the inevitability of death. 'Only those blessed by God go swiftly and without pain,' pronounced the Rai Bahadur. 'Your revered father—I'm told by your driver that he was in good health and passed away having his morning cup of tea. What a nice way to say farewell to the world.' I nodded my head. And took a sip from my glass of whisky.

'When should we have the chautha and uthala?' asked the Rai Bahadur. 'We shall announce it in the obituary columns of *The Hindustan Times* and book a time at Mata Ka Mandir for keertan.'

'You decide the date and the time. I don't know anything about religious ceremonies,' I said, taking another long sip of Scotch.

The family spent an hour with me. By the time they left I was on my third glass of Scotch. I knew they did not think it was the right thing to do during the period of mourning; I did not give a damn about what they thought. The grief was mine, as well as its antidote. Sonu's youngest brother could not resist making a nasty remark as he shook hands with me to leave. He pointed to my glass of whisky and said, 'That's the best thing in which to drown one's sorrows, boss.'

For the next three days no food was cooked in my home. It was sent by the Achint Ram family. Custom required that no fire be lit in a home where there had been a death. *The Hindustan Times* carried the announcement of Pitaji's demise in Haridwar and the chautha-uthala ceremony in Mata Ka Mandir. The Achint Ram family was prominently mentioned under the heading 'Grief Stricken', facing my name, Sonu's and the children's.

I had a stream of callers from sunrise to sunset: my office staff, friends, their wives, and most of all friends and relatives of the Achint Ram's. What time-wasting customs we Indians have evolved! Although I did not attend office during these days, I asked Vimla Sharma to see that everyone else did and to report to me every evening and bring up all the correspondence with her. I spent half an hour every afternoon with her in my study dictating replies.

The coming and going of people came to an abrupt end after the prayer meeting at Mata Ka Mandir. Gloom enveloped my home. The children and servants talked in subdued tones. Sonu and I kept a distance from each other, fully aware that a nasty confrontation was in the offing. She had been stung by my remark that she had driven Father from the house. She was not the kind of person who would let such an observation pass as something uttered in grief. One day she would have it out with me. And I was not the kind of person who would apologize for the sake of peace. We stored up ammunition to fire at each other when battle lines were drawn. I was reluctant to fire the first shot. She looked for an opportune moment to open hostilities.

We stopped talking to each other. I began going to the club straight from the office and returned late. By then Sonu and the children had finished supper and gone to bed. I ate my dinner alone. I resumed sleeping in my study downstairs. My morning tea was brought to me, I bathed and dressed downstairs. Ranjit and Mohini came to see me in the mornings and spent some time chatting with me as I turned over the pages of the morning papers and smoked my cigar. I gave up breakfast as it would give Sonu the chance to question me. We both sensed we were coming closer and closer to a showdown.

Sonu bided her time to let a decent interval elapse after my father's death before she decided to settle scores with me. A month after the obsequial ceremonies were over she sent me a note through the bearer who brought me my morning cup of tea. It read: 'I want to discuss something with you—today. Kindly come home on time—Sonu.'

I could not put off the day of reckoning any longer. I drove back from the office fortified with arguments, determined to keep my cool but not give an inch. My nerves were on edge.

I went upstairs and took my usual chair. Sonu came out of her bedroom and asked the ayah to take the children to play in the garden.

She opened the assault. 'Is this a civilized way to behave towards one's wife?' she asked.

I ran my hand over the new hair sprouting on my pate and did not reply.

'You hate my guts, don't you?' she said firing the second salvo.

'I don't hate anyone's guts,' I replied calmly.

'Why did you accuse me of throwing your father out of the house? Answer me. You know there is no truth in the accusation. He left of his own free will. You said it because you wanted to hurt me. Is that true or not?'

'Not true,' I replied, anger staining my words. 'You cannot deny you made my father—old man, as you called him—feel unwelcome in the house. He was a man of dignity and felt it would be better if he lived elsewhere. How can I forgive you for doing this to the only relation I had on this earth!'

'As far as you are concerned, I can do nothing right. I am always in the wrong!'

'I did not say that. Don't put words in my mouth.'

'You think I am a bitch! You want me out of your way so that you can start fucking other women,' she said in a shrill voice.

'Shut up.'

'I won't shut up. I'll settle this matter one way or the other, once and for all.'

'Do as you please,' I replied. 'I have nothing more to say.' She glowered at me for a few moments, then walked off in a huff to her bedroom. I went downstairs to my study and asked the bearer to bring my Scotch and dinner downstairs. I thought the first round had gone to me.

The second was fought the next day.

Sonu opened the attack. 'I have thought over the matter. I think we should live separately.'

'If that is what you want, you can have it. If you want me to move out, I will do so as soon as I can. If you want to go back to your parents, you can do that.'

'You seem very eager to get rid of me.'

'It is your suggestion, not mine.'

'You want to put me in the wrong all the time.'

The wrangling went on for half an hour. And ended the same way: she went off to her bedroom, I to my study to have my drink and dinner in comparative peace.

I thought the second round had also gone in my favour.

We retired to our entrenched fortifications—for a fortnight or more. The cold war became colder by the day. One Sunday when I had no excuse for going to the office and was peacefully watching TV, Sonu stormed in, switched off the TV and stood facing me. Her face was flushed with anger. 'How can you go on day in and day out ignoring my presence in the house—as if I was piece of dirt. That whore Mrinal takes good care of you, doesn't she? Why would you need a wife!'

'For God's sake shut up and let me watch TV.' I put out my hand to switch on the TV. She slapped the back of my hand and screamed, 'You will do nothing of the sort. I'll teach you how to behave like a gentleman, you filthy lecher!'

I lost my cool and slapped her. I had never before descended to violence. She was stunned. 'You dared raise your hand against me!' she hissed through her teeth, trembling with rage and humiliation. 'I'll teach you a lesson you'll never forget for the rest of your life.'

I knew I had lost the third round, and the battle for supremacy.

It was that day that she reported me to the police and effectively put an end to our turbulent marriage of almost thirteen years.

When I returned from the police station, she had gone off to her parents with the children. I did not bother to visit or call her. She came back over a month later. I ignored her. When I hugged and kissed the children, she said I had no right to do that. I kept quiet. 'You have no right. You did not bother to come and fetch them and their mother,' she said. 'Yes I did not,' I said, looking straight at her. 'I love the children, but I am happier without you.' 'I know that, you bastard,' she shouted. 'But if you want the freedom to bring whores to this house, you cannot keep the children.' It was difficult, but after a few more months of quarrelling, I gave up. I told her I needed a divorce and she could keep the children. Two days later, she took the children and three suitcases full of her things and drove off.

Fourteen
Molly Gomes

After Sonu left with the children, I felt lonely and disoriented, till I decided to advertise for paid lady companions. It was an extraordinary decision. But I am glad I made it because it brought me many moments of joy. My friend, the writer, has already written about my first lady companion, Sarojini Bharadwaj. There is nothing more I can add to that; he has faithfully reported what I told him.

After Sarojini, only Dhanno remained. She served me well whenever I wanted her. But she was no company. We hardly exchanged more than two words. When the coast was clear, I would say chalo— come. She would follow me like a lamb to the bedroom, slip off her salwar-kameez and lie down on the bed. I would do my job to my satisfaction and dismount. 'Bus, sahib—you've had enough,' she would say at the end, wash herself, collect her money and slip out of the rear door. I could not take on another woman till Dhanno was around, and I had no reason to sack her. She opted out of my life in a most unexpected way.

One evening when I returned from office I saw a couple of policewomen and a male sub-inspector sitting in my garden. They had ordered chairs to be laid out for them. A woman was sitting on the ground with her head tucked between her knees. The sub-inspector and the policewomen stood up as soon as I entered. The bearer brought a chair for me. 'What is all this about?' I asked. 'Sir, a complaint was lodged in the police station about thefts in two houses where this woman was employed. We raided her quarters and recovered a lot of stolen property. Stand up and show your face to the sahib,' ordered the sub-inspector.

The woman stood up and uncovered her face.

It was Dhanno.

'Sir, this woman also swept floors in your house. Do you know her?'

'Yes, she is the jamadarni. She comes here twice a day to do the bathrooms and floors. Her name is Dhanno.'

'Have any things been missing from your house? Ishwari, open the bag and show him the items that have not yet been identified by other complainants.'

The woman constable laid out bottles of French perfume and nail polish, a pair of gold earrings, two pairs of ladies' shoes, a couple of saris, two pairs of silk salwar-kameez and a Cartier gold pen. I recognized the pen which I had misplaced somewhere; all the other items were Sonu's. She had accummulated so much that she did not know when something went missing.

I examined the spread of booty on the lawn and said with a straight face, 'Sub-inspector sahib, I don't think any of these items belonged to this house. The little I know of this woman is that she is clean and honest and does her work well. I have no complaints against her.'

'Clean and honest she certainly is not,' snapped one of the policewomen. 'We have several complaints that she was also doing dhanda in this locality—we found a lot of cash in her trunk.'

'Dhanda? What is dhanda?' I asked feigning ignorance.

'Business,' explained the woman constable. 'She's a prostitute as well as a thief.'

'I have absolutely no knowledge about that,' I replied. 'As I have told you, she took nothing from this house and has been a diligent worker. If you like, I can give her a certificate of good character. I suggest you drop the charges of stealing things from this house.'

Dhanno broke down, clutched my feet and wailed, 'Sahib, save me from the police. If they put me in jail my children will starve to death. There is no one to look after them.'

'You should have thought of that when you went around stealing other people's things and whoring,' growled the sub-inspector.

I put my hand on Dhanno's head and assured her, 'Your children will be fed by my servants—don't worry about them. If you want a lawyer to defend you, tell your husband to see me. I will arrange for one. If the magistrate wants anyone to testify to your good character, you can name me.'

The police put Dhanno in their van and took her away. That was the last I saw of the woman. For a few days her children came to the kitchen for their food. Then they disappeared. Their father could not take the taunts about his wife being a thief and cheating on him for money. He moved to another locality.

No one approached me to engage a lawyer on Dhanno's behalf. She had no one to defend her against the charge of thieving. The police dropped the charge of prostitution. She was sentenced to one year's imprisonment. She never came to see me. I missed my gold pen, which I was sure the sub-inspector had kept for himself. Sonu's things were no doubt taken by the women constables. I had to buy another pen for Rs 15,000.

*

Once again I was on my own. My cook found an old jamadarni, a one-eyed widow, to do the sweeping and cleaning now. I had to look for another pro tem companion. I brought out the bundle of letters and photographs of the women who had shown willingness to accept my offer of temporary concubinage.

I went over the pictures and the letters again and again. What exactly was I looking for? The top priority was of course sex. I never seemed to have my fill of it. Once a day was not good enough for me now. Without doubt all the women who had answered my ad would be more than willing to engage with me. I wanted it to be lustful give and take—and in the open: in sunlight, moonlight, starlight. What more? The person had to be of a cheerful disposition; no sulking, no nagging, I'd had more than my share of that. Also, the lady should not try to establish proprietary rights over me. It was important, too, that she be interested in the good things of life: good food, vintage wines, music and the arts. Since I did not read much I did not set much store by literature.

After scanning all the photographs, I settled for one Molly Gomes of Goa. It was her second letter following receipt of my photograph that helped me make up my mind. It read:

> Hi, handsome! this is Molly Gomes again. You wanted to know more about me. Here it is! I'm a trained nurse specializing in physiotherapy. I use massage to treat people who have suffered partial paralysis or have limb ailments. During the tourist season I'm much in demand in five star hotels. I was married once to a foreigner. He was no good at anything; all he wanted was a massage every day. So I chucked him up after a few days. Life is too short to be wasted on a fellow who is good at nothing. Don't you agree? I can speak Konkani, English & Portuguese. My Hindi is not so good. Although a Catholic I have no hangups about religion. I go to church only to please my parents and relations. I tell them that all religions teach you to be good and honest, so what's the big deal about being Christian, Hindu, Muslim or Parsee! I'm also a good cook—I can make spicy Goan curries, prawns, crabs, lobsters & fish. I love music & dancing. I have a cheerful disposition. You'll find me good company. Any more you want to know about me, don't hesitate to ask.'
> Yours lovingly,
> Molly.

From her photograph I could make out that she was short, stocky and dark. She had a broad smile showing a row of pearly white teeth. A bright scarlet hibiscus flower was stuck in her black curly hair.

Why not? I asked myself and wrote back inviting Molly Gomes over. I enclosed an open air ticket —Goa-Delhi-Goa—and suggested that as soon as the peak-tourist season was over, she could avail of my invitation. By the end of January, the tourist traffic from Europe, America and Australia to Goa begins to taper off. Goa becomes oppressively warm for white skins. It was coming to the end of January. Winter was giving way to spring and Delhi was at its colourful best. It was pleasantly cool; every park, every garden and roundabout was a riot of flowers. The perfect time to start an easy, uncomplicated relationship.

Molly did not waste any time. Three days after I had mailed my letter came her reply by telegram: 'Arriving 1st Feb I.A. flight 804. Meet at airport. Love. Molly.'

I talked to my servants. A lady doctor from Goa was coming to stay with me for a few weeks, I told them. She spoke no Hindustani. They were to look after her needs when I was away in office. And not gossip about her with other servants. By now they took a more compassionate view of their master's youthful compulsions and regretted having talked carelessly about Sarojini. I had the guest room done up, put a buff envelope containing Rs 10,000 in cash under the pillow and locked the room. Satisfied with the arrangements, I went to fetch my guest from the airport.

The flight from Goa was on time. I saw the passengers stream in from the entrance gate, pick up hand trolleys and take their positions around the luggage conveyor belt. I had no difficulty in recognizing Molly Gomes. She was as her photograph showed her: short, stocky, muscular, skin the colour of cinnamon. She was wearing a red T-shirt and blue denims and had a large sling bag on her. She looked at the crowd waiting to receive arriving passengers. She could not spot me. I did not wave to her lest I be mistaken.

The conveyor belt began to move—one suitcase after another, holdalls and wooden crates bobbed along to be grabbed by their owners. I saw Molly pick up two suitcases and load them on her trolley. As she handed over her baggage tickets to the airport official I stepped forward to take the trolley from her. 'Hi, there!' she greeted me loudly. 'I was scared you wouldn't be here to receive me. Where would I go?'

'Not to worry. You are in safe hands,' I replied shaking her hand. 'Mohan Kumar at your service.' She had a strong grip, as one would expect in a professional masseuse.

'Who else could it be? You look exactly like your picture, only taller and handsomer.'

'Thanks.'

I pushed the trolley through phalanxes of cab drivers holding placards with the names of people they were to meet. We got to my car in the parking lot, I put her suitcases in the boot, opened the front door for her and lowered the window. I got into the driver's seat.

'Aren't you going to kiss me?' she asked.

'Sure!' I leant over and kissed her on her lips. 'Plenty of time for that,' I assured her patting her on her cheek.

'By Jove its cold,' she said rolling up the glass. 'After Goa this is like the Arctic.'

I turned up my window pane as well. She kept looking at the scenery. 'Much greener than Goa,' she remarked. 'There we have only brown rock, huge wild cashew, palm and coconut trees. Hardly any grass. You have more trees here than I expected, and lots of bushes.' On an impulse I took a detour through West End. She gasped at the spread of flowers on either side of the road. 'This is beautiful!' she said. 'I know I'm going to like this city. You have flowers in your garden?'

'Not many,' I replied. 'A lawn in front with a hedge around it. A couple of pine trees. I don't get much time to look after my garden. A fellow comes once a week to mow the grass and water the lawn.'

We hit the Delhi-Mathura road. Three cars running alongside on each side of the dual highway, scores of phut phuts, three wheelers weaving in and out of the lanes of cars, long halts at traffic signals, petrol fumes making the air thick and grey. 'This is mad! How can you live in this noise and foul air?' she asked. Suddenly she did not like the city, and who could blame her.

'We've got used to it. Some areas of Delhi are worse than this.' At the Ashram crossing I turned into Maharani Bagh. There was less noise, fewer cars, larger bungalows with gardens. I turned towards my house. 'Remember, to the servants you are Doctor Gomes. And no kissing and cuddling in front of them.'

'Right, boss,' she said saluting me. 'From now on I'm a respectable lady doctor from Goa. You must be the world's greatest humbug.'

'That I am,' I replied. I knew I was going to like this natty little chatterbox.

The servants were waiting for us. They opened the iron gates of Ranjit Villa to let in the car. I introduced Molly to my cook and bearer. She shook hands with both and in a nasal Yankee accent said, 'I'm happy to make your acquaintance.' They took her cases to the guest room. Molly followed me upstairs. I showed her round the upper floor and took her to her room. An electric heater glowed red. The room was warm. Extra blankets had been put on her bed.

'You unpack and rest for a while. If you want to have a bath there's running hot water in the taps. I'll catch up with my office work. The bar opens at six-thirty.'

I went down to my study and rang up Vimla Sharma for a report of what had gone on in the afternoon. I told her not to send me any letters that evening. I would deal with them the next day.

I had a fire lit in the sitting room. Thick logs with rock-coal heaped on them. Drinks were laid out. I put on the stereo. Strauss' waltzes. I could not think of anything more romantic.

I went to check on Molly. The door to her room was shut. As I went down the stairs and back to the sitting room, I could hear her singing. Of all things, a popular Hindi film song:

Jab Jab bahaar aayie
Aur phool muskaraaye
Mujhe tum yaad aaye

(Whenever came spring
And flowers began to smile
I thought of you awhile)

It was a beautiful song, though she sang it very badly. But she was clearly enjoying herself, and that made me feel warm and contented. Exactly at 6.30 p.m. she joined me in the sitting room. She was dressed in a golden yellow blouse and a long grey skirt. She wore a pearl necklace, pearl studs in her ears and a thin gold chain round her right ankle. She was carrying two bottles and a large packet of cashew nuts. 'These are for you,' she said handing the bottles to me. 'The finest feni from Goa, distilled at home by my father. One cashew, one coconut. You like feni?'

'I've never tasted it. I'm told it is like firewater.'

'Try some. It's pure, no additives. And these cashew nuts will have to be roasted. This is all that Goa produces; so I got some for you.'

'Thanks. What about a drink? Scotch, beer, gin, sherry or wine?'

'You keep all that in stock? I can see you're a rich, rich man. And what's that money doing under my pillow?'

'Not rich, rich but well-off. The money is advance payment for my part of the deal.'

'Don't make it so commercial. I've come to you for the romance I've missed in my life, not for money.'

'You can have both,' I said as I gave her a peck on her cheek. 'So what's your poison?'

'I'll have what you have.'

I poured out two large whiskys with soda and ice and handed one to her. She took the armchair by the fireplace.

'Now tell me what you do for a living,' I asked.

'I told you in my letter, I am a masseuse. During the tourist season I do at least a dozen massages a day. Apart from the hundred and fifty rupees I charge, I get lots of tips. I help to keep the home fires burning.'

'Is it only women you massage or men as well?'

'Mostly women. Sometimes old men as well. I avoid massaging young men; they get ideas in their heads and want to take *liberties* with me. I tick them off roundly—"Mister, this is not Bangkok or Tokyo where you can have a woman for a massage and a fuck." I don't mind old men. Occasionally one will grab my hand and put it on his sorry-looking ancient dick. "Mister," I ask him, "you want me to massage this as well? It has no life left in it," and I shake the limp little thing to show the oldie what I mean.' She laughed and added, 'Many plead with me! "Shake it a little more and it will come alive." I tell them, "I can shake it till kingdom come and nothing will happen to it," and they look at me as if I've kicked them in the teeth. Can you believe it, the same old fogeys ask me to massage them again and again, go through the same drill and give me large tips!'

'You won't have that problem with me.'

'I hope not. Or I'll take the next plane back home.'

She reminded me of Jessica Browne; no hang-ups about anything.

In honour of 'Dr' Gomes my Mug cook had prepared Goan prawn curry and rice. I opened a bottle of Grover's white wine. We had our dinner by the fireside. Molly complimented the cook. 'Better Goan food than I have at home,' she said. The Mug had indeed excelled himself. After caramel custard, we had coffee and cognac. The bearer cleared the plates. I saw the servants out and latched the back door. I went out into the lawn and performed my ritual of urinating against the hedges. It was chilly. I started to shiver. I quickly went indoors to be near the fireplace. I put another couple of logs in the fire and stood before it, warming my hands.

'What do you do after dinner?' she asked.

'I usually smoke a cigar before going to bed, but I'm not in the mood tonight.'

'It's so much nicer here than in the bedroom. More comfy, more cheerful. Let's stay here till the fire burns out.'

'As you like. It will keep going for quite some time.'

We ran out of conversation. Molly got up from her armchair and came over to me. Without another word she slipped her blouse over her head and undid her bra. Two beautiful rounded breasts with black nipples emerged. She rested her arms on my shoulders and put up her mouth. I glued my lips to hers and fondled her breasts with my warm hands. She unbuckled her skirt and let it drop to the ground, then undid my belt, pulled down my trousers and felt my penis. Like the other women her first reaction was of awe and wonder. 'Man, I've never seen anything of *this* size before. And believe me I've seen quite a few.'

This woman gave me a lot of confidence. I was in no hurry to get on with the act. We lay down on the carpet and fondled each other. She certainly was a skilled masseuse. She nibbled the lobes of my ears, pressed her thumbs into the back of my shoulders, ran her fingers over my belly, middle, thighs and shins, down to my feet. She rubbed my toes and my insteps. Not a part of my body did she leave untouched. It was relaxing, soothing. 'If you go on like this, I'll fall asleep,' I murmured.' She came up over me, kissed me passionately and said, 'Darling, you go to sleep, I'll do all the love-making.'

Indeed! She effortlessly slipped my organ into her vagina. 'Now we can go to sleep as we are.' She pretended to doze off. Only the twitching and milking of my organ assured me she was wide awake. It was blissful; it was prolonged. We took turns being on top of each other. We went on for an hour before I rolled over, bringing her under me and asked, 'Are you ready?'

She nodded and replied, 'I've been ready for a long time.'

I began to pump into her. She crossed her legs behind my back and heaved up each time I plunged down. 'Harder!' she cried. 'For God's sake, don't stop!' she screamed. I put all I had into her. She slapped the carpet with both her hands and cried loudly, 'Oh God, this is heaven heaven heaven—'

We climaxed together. Her legs loosened their grip on me. She lay back utterly exhausted. Nothing in life gives a greater sense of fulfilment than the satisfying coupling of male and female.

We lay side by side for a long time before she said, 'Don't move. I'll be back in a jiffy.'

She went to her bedroom, stark naked as she was. She came back with a towel soaked in hot water. She towelled my penis and thighs with loving care and wiped away drops of semen and vaginal fluid. With another end of the same towel she rubbed my anus and the cleft between my buttocks. She threw the towel aside and lay down beside me.

'That was nice, wasn't it?'

'The best I've ever had,' I acknowledged truthfully. 'You are an artist. You deserve a summa cum laude for specialization in sex.'

'What's summa cum, whatever it is? Doesn't sound very right to me!'

I told her.

'And you? How many summa cums did you get in America?'

'Only one, in computer sciences. Only pluses from the women.'

'Did you have lots of them?'

'Quite a few. And you? Lots of men?'

'Not lots but some. I live in a strict Catholic society. It was while working in five star hotels that I occasionally agreed to have sex with some foreigners. I didn't enjoy it very much. I felt dirty at first when they pressed dollar bills into my hands after they had finished, but after a while it seemed quite normal; I didn't feel like a whore. Nothing like being made love to by you, though. Don't you use condoms?'

'I do, but I forgot to use one tonight, I'm sorry.'

'What if I get pregnant? I wouldn't mind having your baby, but what will people back home say? They'll call me a slut. Even the priest of our church will not forgive me. And you won't marry me.'

'Why don't you douche yourself?'

'Don't worry, sweetheart!' she said patting my cheek. 'I'm on the pill and I will be as long as I'm with you. It's not much fun with a condom.'

I kept feeding the fire. We spent the night on the carpet. We made love three times.

Molly shook me awake. It was broad daylight. 'Somebody's banging on the back door,' she said as she picked up her clothes.

'It must be the servants. By God, I've overslept.' As she ran to her bedroom I got into my dressing gown and hurried downstairs to let the servants in. 'I went to bed very late,' I said by way of explanation. 'I'll have my morning tea in bed, give memsahib hers in her room.'

I ran up and unmade my bed to make it look as if it had been slept in. I knocked on Molly's door and shouted, 'Morning tea. You want it in bed or will you join me?'

'I'll be out in a second.' When she came out, she had washed her face and was full of pep, singing, 'O what a lovely morning, O what a lovely day.' She greeted the bearer and the cook. She beamed a mischievous smile at me and asked, 'And how are we this morning? Slept well?'

'Sleep of the just. Only fucked out.'

'Mustn't use bad language,' she admonished, raising her index finger like a school marm. 'Say thank you ma'am for a very pleasant evening. And what's the drill for the day?'

'I'll be off to my office in an hour. The driver will bring the car back for you. His name is Jivan Ram. He'll take you round the city or any place you want to visit; shopping centres, monuments, museums, picture galleries. He should pick me up from the office around six.'

'You know what? I'd like to go with your cook to get things for dinner. This evening I'll cook for you.'

I spent the day in the office. My mind was not on my work. I kept going over the night's love-making with Molly Gomes. I kept yawning and wasn't paying attention to what my staff had to say. At lunch break I ordered soup and a sandwich. I told Vimla Sharma not to put through any calls or let anyone in till I asked her to do so. I stretched out on the sofa and fell fast asleep. I had three hours of deep slumber. I washed my face and rang for tea. I was much refreshed and went through the correspondence, signed letters I had dictated. By six o'clock I had cleared my desk and was ready to go home.

Molly was upstairs. As I went up, I heard loud music being played on my stereo with Molly's contralto in full flow. It was some kind of opera. It was not one of my cassettes, I had'nt got to the stage of appreciating operatic music. Molly heard my footsteps, toned down the music and greeted me from the top of the stairs. She bowed low and exclaimed, 'Welcome home, Mr Kumar! I trust you had a good day at the office?' She courtesied again and asked, 'How do you like my new get up? I bought it this morning.'

She was dressed in a salwar-kameez with a bright red dupatta thrown about her shoulders and a red bindi on her forehead. 'I thought instead of looking like a kaala Catholic memsahib from Goa, I should look like a Punjabi Hindu shrimati when I'm in the company of Shri Mohan Kumar.'

'It looks very nice on you,' I replied. 'I expect anything you wear looks nice on you. You have the right kind of figure.'

'O thank you, sir,' she replied and again courtesied to me. 'Your cook took me to some place called INA Market. Just about everything in the world was available. We examined lots of fish; rohu, salmon, pomfret, hilsa. Also lobsters, shrimps, prawns. I settled for crab. And I have cooked it with my own dainty hands—Goan style, with a little wine. Hope you'll like it.'

I took off my coat, tie and shoes, slipped on a woollen dressing gown and slippers. I asked the bearer to light a fire in the sitting room and put out the drinks.

'What else did you do besides shopping and cooking?'

'Slept—three hours, may be four. You knocked the hell out of me last night.'

I was pleased to hear that. 'Me too,' I replied. 'I slept on the office couch all afternoon.'

'Learn a lesson from that, dear sir. Like anything else, fucking should also be done in moderation,' she said. 'In any case I have the curse on me. I'm relieved you did not make me pregnant. So no messing with me for the next four days—unless you want a messy job.'

I was relieved. I did not want her to think I could keep up the pace of the first night every day. 'Okay,' I replied. 'A four-day enforced holiday from sex. You get over your period, I'll replenish my stock of semen. Then we'll regulate our love-making. Not too much, not too little.'

Molly had cooked a wonderful meal: the mulligatawny soup was as peppery and hot as it should be, crab as succulent as I had ever tasted it, caramel custard (which we Indians are stuck on because it was the dessert of the Raj days) tastier than that made in the States or in England. I complimented her. 'You seem to be good at everything.'

'What exactly do you mean by *everything*? We are only talking about food here,' she said with a laugh.

'By everything I mean everything—including you know what.'

'I'm not dense. I also stitch my own clothes and I can mend a fuse. Living all by myself on a limited budget I have to do everything myself.'

We sat by the fire for a long time. She chatted away merrily about her life in Goa, her parents and brothers, nephews and nieces—all with Portuguese names: De Souza, De Mello, De Sa, Miranda, Almeida and so on. You would have thought Goa is entirely Portuguese Catholic. 'As a matter of fact, Hindus outnumber us,' she informed me. 'Also much richer than us Catholics; millionaires like Salgaokar, Chowgule, Dempos and a dozen others are Hindus. Rich, rich, rich. Big, big houses but no style, no class, no fun. We enjoy life: drink, dance, sing, and eat well. They just make money, worship the tulsi plant and visit the Mangesh temple on holidays. Though they outnumber us we have many more cathedrals than they have temples. Christians attend mass more regularly than Hindus do puja in their temples. We look down on Hindus and don't intermarry with them.'

'So you look down on me and will never marry me because I'm a Hindu.'

'Don't be silly! I didn't mean you! You are different.' She leant across and kissed me on my nose.

Since Molly was out of action and we had to do more talking, I asked her casually, 'Your name sounds more English than Goan or Portuguese. How's that?

'It's a short name they gave me when I joined the nursery class of a convent run by Irish nuns. At birth I was christened with a name a yard long—Maria Manuela Francesca Jose de Piedade Philomena Gomes . Try saying that in one go and you'll be out of breath. Molly is short and jolly. I like the name. Will also go nicely with yours if you decide to make an honest woman of me. Senora Molly Mohan Kumar. What do you think?'

I did not want to pursue that line of thought. Much as I was infatuated with Molly, our only bonding was based on lust, and lust loses its frenetic pace as soon as the partners slip wedding rings on each other's fingers. Molly sensed my unease and said with a light laugh, 'Not to worry, love, I have no desire to change my name from Gomes to Kumar.'

After a pause and a sip of Scotch I dared to ask her the question which had been uppermost in my mind: 'How old were you, Molly, when you lost your virginity?'

She was, as usual, sitting on the carpet at my feet. She looked up, transfixed me with her large eyes and snapped, 'Why do you want to know? If you tell me how and when *you* lost yours, I might tell you when I was deflowered and by whom.'

'Okay,' I said. I had no problems talking about my sex life, and if it made her less angry about having to talk about her own, so much the better.

It turned out to be a pleasant evening, as we recounted our past. I told her about Jessica Browne.

'What did she look like?' interrupted Molly.

'Complexion much like yours, coffee and cream. A lot taller, athletic. She was a tennis champion. Full of beans . . .'

Molly interrupted me again. 'Did she make the first move or you?'

'She did. We'd been going out for some days, holding hands and kissing. One evening she asked me to have a drink in her digs. We'd had a drink each when I complimented her on her figure. "Want to see what I really look like?" she asked, and before I could say yes, took off all her clothes and stood stark naked before me. She slowly turned around to show me her behind as well. I had never seen a naked woman before. I tried to grab her in my arms but she pushed me back and said I couldn't till she'd seen what I had hidden behind my clothes. I took off my clothes, and she gasped at the sight of my tool——she didn't notice my flat stomach or my broad chest. Nothing, just this!' I made a face and slapped my crotch. Molly giggled and patted my member lovingly. It was fully roused and straining against the fabric of my trousers.

'Did you make love?' she asked.

'Yes.'

'How many times?'

'All through the night. Four times, I think, with short intervals. I was twenty, she was a year older. But enough! Now you tell me about your first time.'

'Oh, all right,' she relented. 'I was fourteen, still at school. Of course, I knew the difference between boys and girls. I had many male cousins and even as children we used to show each other what we had between our thighs. The boys were great show offs. They'd show us how far they could pee. Once in a while they'd show us their erections and boast how they could "puncture" our pussies with them ramrods. I could not wait for that to happen—a dirty little girl I was, you see. But it wasn't one of those boys who finally did it to me. It was my own uncle, my mother's younger brother, a good twenty years older than me. Beast! Took advantage of poor, innocent me.' She laughed as she said this, but it was a mirthless laugh. 'Anyway, it happened one afternoon when he came to call on my parents and they were not at home. I was still in my school uniform—short frock which ended above my knees, barely covering my thighs. He kissed me, as he always did, but this time on my lips. He sat down on the sofa, pulled me onto his lap and started kissing the back of my neck and my ears. I could feel his prick getting stiff and large against my bum. He began to fondle my breasts, then squeeze them roughly. He was all out of breath. I knew he was up to no good and should have stopped him. But I was pretty worked up too by now and let him go on. He put me on the sofa, pushed my frock up and pulled my panties down roughly.

'Then he fumbled with his trouser buttons, managed to get his fat dick out and shoved it in me, all in one go. He was an impatient man. It hurt and I screamed in agony. He pulled out after a few violent thrusts and spilt all his gooey stuff on my thighs. He made me promise I wouldn't tell my parents, or they'd kill us both. Of course I didn't tell them. Dirty little girl, as I told you. I didn't even tell the padre at confession. I told nobody. You're the first person.'

'Couldn't have been much fun,' I said. 'When did you first have sex that you enjoyed?'

'Enough for one evening,' she replied. 'When you tell me about your other women, I'll tell you of the men in my life.'

The fire died down. I went downstairs to urinate in the garden (I noticed I could still 'pee' quite far) and bolt the doors. I came up. Molly had her arms outstretched above her head and was yawning with her mouth wide open. I tickled her armpits and hoisted her off the ground. She squirmed with unconcealed delight and kicked her legs in the air. I took her to her room and dropped her on the bed. I kissed her on the lips and said, 'Good night, and sleep well. Keep the door open, just in case I change my mind. I'll keep mine open in case you get frightened being alone in the dark and want to cuddle up with me.'

That night we slept in our respective beds. I was up at my usual hour to let the servants in. I had my morning tea alone as Molly was not in the habit of taking bed tea, then read the papers. I was reading my office files when she came out. She sensed I did not want to be disturbed and quietly went back to her room.

It was odd that though I had no pressing desire to have sex, I wanted Molly to be around. I knew sooner or later people would begin to gossip about us. Molly was far from her home, so it would not affect her. Delhi was the capital city of gossipmongers and my new lady friend would provide plenty of fodder for my nosey friends. I decided to ignore them and take Molly out with me wherever I went. Whose life was it anyhow?

On some excuse or the other I started leaving the office an hour earlier than my usual time. I would send Jiwan Ram off and come home to take Molly out for a drive. The first evening she asked, 'Aren't you earlier then usual?'

'I thought I'd show you some of our parks. They are at their best this time of the year—full of flowers. They'll be gone in a few days.'

She got into her grey skirt and walking shoes. I took the route from India Gate through Rajpath upto Rashtrapati Bhavan, then the side road to the Ridge and on to Buddha Jayanti Park. There were lots of cars and scooters in the car park. As we entered the garden we were welcomed by masses of bright red salvias on either side of the pathway. Then there were beds of violets and cosmos. I did not know much about flowers, nor do I now, but I liked going to Buddha Jayanti because it was a large spread of undulating lawns and clusters of the same kind of flowers in every bed. It also had trees planted by visiting dignitaries with plaques bearing their names and dates of planting. We walked hand in hand down the leaf strewn paths that run from one end of the Ridge to the other through a forest of flame trees: the flame tree in flower is a sight for the gods.

Molly knew a lot more about the flowers and trees than I did and loved showing off her knowledge. After an hour of strolling around she turned to me and said, 'I'm tired. I shouldn't be doing so much walking when I have the curse on me. I feel damp and dirty inside. I need to change my pad.' We went to the restaurant in the park. She went to the bathroom to clean herself and change her sanitary pad. By the time she came out the waiter had laid tea on the table. I had ordered plates of samosas and patties. I knew she had a healthy appetite.

I nibbled at a samosa; Molly polished off the rest. The sun went over the ridge and a deep shadow spread over the lawns and flower beds. People began to leave as it had also became chilly. 'Time to go home,' I told Molly as I paid the bill.

We got back to our car. 'Are the other Delhi parks like this one?' she asked as I took the homeward route.

'Not as large but equally beautiful. Tomorrow I'll show you the Lodhi Gardens. There are several beautiful monuments there.'

The next evening I again left office an hour earlier and took Molly to the Lodhi Gardens. I parked the car near the side entrance of the India International Centre and we entered the park through the turnpike facing the ancient mosque with a dome shaped exactly like a young woman's bosom with a nipple on top. Bauhinias were in flower; choryzias were shedding their petals. This time I told her gently, 'Molly, no holding hands here. There are likely to be people who recognize me and they'll be curious to know who my lady friend is!'

'Right, boss, no holding hands. Respectable distance will be maintained.'

We went across the park to the tomb of Mohammed Shah Tughlak, to the green house and then back, round Sikandar Lodhi's fortified mausoleum and on to the India International Centre for tea. We stopped for a while by the lily pond. Six blue water lilies bloomed amidst a lot of flat brown leaves. Every one who came to the Centre first paid homage to the lilies. One chap who had the audacity to piss in the pond in broad daylight was promptly expelled and his membership cancelled.

I ordered tea and cakes and found a table for two. The place filled up. A few people raised their hands in greeting. A fellow I knew came up to our table. 'Long time no see,' he said eyeing Molly. I knew the bugger was more curious to know who she was than why I had not been around for so long. I introduced her. 'This is Dr Gomes. She's on a short visit to Delhi.'

'Nice to meet you,' said Molly taking his hand.

'The pleasure is entirely mine,' said the nosey bastard. 'And where have you come from?'

Before she could answer, I interjected, 'Doctor Gomes is from Bombay. She's staying with friends in Delhi.' The fellow wouldn't move, so I decided to be rude and shake him off. 'See you sometime,' I said and turned to Molly.

He took the hint and returned to his table.

Back in the car, Molly said to me: 'You're as straight faced a liar as I've ever met. Dr Gomes from Bombay staying with friends in Delhi! Indeed! Only I happen to be Molly, the masseuse from Goa, staying with Mohan Kumar who wants a new woman to fuck every two days.'

'Not days but months,' I said leaning across and kissing her on the ear. 'And you perhaps for many years. You are just the kind of woman I've been looking for.'

'Thanks a million.'

She switched on the car stereo. I had cassettes of both Eastern and Western music. She put on Beethoven's Emperor concerto at full blast. For a change she did not want to talk but listen in silence and perhaps ponder over what she had let herself in for. I left her to her thoughts. Perhaps I had hurt her feelings by lying about her. What else could I have done? I would try to explain it to her later.

When we reached home she ran up the stairs ahead of me and went straight to the kitchen to see how the dinner was coming. With the Mug cook's broken Bengali-English and her more than broken Hindi, they managed to say a lot to each other. She even managed a dialogue with the bearer in the style of the Ango-Indian memsahibs of Hindi films. In two days she had won the hearts of my servants. And mine.

She joined me at the fireside. I poured out drinks. 'How did you like Lodhi Gardens?' I asked to get her talking again.

'Beautiful! We don't have anything like it in Goa. No parks, only old Portuguese forts and cathedrals,' she said screwing up her face. 'But we have beautiful beaches—dozens of them, and a clean, warm sea. You can lie on the sand soaking in the sun. That's what most foreigners come to Goa for. Our spoilsport police don't allow them to expose themselves in public, so they lie stark naked on the hotel lawns, on their backs and then on their stomachs, roasting themselves like we roast chapatties. Their white skins can't take too much sun, so they smear all kinds of lotions to turn brown without getting sunburnt. You can tell who has exposed himself or herself completely and who hasn't. Those who have, turn brown all over; those who covered their boobs and pubes have bands of pale flesh on their breasts and bums. They look funny, like zebras,' she laughed. 'You don't get much sun in your house, only in the garden. You should do some sun-bathing. It's very good for your health.'

'I have a terraced roof with low walls all round. At times I go up to do surya namaskar. On winter days I occasionally take up a canvas chair and sit in it for an hour or two.'

'Not good enough,' she said firmly. 'Get a thick mattress with a pillow. And put a door with a bolt on the outside so you can strip yourself and let every part of your body be kissed by the sun's rays.'

It was an attractive idea she had put in my head. I decided to get a carpenter to put a latch on the outer side of the door which opened out to the roof. And instead of one I would get the servants to put two rexine mattresses there. My imagination began to run riot about what Molly and I could do on the roof. The prospect cheered me up.

'What are you smiling about?' Molly asked.

'What—nothing,' I replied.

'You were thinking dirty thoughts. I can tell by the look on your face, naughty boy!'

'Never mind,' I laughed and changed the subject: 'What did you think of the India International Centre? It's the most sought-after club in Delhi. Good library, good restaurants, reasonable accommodation at reasonable rates. Something is always going on there in the evening: dance and music recitals, lectures, foreign films. I know many retired people who spend their entire day in the Centre.'

'It's no fun being at places where everyone knows everyone else. They want to know who a member has brought with him,' she said. 'Like that nosey friend of yours.'

'That's true of all clubs. A newcomer rouses curiosity. Next time I'll take you to the pub. It's a small, cosy place. Tipplers are too involved with tippling to bother about others.'

Molly was mollified. She slipped a disc of dance music into the stereo system. It was a tango. 'Shall we dance?' she asked extending her arms towards me. 'This is my favourite tango—"Jealousy".'

'I haven't danced much and I'm clumsy on my feet. You teach me.'

I got up and put my left arm around her shoulder. She had to guide me. I stepped on her toes a couple of times. She pushed me back on my chair and went through the steps all by herself, turning and twisting, long steps, short steps, till the music was over.

'I thought you were good at everything,' she said collapsing into her chair. 'You can't dance for nuts. I'll teach you a few steps: waltz, fox trot, quick step and that sort of old stuff, then some rock-n-roll, twist and modern stuff. Didn't any of your American women teach you how to dance?'

'There's not much of that on American campuses. Those interested go to dancing joints.'

'We Goans have it in our blood; everyone knows how to sing and dance. You should come over during Christmas or carnival time. The taverns are full, feni flows like the Zuari river, couples spend nights on the beaches making love . . . There's no place on earth like Goa.'

Her cheerfulness had returned. She chatted away during dinner. After dinner we sat in front of the fire; I on the armchair, she on the carpet, resting her head between my legs. We told each other with absolute candour about the affairs we had had. Hers were almost entirely with the whites she met in the health club or gave massages to in their rooms.

'I can't afford to sleep around with Goans. It would soon get around and I'd be branded a slut. With foreigners there's no such danger. And although they paid me, I did not feel I was whoring because there was no talk of money beforehand, no bargaining. Everyone gave me a tip after a massage. If I gave them more than a massage, the tips were not a few hundred rupees but a few thousand— you can't let that kind of easy money go. But my motto is: Have fun with the whites, marry only a Goan. Did you ever pay for sex?'

'Never,' I replied. 'On the contrary many women gave me expensive presents after I had bedded them.'

'I say, you're special! You should have been a gigolo, then. I expect with a thing that size you'd have women willing to pay you a fortune to put it inside them,' she laughed. 'And I get it for free—get *paid* for it in fact, imagine! Oh, but of course it isn't sex that you're paying me for. You *never* pay for sex, do you?'

She was pulling my leg, but I enjoyed it. I enjoyed everything about that evening. Far from resenting what the other had done, we had become closer after our confessions. We looked forward to getting even closer.

I played with her hair till the fire died out. 'I know it's not the right time for you to be made love to,' I said standing up, 'but can't we be in the same bed to keep each other warm? The nights are frosty and cold.'

'I was thinking about the same,' she replied. 'But no jiggery-pokery. Yours or mine?'

'I prefer mine. I get up early to let in the servants. I can lift you bodily and put you in your bed. You can sleep late.'

She nodded her head.

I went down to do my usual business in the garden and lock the doors. When I came up Molly was already lying in my bed. I brushed my teeth, changed into my night clothes and slipped in beside her. I took her in my arms and cupped her breasts in my hands. She pushed herself closer in my embrace and mumbled, 'Thus far, no further.'

We spent the night in each other's arms, enveloped in the warmth of our bodies. When two bodies have settled their equation, they can derive as much pleasure from simple physical contact with each other as they can from sexual intercourse. When I got up in the morning, she was still fast asleep. I went into the kitchen and put the kettle on the gas fire. I got out two rubber hot water bottles from my almirah and filled them up with boiling water, went up and put them in her bed to take the chill out of it. A few minutes later I picked her up, plonked her in her warm bed and covered her with an eiderdown. She murmured, briefly disturbed, then turned round and was back in her dreamland. I went down to unlock the doors and was back in my bed before the servants arrived.

I had my morning tea, read the papers, bathed, dressed for work. I had my breakfast alone. I was smoking my cigar when Molly emerged from her bedroom rubbing her eyes, stretching her arms above her head and yawning. 'Good Lord! What time is it?'

I glanced at my watch and told her, 'Eight-thirty. I'll be leaving in a short while. It's Saturday, half day at work, so I'll be back home for lunch. I can take you out shopping in the afternoon. You should buy a few more pairs of salwar-kameez if you mean to wear them when we go out, or perhaps a few saris.'

'Will you believe me when I say I've never worn a sari? I don't know how to. Anyhow, it's a clumsy dress. A working woman who has to jump in and out of crowded buses, ride scooters or cycles and work in massage parlours can't afford to have all that drapery round her person. Salwar-kameez is more practical, better than a skirt, more elegant than jeans.'

'Okay, I'll take you to ready-made salwar-kameez shops.'

Before leaving the office that afternoon I cashed a self cheque as I did not want to use my credit card to pay for women's clothing. I was back home in time for lunch. Again it was Molly's cooking. A very sensible menu, light and tasty. Clam chowder followed by pomfret with mayonnaise sauce. No dessert.

Two hours later we set out on our shopping expedition. First South Extension market, then Janpath, and finally the state emporia with dresses and handicrafts, supposedly genuine, from the different states of India. Besides four pairs of salwar-kameez Molly bought a lot of other things like blouse pieces and cosmetics. I picked up two boxes of Havana cigars from M R Stores. I blew up a lot of cash. We went to Gaylords to have tea. In between munching sandwiches and hot pakoras she put her hand on mine and asked, 'Are you as generous with all your women?'

'If they are generous with me, I'm generous with them. So far you've been the queen of generosity so I grudge you nothing.'

She pondered over what I had said, then resumed attacking the sandwiches and pakoras till none were left on the plates. 'I'd like a smoke,' she said. 'Do you have a cigarette on you?'

'I switched to cigars some years ago—much nicer. I'll get you a packet. What kind?'

'Any—Goldflake, Charminar. I can't tell the difference. When I'm tired, I like a smoke.'

I gave the waiter a twenty-rupee note to get me a packet from the vendors outside. She lit her cigarette, inhaled and sent the smoke streaming out of her nostrils. 'When I have the curse on me, I tire quickly,' she said, fanning the thick curls of smoke away from my face. 'For two days I bleed like a pig being slaughtered. On the third day it's much less. By tomorrow I should be right as rain. And at your service.'

She winked at me just to make sure I had understood.

By the time we came out of the restaurant Connaught Circus was bathed in grey twilight. Drowning the roar of traffic was the screeching of thousands of parakeets and mynahs settling down in trees for the night. As usual there was heavy traffic on the road leading to Maharani Bagh. It took us almost forty minutes of bumper to bumper driving to reach home.

There was a log fire in the sitting room. Drinks had been laid out. After the hours of shopping even I felt tired. I took a hot shower, got into my night clothes, woollen dressing gown and slippers. Molly did the same. When she emerged from her room, she looked fresh and cheerful. She brought parcels of her shopping with her and spread out the pairs of salwar-kameez she on the carpet. 'Which do you like best?' she asked.

'I don't know; they all look nice to me.'

She picked up the kameezes in turn and held them against her chest, turned sideways to examine herself over and over again. She folded each item carefully and took them back to her room. I poured her a drink. She put on the stereo when she returned, this time a Tchaikovsky waltz. 'Too tired to dance,' she announced, 'but music goes nicely with booze.'

We drank, listened to music and chatted. We had our dinner by the fire.

'Can we sleep together again?' she asked. 'I'm still not quite clean, by tomorrow morning it should be over. Messy business! Will you tell me why God put this curse on women and not men? Seems so unfair.'

'I haven't a clue. I'm told though men don't menstruate they have a menopause when they turn fifty. Some begin to behave very oddly. They have a final bout of womanizing, pawing young girls, using bawdy language or exposing themselves. Others turn religious and waste hours in pilgrimages and prayer.'

'Yes, that's true!' agreed Molly. 'Women at least know that after they've had their menopause, they can't have children. Even their appetite for sex wanes. But men seem to get randier. Even if they can't get their peckers upright and hard they try to poke them into women. Have you seen a fifty-plus man squirming with lust? It's the saddest sight. So disgusting! They make such fools of themselves. I feel sorry for old men. They never learn to leave their limp old dicks in peace.' She laughed uproariously. 'Now to bed. Yours, I expect? And nothing doing this night as well. Just cuddle and go to sleep.'

It was the same as the night before. We snuggled into each other, kicked the hot water bottles out of the bed and slept with the warmth of our bodies.

*

It was Sunday. No office. I slept longer than usual. I picked up Molly, carried her to her room and tucked her into her own bed. 'Sleep as late as you like. It's Sunday. It will be a late breakfast—early brunch. Take your own time.'

She mumbled something I couldn't make out and turned over and went back to sleep.

I opened the doors, picked up the Sunday papers lying in a heap by the gate and went back to my room. I switched on the electric radiator and got back into bed to read the papers. The bearer brought me tea. In half an hour I had run through the six papers and their colour supplements. There was nothing much to read. I went up to the roof to check the arrangements. The two rexine mattresses were lying next to each other, drenched in dew. I walked round the roof. It was higher than the roofs of the other houses. I could see my neighbours, they could not see me. The rooftops were a forest of TV and dish antennae as far as the eyes could see. While strolling around in the chill morning, it occurred to me that I had missed out on my surya namaskar for many days. I stood facing the rising sun and went through all the motions. I felt the better for it.

I bathed, changed into a sports shirt and slacks and put on a thick sweater against the cold. Molly emerged from her room after ten, freshly bathed and in one of the salwar-kameez sets she had bought the day before. 'How do I look?' she asked looking down at her long shirt.

'Very nice! I suggest you wrap a shawl around you. This weather can be very treacherous.'

She went back and came out with a hand-knitted woollen scarf, which barely covered her front. We sat down in front of the electric radiator. I lit my cigar, she lit her cigarette.

'It promises to be a bright, sunny day. The mattresses are on the roof and I've got a bottle of herbal oil to put on my skin. We can sunbathe all afternoon till the sun goes down.'

'That will be lovely,' she replied.

We had a light brunch: hot Chinese sweet-and-sour soup and ham sandwiches. The servants cleared the table and left for their quarters.

'Come and take a look at the bandobast,' I said and led her by the hand up the stairs to the roof. The sun was bright and warm. It had dried the dew on the mattresses. A bottle of herbal oil was warming itself in the sun. Molly walked round the roof to make sure that no one could see us.

'You get into a light dressing gown,' she ordered, suddenly very professional and in command, 'I'll get into my working clothes'.

We waited to let the sun get warmer. When we went up again, it was exactly overhead. And no breeze. 'Perfect for sun bathing,' pronounced Molly. 'Take off your dressing gown and lie down on your stomach.'

I did as I was ordered. She took off her cotton nightie and tossed it on the ground. Not a stitch of anything on her except the gold chain round her ankle. She came over and sat on my back—astride, as if riding a horse. I could feel her pubic hair tickle the base of my spine. With both her hands she kneaded my spine from bottom to top, over and over again. She pressed her thumbs hard into my shoulder blades, then twisted them, rinsing out all the tension. She filled her palms with warm herbal oil, smeared it on my back, and repeated the process: up the spinal cord, behind the neck to the base of the skull, round the ears, down to the shoulders and back to the base of the spine. She got up, stepped over me twice and again sat down on my back, this time facing my feet. She put more oil in her palms and went over my buttocks and between them, circling my anus lightly, then to my thighs, legs, ankles, down to every toe. This went on for almost half an hour. It was very soothing and sensuous. Every inch of my body was aching to be ministered to by her loving fingers. She stood above me and ordered, 'Turn around.'

I turned around and lay on my back. I got a worm's eye view of her thighs and what they concealed. She sat down on my stomach. She ran her fingers round my nipples. I had not realized a man's nipples could be as sensitive as a woman's. She poured oil on my chest and with open palms rubbed it into my torso many times. Once again she changed positions; now her buttocks were towards my face. As she stretched forward and back, her pubic hair grazed the line of hair running down from my navel to my groin. She slapped a liberal palmful of oil beneath my testicles and rubbed it into my inner thighs, down to the ankles and the feet. She had to lean forward to massage my feet and I had a splendid view of her anus and pubic fluff. I began to react. My penis sprang to full life and slapped against her thigh as it did so. She slapped it down and away. 'Patience!' she admonished.

The massage went on for an hour. I can't recall ever having experienced anything more pleasurable and sensual—even more than sexual intercourse. She wiped her oily hands against her sides and lay down on her mattress, face down. This time I went over and sat astride her, my balls caressing the small of her back as I moved. Though I had not massaged anyone before, I imitated her. I massaged her body from her neck to her toes, first the rear then the front. I glued my lips to her nipples in turn and slowly entered her. It was heavenly. I stayed inside her a long time, both of us motionless. Then I pulled out and asked her to turn around. She lay on her stomach with her legs wide apart. I positioned myself between her thighs and began to massage her buttocks. Come to think of it, a woman's buttocks excite a man more than any other part of her body— more than her lips or breasts or her pussy. And Molly's were beautifully rounded and firm. I found them irresitible and slowly entered her cunt from the rear. She gave a long sigh of pleasure and let me go further and further into her. We did our best to prolong our bliss. Every time I felt I was coming I pulled out and sat still till the crisis had passed. Then we resumed our search for the ultimate truth of bodily existence: at times she pressed into me from above with my hands squeezing and pressing her buttocks to urge her on; then I on top with her nails stuck into my posterior. When neither of us could hold out any longer, we went at each other like wild animals, tearing and clawing each other's flesh. The climax was the most prolonged that either of us had experienced in our lives.

No words were spoken. Words were superfluous. We lay on our mattresses and let the sun dry up the oil on our bodies. We had been at it for almost three hours.

After worshipping the sun with our bodies in our own unique way, we went downstairs to cleanse ourselves of the oil on them. I fetched two loofahs and gave her one to run over her limbs after she had soaped herself. There is nothing better than a loofah to scrape oil or dirt off one's body. I felt cleaner than ever before. I got into my woollen dressing gown, switched on the electric radiator and lit a cigar. Molly joined me a few minutes later and lit a cigarette.

'That was heavenly,' I said. 'Don't you think so?'

'Never known anything better in my life,' she replied with a smile. 'But let's not try to repeat it?'

'Why on earth not?'

'This kind of love-making in which every part of your body makes love to every part of your partner's is a once-in-a-lifetime experience. Dwell on it in your mind, never try to relive it in action. It will be a great disappointment.'

*

Molly was by no means good-looking by north Indian standards: too dark, too short. Behind my back my friends' wives would ask, 'What on earth does he see in her? With his money and looks he could have got a much better looking and well-educated girl for the asking.' And their husbands would smirk and reply: 'She's probably very good in bed. You don't have to have fair skin and a BA degree to be a good lay.' And the wives would snort, 'As if that is all that matters in marriage. Any wife can be a good lay if her husband knows how to lay her.' And more of such claptrap.

I wasn't sure what Molly would think of a long-term commitment to me. The way she talked gave me the impression that she missed Goa very much. I could not very well ask her how long she meant to stay, as she might construe it as my wanting to get rid of her—which was far from the truth. I had enjoyed her being with me better than the company of all the other women I had known. But for how long? I knew she wrote to her mother every week: the letter was meant for the entire family. She received no post as, very sensibly, she had left no mailing address. One evening I asked her, 'What did you tell your parents back home when you left for Delhi?'

'I said I was going to treat an old woman suffering from partial paralysis. I told them I didn't know how long I would be away because

I had no idea how long this lady would need my services. Perhaps you can tell me. I know you won't marry me, and I don't want to marry you either. It would never work. So I'll stay as long as you want me around. Don't make it too long as it will create problems for both of us. Also don't make it too short as that will hurt my feelings.'

How much truer and matter-of-fact could anyone be! I was overcome by her candour and gave her a kiss of gratitude. 'Molly, you are the nicest girl I have ever met,' I told her truthfully. 'I think I'm falling in love with you.'

'Cut out the crap about love,' she snapped, surprising me with her sudden fierceness. 'You just enjoy being fucked by me. You'll soon tire of it. I have an insatiable appetite for sex, mister. You won't be able to cope with me for too long. Yes or no?'

She laughed uproariously.

'Yes or no?' she repeated, waiting for an answer.

'No,' I replied. 'You may be a lot younger, Molly Gomes, but I'll match you fuck for fuck till kingdom come.'

'Amen!'

*

Molly stayed with me for three months. It was becoming a little awkward for both of us. I was asked by more than one of my friends whether there was any truth in the rumour that I was planning to marry a Goan lady doctor. I denied it vehemently and replied: 'She's treating a paralytic who needs daily therapy.' They would go on to ask, 'How did you get to know her?' I did not like that kind of interrogation. Molly also felt that her family and friends in Goa would be wondering why she had been away so long. She might also be losing her business contacts with five star hotels. 'If my regular clients don't find me they'll find others. How will I earn my bread and butter?' she asked.

I left the decision to her. It was she who finally asked me to book her on a flight to Goa.

'Molly, must you go? And so soon?' I protested.

'I think I must,' she replied, 'and it's not as soon as you think. It's been a full three months and a little more. All good things must come to an end one day, Mr Kumar. As does life.'

Although the foreign tourist season was ending, many Indians were availing themselves of cheaper rates offered by hotels. My travel agent was able to get a seat for her, executive class, on a flight a week later. It left Delhi at a reasonable hour, 11.30 a.m. When I handed her the ticket, she clung to me. We made love. We made love every day of the week left to us. 'I must give you your money's worth,' she said one day after a prolonged session in bed. 'You are worth a lakh of rupees every time,' I told her.

'Oh yeah? Then you owe me at least eighty lakhs. I've kept a count in my private diary but I won't charge you a single paise more than we bargained for as I've got more out of you than I got from any other man in my life. My womb's got a tankful of your seed. All wasted. Not one bambino.'

We made love the morning she was to leave. I drove her to the airport. As her flight was called, I embraced her and gave her a passionate farewell kiss. 'Molly, promise you'll write. We must keep in touch for as long as we can.'

She did not make any promise. Just waved to me and was lost in the crowd queuing up to go through the security check.

Molly did not write to me. The letters I wrote to her remained unanswered.

Fifteen
Susanthika

It took me a long time to come to terms with life without Molly. Separation is always harder on the one left behind than on the one who goes away. More so in my case as Molly had filled my life to overflowing and the emptiness she left behind was excruciatingly painful. Many a time I thought of flying to Goa and looking for her in all the hotels there. It was not an impossible task. But I held myself back. I had nothing really to offer her and my presence would embarrass her. Her family and friends would rightly conclude that her visit to Delhi was not professional but for other reasons not acceptable to them. And I remembered what she had told me on the rooftop after the best sex I had had in my life. Never try and repeat this, she had said. She would rather we never met again; she would not risk disappointment. Gradually I reconciled myself to the idea that I would not see Molly any more. Her image receded into a misty haze till it became a memory, a very sweet memory.

*

After I got my divorce, I felt that I had been freed of Sonu and could lead my life the way I wanted to. I had not reckoned with her vindictiveness. Whenever I went to the Gymkhana or the Golf Club, I could sense a change in the attitude of my friends and their wives towards me. They stared at me as if they were seeing me for the first time. The men made snide remarks calculated to hurt or irritate me. On one occasion a fellow slapped me on the back and said, 'Yaar Mohan, you chhupa rustam (hidden champion), we hear you're a tees maarkhan (one who knocks down thirty at a time); the Muhammad Ali of sex.' I tried to laugh it off. On another evening one of the women in the circle I joined for a drink asked, 'Mohanji, I hear you are already planning to get married again. Is that true?'

'I haven't heard about it,' I retorted, 'so it must be true.' She got a bit flustered and went on, 'Forgive me if I said the wrong thing. But everyone tells me you are going to marry some lady doctor from the south.'

I knew she was referring to Molly. I countered her by replying, 'I will be obliged if you could introduce me to this lady doctor from the south. I'd like to get to know her before I marry her.'

Sonu was undoubtedly responsible for the gossip. Her servants must have got to know from mine that a woman who passed off for a lady doctor was staying with me. My sour ex-wife would not miss any opportunity to make my life public. She must have worked overtime to get the Delhi gossip mills working furiously. I went to the clubs to relax among friends. I left them more tense, with the whisky turning sour in my stomach. Sonu succeeded in giving me the reputation of a compulsive womanizer. Although many young women eyed me with a mixture of desire and curiosity, I knew they would never have the courage to step out with me. In their parents' eyes I was simply a lafanga—a no good loafer who consorted with women of 'loose character'. It was the loss of normal human dignity that bothered me. There was nothing dirty in what I did, but their looks and remarks made me out to be a filthy sex maniac. Gradually I stopped going to the clubs and turned down invitations to parties. I stayed at home, drank alone, listened to music or watched TV. I wallowed in the misery of one whom no one loves. For a time I quite enjoyed my loneliness.

I wondered if my experiment of taking on mistresses on a short-term basis had been successful. It might have been if Sonu had put me out of her mind and stopped persecuting me. On the other hand if it were not Sonu it could have been someone else, male or female, who resented my having a good time. But what was the alternative to the clandestine affairs I had been having? How could I openly have a woman companion whose parents, brothers, sisters, ex-husbands would accept her having an affair with a divorced man and not get upset with her? I could not think of a way out of the impasse because I needed sex on a regular basis, with a change of partners every few months. I did not relish the idea of visiting brothels or having call girls who serviced many men every day: my woman had to be exclusively mine for the time she was with me. I had no right to tell her what she should do with her life after she left me.

I also realized that the sort of relationship I sought with women made me a social outcast. I did not like that. I wanted to regain respectability, but how was I going to do that in a society which could not accept my enjoying intimacy with unattached and willing women?

During Molly's stay in Delhi I had missed out on my monthly visits to Haridwar. I felt bad about it because the Ganga had in some mysterious way become my spiritual sustenance. My father had died by its banks; his ashes were immersed in its waters and in his later years a daily dip in the river had meant more to him than visiting temples and gurudwaras. I had inherited some of the reverence for the mother of all rivers from him. A post card from the secretary of the ashram where I had retained my father's room enquiring about my health and asking me why he had not had my 'darshan' for some months helped me make up my mind. I consulted my diary which had a lunar calendar and wrote back to say that I would be there for the next full moon.

I had often spoken about the aarti at sunset to my friends at cocktail parties. 'If you want an experience of living Hinduism, you won't get it from the sacred texts or by visiting temples, you will see it in Haridwar, in the worship of the Ganga at sunset,' I told them. Many of them had asked me to take them along the next time I went there. Amongst them were quite a few foreigners whose idea of 'doing' India was confined to visiting Agra, Jaipur, Varanasi, Khajuraho and the temples in South India—all monuments, no people. At one such embassy party where I was holding forth on my pet topic, one person avidly taking in everything I was saying was a young, darkish, slightly built woman in her late twenties. I had never seen her before and could not make out whether she was Indian, Pakistani or Bangladeshi. She was none of these. She introduced herself: 'Hello, I'm Susanthika Goonatilleke from the High Commission of Sri Lanka. I was very interested in what you were saying about Ganga worship. How does one get to Haridwar? Is there anywhere one can stay overnight?'

We broke out of the circle and took two chairs next to each other. I told her of the route to take, the towns she would pass on the three-and-a-half-hour journey. 'There are a good number of bungalows and a government tourism hostel, but you'll be more comfortable in the guest house of Bharat Heavy Electricals, which is a few miles before Haridwar. Haridwar is a holy city and there's strict prohibition—no alcohol and no meat. But the BHEL guest house is outside municipal limits. And I'm told it has a very good cook. I'd advise you to book a room well ahead of time. I'd suggest you spend two nights there near the time of the full moon. You should not have much problem getting accommodation. If your husband writes to the the General Manager at BHEL, I'm sure he'll be honoured to have you as his guests.'

'I'm not married,' she said. 'I'm only the second secretary in the High Commission, but I'll try to get the High Commissioner's private secretary to speak to the GM of Bharat Heavy Electricals.'

'It would be advisable to have a guide to escort you. The place teems with beggars, priests, paandas, astrologers and sadhus—some of them with nothing more than ash smeared on their bodies. A single young woman going about the ghats would not be a good idea.'

'Where will I find a guide?'

'I'd be happy to show you around. I try to go there every full moon night. I have a room in an ashram. Unfortunately the ashram does not allow women visitors. I've promised to take my cook and bearer with me the next time I go, but we could fit you in our car.'

'Car's no problem, I have one with a chauffeur. We can follow you all the way. Will your wife be going with you?'

'I'm a divorcee. If that matters to you, I'll find you another escort.'

She smiled and replied, 'Your being married or divorced is of no concern to me. I'd be happy to go with you and your servants. How do I get in touch with you? I didn't even get your name.'

I fished out a visiting card from my pocket and handed it to her. She took one of her own out of her hand bag and gave it to me. 'I have a long unpronounceable name, so my friends call me Sue. But I'm not a Christian, I'm Buddhist.'

'I've never met a Buddhist. I hope you'll tell me something about your religion and your people.'

The full moon night was ten days away. I was in two minds about ringing up Sue whatever she was and having to explain my business to her private secretary before she put me through. I asked Vimla Sharma to inform Sue. She rang me up the next day and told me she had got a room in the BHEL guest house. I gave her details of the journey. She was to come to my bungalow in Maharani Bagh by eleven in the morning. I would be carrying a packed lunch for us to have on the way. We would reach her guest house by half past three. I would go to my ashram and send my car to fetch her around half past five and drop her back in time for dinner. If she wanted to bathe at Har Ki Pauri she could do so the next morning. She could return to Delhi whenever she wanted. I made it sound as matter of fact as I could.

*

Susanthika Goonatilleke's large Japanese Toyota bearing a blue diplomatic corps number plate drew up outside Ranjit Villa exactly at eleven. Jiwan Ram opened the iron gate to let it in. We were already packed and ready to go. I instructed my one-eyed jamadarni to look after the house while I was away, to not let anyone in, nor answer the door bell.

Jiwan Ram and the servants went ahead in my car; I sat with Sue and followed them. I had instructed Jiwan Ram to pull up at some nice secluded stop at about one for lunch.

On the way we got talking about each other. I asked her why she was unmarried. Of course I threw in a few compliments with my query: an attractive, intelligent girl in the diplomatic service, etc. She accepted the compliments with good grace and replied, 'I don't quite know why; it just did not happen. Perhaps Mr Right did not come along,' she said shrugging her shoulders.

'You've never had anyone you were serious about?' I asked, a little incredulous. 'Yes, I had a boyfriend, the son of a tea planter. He believed in good living, partying, drinking and dancing through the night. There are quite a few of that type in Colombo. I knew I would not fit into that kind of life. Then I qualified for the diplomatic services and that decided things for us. Delhi is my first posting. I've already done a year, another two to go before I'm posted back to Colombo or sent to another embassy. Maybe London or Paris or New York—anywhere. Diplomats are like rolling stones, here today, gone tomorrow. No permanent stay anywhere. The day I marry, I'll quit the service and settle down somewhere. And what about you? I'm told you're quite a ladies' man. And rich.'

'Where did you pick up that gossip?' I asked. 'Just because my marriage didn't work out doesn't make me a no-good philanderer. I come from a lower middle-class family. I started from scratch and made whatever I have myself.'

She put her bony little hand on mine. 'Don't take my words seriously. I was teasing you. You were at Princeton and the only one to get a summa cum laude in your final examination. Right?'

'Right. How did you dig up all that information?'

'I didn't have to do much homework. Just about every Indian I met at the embassy parties seemed to know about you and hold you in high esteem.'

'That's nice to know. All I hear is nasty gossip about my broken marriage.'

'Envy, that's for sure,' she remarked. 'A handsome young man from a poor family who becomes a topper in a prestigious American university and earns a million before he's forty is bound to rouse a lot of jealousy and rancour. I wouldn't bother with such types.' Once more she put her bony, cold hand on mine. I noticed how thin her wrists were. She was even more slightly built than I had first thought. High cheek bones, thin dark lips, small breasts and a smaller behind.

Her head would just about reach my chin. But her eyes sparkled as she spoke. She was highly intelligent and animated.

Jiwan Ram pulled up under a cluster of mango trees a few yards off the main road along the Ganga canal. The sun was right above us. It was uncomfortably hot. A gentle breeze blew over the canal towards freshly harvested wheat fields. There was a village at a distance but no sign of humans or cattle. We made ourselves as comfortable as we could. Jiwan Ram opened the hamper he had brought. It had a variety of sandwiches and cans of chilled beer. 'I don't usually drink in the daytime but I'm hot and thirsty,' she said accepting a can from me. She gulped the beer down and exclaimed, 'Delightful! Nothing could be better than ice-cold beer on a dry hot afternoon.'

We munched our sandwiches. Jiwan Ram and the servants sat on the canal bank gobbling parathas and potato bhujia. Sue and I resumed our dialogue.

'Are you a practising Buddhist?' I asked her.

'I don't know what you mean by practising,' she replied. 'I rarely go to a temple and I don't pray very much. But I'm a Buddhist because I like what I've read about the Buddha's teachings. To me it makes more sense than the teachings of other great masters. All the world's religions have taken something from Buddhism. I'm sure there must be as many non-Buddhists who revere the Buddha as do practicing Buddhists.'

'I attended classes on comparative religions at Princeton,' I told her, taken back over fifteen years to those days. 'Our professor laid a lot of stress on Dukkha—sorrow, all-pervading sorrow—in the teachings of the Buddha. His way of overcoming it was to overcome desire: desire for food, sex and the good things of life. I found that hard to accept. The strength of Hinduism lies in the fact that it is a happy religion. Our rituals allow lots of fun and frolic, drinking, dancing, gambling, flirting. I go by that rather than fasting, penance and that sort of thing.'

'You call having fun and frolic religion?'

Before I could answer her, Jiwan Ram came to pack up the hamper. It was another hour's drive to Haridwar.

'We'll continue our argument another time,' I said standing up and brushing the dust off my trousers. She held up both her hands for me to haul her up to her feet. She could have got up herself; I guessed it was a gesture of friendship. I went further and brushed her posterior of dust and dried grass that had stuck to her sari. 'Thanks,' she said giving me a winsome smile. We got into her car and followed Jiwan Ram to the BHEL guest house.

The caretaker was awaiting the arrival of the VIP guest. He was impressed by the size of the car and its diplomatic corps number plate but was evidently not impressed by the diminutive dark lady who looked like any college girl from the south. Her bossy manner put him in his place. 'Driver, put my bag in the room allotted to me,' she ordered. Then to the caretaker: 'Can I have some tea?'

I did not go to inspect Sue's room. I simply shook hands with her and said, 'My driver will come for you at five-thirty—about two hours from now. Pick me up from the ashram and we can have an hour strolling along the ghats and then watch the aarti at sunset.'

She did not protest against being left alone.

At the ashram I had my room opened and everything in it dusted. I was served highly sugared tea in a brass tumbler. I had a lota bath and changed into fresh clothes and awaited Sue. Jiwan Ram was a stickler for time. He drove in exactly at five-thirty. Sue's driver was also in the car. 'He insisted on coming with me to have Ganga darshan. He also wants to come in the morning to bathe. I hope you don't mind.' Sue had a camera slung on her shoulder.

'The more the merrier,' I remarked.

We crowded into my car and proceeded to the point nearest Har Ki Pauri. I assumed the role of guide and protector. I shooed off beggars, paandas, and subscription collectors. On the main ghat the servants stayed a discreet distance behind us. Sue had her camera ready all the time: temples, sadhus, paandas, cows, pilgrims, river, landscape—it was snap, snap, snap all through. She had no time to talk to me. I found her behaviour somewhat off-putting.

Sue noticed my irritation and put her camera in her bag. 'These pictures will remind me of my pilgrimage to the Ganga. I must take some of you with the river in the background.' I did not say anything.

The sun had gone over the western range of hills. It was time to find a good spot near the clocktower facing Har ki Pauri. I led her with my arm round her shoulders and with a succession of 'excuse-me's' we pushed our way through to the front row—in such places size and 'Sahib English' command obedience. The pageant of lights and sounds began. I kept a protective arm round Sue's shoulders throughout the waving of candelabras, the chanting of shlokas and the clanging of bells. She did not seem to mind: on the contrary, she rested her head against my chest. And when the aarti ended she looked into my eyes and mumbled, 'Bewitching! Thank you ever so much for letting me come with you.'

The crowd began to disperse. We stayed by the river for a while, strolled on the ghat, enjoying the moonlight and cool breeze. We went through the brightly lit bazaar to reach the car. 'What next?' asked Sue as we took our seats.

'I to my ashram; you to your guest house. No women allowed in the ashram. Nor any alcohol in the holy city.'

'Both allowed in the guest house. You told me it is off limits. I've brought a bottle of Scotch and some soda, would you care to join me?'

'Can I have a rain check on that?' I asked. 'I would like to get up early and take a dip in the river in memory of my father. He never missed the opportunity to wash away his sins. Mine need a lot more washing.'

'Why can't I come too? I may not bathe, but I would like to see the spectacle,' she said.

'Sure! If you can join me at the ashram at five tomorrow morning I'll take you along. But no photography allowed.'

I and my servants got off at the ashram. Jiwan Ram drove Sue and her chauffeur to the BHEL guest house. I felt bad at having turned down Sue's invitation so brusquely. I had not told her that I had my own Scotch and soda in my room—prohibition or no prohibition.

Early the next morning she arrived at the ashram to pick me up. Daylight had just begun to lighten the sky. She was in salwar-kameez and carried a sling bag with clothes. 'I decided to give the holy Ganga a chance to wash away my sins. I'm not a Ganga worshipper, but she may extend her cleansing properties to me,' she said with a laugh.

We were at different sections of Har Ki Pauri. I could see Sue divest herself of her salwar and wrap a towel round her waist. She took off her kameez, but kept her bra on. Some women had less on them than her. She was the smallest of the lot. I turned my gaze away. I recalled my father offering water to the rising sun and submerging himself in the water a few times. He used to name the people for whom he was performing the ritual by proxy. I offered two palmfuls of water to the sun and ducking into the stream I could only think of a few people who had been close to me: Jessica, Yasmeen, Sarojini, Molly, my father and my children—seven dips in all. It was very refreshing. I turned around to see how Sue was getting along. She had put on her petticoat and had a towel round her shoulders, covering her breasts. Clearly she had got bolder and taken her bra off before the dip. With a second towel she was rubbing herself between her legs. She felt secure among the many women in different stages of nudity. She towelled her small breasts and slipped on her bra.

Then she draped her sari round her, Sinhalese style. We found our way to our cars. I wasn't sure if Sue meant to return to Delhi or spend another day in Haridwar. I asked her. 'I booked the rooms for two nights and days. I thought I'd see all there is to see around here and go back with you,' she replied.

'It will be too hot to do any sightseeing,' I said. 'It would be wiser to stay in your air-conditioned room during the day. I have to make do with an old ceiling fan which only churns up hot air. We can go to the ghats again in the evening. This time without a camera. And if I may, I'll join you for a drink in the evening.'

We returned to our respective abodes.

I gave my servants money to take Sue's driver with them to a film on some religious theme showing in a local cinema and for their evening meal in a dhaba. Soon after sunset I drove to the BHEL guest house and was shown to Sue's room. She had Scotch, soda and a bucket of ice cubes laid out on the table. She was smoking a cigarette.

She had not smoked on the way, not even after the picnic lunch by the canal. She was obviously doing so to soothe her nerves. She got up from her chair and instead of shaking hands greeted me with a kiss on both cheeks. 'This is to thank you for bringing me with you. It was a memorable experience. It will stay with me for the rest of my life.'

She stubbed her cigarette out and said, 'You do the honours while I rinse my mouth and get the awful cigarette smell out of it.'

She took a long time in her bathroom. I was not sure what she had in mind but as a precaution latched the door from the inside. I poured out two whiskeys and waited for her to join me.

'So what did you do all day?' she asked as she came out.

'Nothing much,' I replied, 'it was too hot to go out. I read papers, magazines, ate and snoozed, and the day was gone. And you?'

'I had the driver take me around Haridwar and up the higher reaches of the Ganga. He didn't know his way about. So we came back. I loafed in the bazaar for a while to see if I could buy something. There was a lot of junk. And shopkeepers would not believe I can't understand Hindustani. I had to point to myself and tell them, "From Sri Lanka." The invariable response was, "Oh, Lanka: land of Ravana." That's all that most Indians know about my country.'

'That's all I know too, besides of course that Sri Lankan Tamils are fighting for Eelam and cursing us Indians for not supporting them . . . . I don't understand why people of different nations hate each other so much. Do you hate us?'

'No,' she replied. 'The Buddha said hate kills the man who hates. I don't hate you, you don't hate me. That's all that matters.' She took my hand and put it against her lips. In return I drew her bony hand towards my mouth and kissed it.

'That's like signing an India-Sri Lanka Peace Treaty,' she said with a soft laugh.

I did not let go of her hand; she did not try to withdraw it. After a while she said, 'Mr Kumar, I'm told most women find you irresistible.'

'Do you?'

'Well, I'm not quite sure. You're a handsome chap and have a way with women. I don't blame them if they fall for you.'

'You haven't told me if *you* have fallen for me.'

'Why do you think I invited myself to Haridwar? But I don't know if I am the kind of woman you fall for. I'm not much to look at. Too dark and too skinny for the tastes of most Indians.'

'I've seen more of you than you know. I had a quick look at you when you were changing from your salwar-kameez into a sari. Everything in miniature but in the right proportions. You have quite a nice figure.'

'Thank you. I thought you went to the holy river to cleanse yourself of libidinous thoughts.'

'Also to seek her blessing for success in a new venture.'

She put her glass of whisky aside, came over and sat in my lap, put her arms around my neck and kissed me. We stayed that way for some minutes. Then I took over. I placed her head on my right shoulder, made her open her mouth to let my tongue explore. I put my hand inside her bra. It was very tight. The buttons at the back snapped and her breasts were freed of their confines. I took her small, firm breasts in my mouth, first one, then the other. She put her head back, shut her eyes and 'aahd' and 'oohd' with pleasure as she kept ruffling my hair with her fingers. She felt my member rise and throb under her. She stood up and tapped it with her bony hand. 'He's getting impatient for action. Come.' She took my hand and led me to her bed. She lay down on her back and pulled her sari up above the waist. She wore no panties. She had planned it all. I was surprised to see how big her cunt was. She had obviously had plenty of sex. As I mounted her, she expressed no surprise about the size of my penis as most other women had: she simply guided it in with her fingers and said, 'It feels like Ashoka's pillar entering me. I like it. Put in all you have.'

I did. She squirmed with pleasure. As she felt her climax coming, she asked, 'Don't you have a condom?'

'No,' I replied, 'I didn't expect to use one on this visit.'

'Then for God's sake don't come inside me. I can't risk a pregnancy. I know it won't be much fun for you, but this time, for my sake.'

She climaxed with her teeth dug into my neck and her hands clutching my hair. I pulled out just in time and squirted my semen on her thighs.

'My thighs are sticky, my sari is crumpled, and you've snapped the buttons of my bra, but it was worth it.'

After showering herself she came out and lay naked on the bed beside me. She took my flaccid member in her hands and said, 'It's massive. No wonder women fall for you. We'd better get dressed. I'll order dinner to be brought to the room.'

We got into our clothes. She rang for the bearer, told him to serve dinner.

While waiting for dinner I thought I'd get to know a little more about Sue. I asked her, 'I know very little about you except that you're a diplomat so you must be very clever. And you're a liberated woman, of course.'

'Well, I come from a large family: tea planters. I was a clever cookie, so I passed the civil service exam and opted for the foreign service. As for being liberated, yes I have no hang-ups about sex. If I like a chap and he likes me we get into bed. Nothing wrong in that, is there?'

'Not at all,' I replied. 'When two people want to get close to each other, sex should be their top priority. When did you lose your virginity?'

'Now you're being very nosey. But I'll tell you. I was sixteen. Nothing romantic about the deflowering. My own uncle, my father's younger brother. The usual thing, you know, a close relative whom you trust. It seemed harmless enough at first—kissing and cuddling, that sort of thing. Then he thought he'd got me worked up and started playing with my breasts and stroking my crotch. I got frantic and before I knew it he had me under him on the floor and tore into me. I almost told my parents but held back because I realized I had led him on. I taught the fellow a lesson by seducing his fourteen-year-old son, my cousin. The boy got so besotted with me he started writing me love letters and poems. I let him to do it a few times but then he wanted to marry me. He went and told his parents that we were in love and wanted to get married. His old man quickly took the boy away from Colombo and put him in a boarding school far from the city. It's not very difficult for a girl to seduce a man. I know I can get any man I want because men are ever willing for sex. I got you.'

'We got each other,' I countered. I told her about Molly who was also 'deflowered' by her uncle when only fourteen. 'It's amazing how many girls are initiated into sex by their older relations or their parents' friends,' I observed. ' Well, it's the same for boys,' said Sue. 'They're seduced by their aunts or older maidservants. When the sexual urge becomes too strong in young people and it's obvious that they can barely contain it, an experienced older person finds it easy to exploit them.'

'And are you experienced?' I asked bluntly. 'I mean, have you had many affairs?'

'Quite a few. And I had a steady boyfriend for some years. I've told you about him. Neither of us wanted to get married, so there was no heartburn on either side. What about you?'

'I was a virgin till twenty. It was a black girl at university who initiated me into sex. Thereafter I had many affairs. Sex is the greatest thing in a human's life. The more varied it is, the more enjoyable. Don't you agree?'

'Yes and no. I don't think one-night stands count. A relationship has to be of reasonable duration with the same person to be fulfilling. Both can sense when the excitement has gone out of it. Then it's time to call it quits and take on a new partner. I hope we'll be able to meet off and on while I'm posted in Delhi.'

'I hope so too. We haven't really begun. You can't really enjoy it if you're scared of being interrupted, found out, or afraid of getting pregnant.'

'I'm sorry,' she said taking my hand. 'The next time I promise you more satisfaction.'

We left Haridwar early the next morning. We could have gone in our own cars and at different times, but we decided to travel together. I in her car, the servants in mine. Occasionally she stretched her hand towards me and we entwined our fingers tightly. After we crossed the Yamuna, she kept carefully noting landmarks which led to Maharani Bagh and my house. Her car pulled up outside the gate. She did not want to come in. 'I'm late for office. I must go home, change and get to work. Don't ring me up at the High Commission or my flat as all calls are monitored. It you have a direct line in your office I'll get in touch with you. I don't want to ring up your home, your servants will recognize me.'

I gave her my direct number at work. She rang me up the next day. 'Hi there! Know who this is?'

'Sue—something, something unpronounceable! What can I do for you?'

'What are you doing next Saturday? We have the day off.'

'I have a lunch date with a lady from the Sri Lankan High Commission. We work half day on Saturdays and I'll give the servants the afternoon off. I'll be home in the afternoon by one-thirty.'

'Okay, okay. Expect your Sri Lankan date at one-thirty sharp.'

Saturday morning I told my cook to make something cold and put it in the fridge as I might be later than usual. I also gave Jiwan Ram the weekend off. When I got back home at noon, the house was quiet as a tomb. I switched on the bedroom air-conditioner and checked the contents of the fridge. Fish, potato and cucumber salad. Also several cans of beer.

Sue was punctual. She did not come in her embassy car but in a taxi. From the balcony I saw the cab slow down outside Ranjit Villa and pull up in front of my neighbour's. I saw Sue pay off the driver, open her parasol to cover her head against the midday sun and gingerly walk back into Ranjit Villa. Before she could ring the bell, I opened the door to let her in. 'Hi there!' she said as she folded her parasol and put it in the coat stand. 'It's hot as hell; I'm sweating all over. Thank God your house is cool.'

'I've switched on the AC in the sitting room.' I led her by the hand into the cool sitting room. Besides the AC, the ceiling fan was on at maximum speed. She collapsed in an arm chair, stretched her hands behind her and said, 'Let me cool off.'

'Glass of iced beer?' I asked.

'That would be nice.'

I opened two cans of chilled beer, poured their contents into crystal glass tumblers and handed her one. She turned the frosting glass in her hand and exclaimed, 'Lalique, tres chic! Mr Kumar, you are a man of expensive tastes.'

'Yes, ma'am. You see, it results from the company I keep.'

'Flatterer!' she screeched. 'I bet you say the same kind of thing to all the women you entertain with we-know-what designs.'

'Not solely my designs,' I protested, 'mutually-agreed-upon designs.'

'True. The fly inviting herself into the spider's web.'

We finished our beer. 'Would you like a bite? The cook's left some fish mayonnaise and cold salad in the fridge.'

'Are we not getting our priorities mixed up? Lunch can wait.'

She stood up. I took her by the hand and led the way to my bedroom. 'I'm sticky with sweat. I'd like to get out of these clothes first and take a shower.'

'Not a bad idea. I'll join you.'

We stripped and went into the bathroom. I turned on the shower, took a cake of scented soap and rubbed it over her body—face, neck, breasts, stomach, between her thighs, on her small buttocks, down to her ankles. Under the cascade of water she gently took my member in her hands and remarked, 'You really are the biggest I've ever seen. I did not notice it in Haridwar. Let me soap it for you.'

She wasn't tall enough to soap my neck, so she concentrated on my middle—rear and front. It was exquisite. We rubbed each other dry, tossed the towels on the floor, went into the bedroom and lay down on the bed.

'Get me a few cubes of ice from the fridge, I'll show you the Sri Lankan boob trick,' she said.

I did not know what she was up to, but got her a tray of ice nevertheless. She put some cubes in a handkerchief and asked me to rub it against her breasts. As I did so, her breasts began to stiffen and her nipples turned into hard black berries.

'I know you men like them hard,' she said. 'Now you can warm them with your mouth.' I did so, kissing and sucking and biting till she slid up and pressed her lips hard onto mine. We were lying on our sides; she put one leg over mine and with one bony hand guided me into her. I could not enter her fully in that position. 'Come over me,' she ordered as she lay flat on her back and raised both her legs. I went into her again. 'All of it,' she cried hoarsely, again and again. 'All of it. 'Nothing to worry about this time.'

I rammed into her. She was small but had no problem taking all I had. Every time I plunged into her she thrust her pelvis up to receive me. I bit her little breasts savagely. She egged me on. 'Bite them harder and give me all you have.'

I did. We came in a furious frenzy. 'By God, that was the greatest fuck I've had in my life,' she said lying back exhausted. 'And you?'

'It was great,' I replied. I did not want to be disloyal to women who had given me as much pleasure, most of all her predecessor, Molly Gomes. 'It was great,' I repeated. Perhaps she understood that it was not the greatest.

*

We set up a regular schedule of meetings. Our code word was 'Operation Colombo'. She came over almost every Saturday—a holiday for her, a half-day for me. I would give my servants a half-day off and tell them not to return before five as I might be having a late siesta. Mid-week she would get me on my direct line and ask, 'Okay for Operation Colombo?' and I would reply, 'All set.' By the time I got back home, the servants would have left. I would be on the lookout. A taxi would stop next door. A small lady would step out, open her parasol and walk into Ranjit Villa. Her greeting was invariably the same: 'Hi there!' The only variation we made in our weekly meetings was whether it would be chilled beer and a cold snack before bed or bed before chilled beer and a cold snack. We would shower together in the nude and dry each other. I would then pick her up in my arms— she was a feather weight—and lay her gently on the bed and stretch out beside her. We made love at a leisurely pace—almost an hour of foreplay till she said, 'Come, I'm ready.' I would enter her and steadily work her up till she clawed my neck and head with her nails. I would then let her have all I had stored up during the week. Almost invariably we climaxed at the same time. We would have another clean-up shower and get back into our clothes. She would stay with me while I smoked my cheroot. I would drop her near a florist at the entrance to Shanti Niketan where she lived in a flat rented by her High Commission. She would step out of the car, open her parasol and glide out of view. She never invited me to her apartment.

Occasionally we ran into each other at diplomatic receptions. She kept a straight face when we were introduced to each other: 'This is Miss Sue Goonatilleke of the Sri Lankan High Commission. This is Mr Kumar, a businessman.' She would greet me with a namaste and always add, 'Nice to meet you, Mr Kumar.' And if we shook hands only a gentle squeeze, invisible to all others, betrayed the fact that we knew each other better, much better.

It was amazing that our two-year-long intimacy did not become a topic for gossip. The credit for this goes entirely to Sue. Most in my circle of friends came to the conclusion that at long last I was going straight. It was a simple formula: if you fucked and were found out you were debauched, a goonda, unacceptable to society; if nobody got to know about it, you were a respectable citizen. In the two years I had sex with Sue, my image changed from that of a sex maniac who paid all kinds of women for their services to a man of impotent respectability.

It was also strange that though Sue and I enjoyed each others' company neither of us used the word love in our endearments. Our bodies craved to be locked into each other, her yoni ached to receive my lingam—the cosmic union! Our bodies spoke to each other— endearing words of how loving and lovable the other was. Perhaps at the back of our minds was the knowledge that our relationship was not for ever and could soon come to an end.

The end came sooner than I expected. Sue's third year in the Delhi posting was about to finish. She hoped her ministry in Colombo had forgotten about her posting in Delhi. It had not. She received orders of transfer to the Sri Lankan consulate in New York. She was given a month more in Delhi, following which she would need to return to Colombo for another month for briefing before proceeding to her new posting. She told me this as casually as saying, 'I will not be able to make it next Saturday.'

'What will we do?' I asked in dismay.

'We will make love as long as we can,' she replied calmly. 'It was good being with you. We knew it was not for ever. We must have no regrets.'

We made the best of the three Saturdays that remained to us. Our love-making was more intense, the last one deliberately prolonged as if it was for eternity. When she was about to leave I gave her a pearl necklace and a gold ring with a blue sapphire. She made me put the necklace round her neck and slip the ring on her third finger. Her eyes brimmed with tears. I kissed them away.

'You will keep in touch, won't you?' I pleaded.

'Of course I will. I'll write to you when I can and may be ring you up from New York to tell you how I'm doing. You must write to me as often as you can.'

When I dropped her at the Shanti Niketan turning after our last meeting, her parting words were: 'Operation Colombo, complete success.'

Bless her!

*

Sue rang me the day she arrived in Colombo, and again when she left for New York, and then from New York the day she moved into her own apartment. I did not ring her up. Perhaps her calls were monitored even there. We wrote to each other every week. We used words of love we had not used while making love. So it went on for some months. I felt closer to her than I did when she was living only a few kilometres from me and was available once a week. Then I began to miss her calls and her letters became shorter and less frequent. She always had a valid excuse: she had to go to Washington for a briefing or she had far too much work. Six months later she informed me that she was engaged to marry a fellow Sri Lankan diplomat posted in Washington and we should stop writing or calling each other on the phone. She assured me that she would for ever keep a secluded corner in her heart for me, and love me as she had from the day we first met.

It would not be honest to say I was devastated. But I was deeply saddened. Eventually, I reconciled myself to losing her: losing a woman is not the end of all there is. While there is life, there is hope. I was not yet fifty and had much to look forward to.

A strange feeling of lassitude bordering on lethargy overtook me. I did not want to do anything. I lost interest in my business. It went on nevertheless. I had no desire to go to Haridwar anymore. The two persons with whom it had come to be closely connected in my mind— my father and Sue—had gone out of my life. I wrote to the ashram secretary, saying that I would not need the room any more and it could be let out to anyone who wanted it. I posted the key of the room to him.

About this time I wanted to see my children more often. They were not receptive to my advances. Sonu had thoroughly brainwashed them. I was a bad man who had done the dirty on their mother. They were allowed to come over to see me whenever I asked but I could see that they did not enjoy their visits and wanted to get back as soon as I let them. I gave them expensive gifts; they accepted them without enthusiasm. I asked them how they were doing at school. The usual answers were 'Okay' or 'So, So'. Ranjit had not inherited any of my mathematical gifts and often failed in his arithmetic, algebra and geometry exams. Mohini showed a little more affection for me but was scared of her brother sneaking to her mother. Once I asked Ranjit what he wanted to do when he grew up. He replied, 'I don't know. Something or the other.' I told him I had a running business which he could take over. He replied, 'If I go into business, I will start something of my own.' When I told him that the house was registered in his name and would become his after me, he just looked around with disdain. 'Daddy, what are you going to give me?' asked Mohini. 'The same as your brother, paisa for paisa. Shares in my company, cash and jewellery for your wedding. If you want a house, I'll buy you one before you are twenty.' She was satisfied. 'Can we go home and tell our Mummy?' I knew they wanted to get away. I let them go.

The idea of inviting another woman to be my mistress no longer appealed to me. I scanned the photographs and letters of the remaining six or seven who had responded to my invitation and tore them up.

I had become irregular in my surya namaskar and had begun to develop a paunch; my hair started turning grey. I often forgot to recite the Gayatri Mantra. I became like a rudderless boat adrift in an endless ocean.

To fight the feeling of emptiness and the restlessness that came upon me in the evenings, I took to recording the events of my life. This is what you have read—not exactly as I put it down, because I've asked my writer friend, Khushwant, to tinker with these words a little; I am no writer. He can do what he likes with these pages; I have been comforted by the memories of the women I have loved in my own way. That much is enough.

III

The Last Days of Mohan Kumar

Sixteen
A Bai in Bombay

The most difficult thing Mohan Kumar had to deal with in his adult life was the loss of his sex drive. This happened about a year after his affair with Susanthika Goonatilleke ended. Even when he fantasized about the women he had enjoyed and others he fancied, there was no stirring in his groin. He tried the wildest of fantasies and looked at pictures of naked women in *Playboy* and *Debonair* to induce erections. There was no response. He did not like this. Sex was the most important thing in his life: with the sex urge gone, there was little left for him to look forward to. However, after a while there was a mild compensation: he paid more attention to his business and began to socialize more than before.

But he could not accept impotence as natural in a man not yet fifty who had lived such a full sexual life. He tried tonics—ayurvedic, unani. He went to health clubs for different kinds of massages: Kerala, Ayurvedic, Swedish, and simple maalish by pehalwans (wrestlers). He felt the better for them but they did not reactivate his libido.

Kumar's business took him to Bombay. He checked into the Taj Mahal Hotel near the Gateway of India where he usually stayed. After calling on his business associates he returned to the hotel in the evening. He sat in the lobby watching the coming and going of guests and visitors. How very desirable some of the girls looked in their slinky saris or tight-fitting jeans, flaunting their big breasts and wiggling their buttocks as they walked past!

He went to his room and took out his bottle of Scotch. He asked the room bearer to fetch him a bucket of ice cubes, a couple of sodas and some snacks. The bearer rang up room service. A few minutes later another bearer arrived carrying the things Mohan had ordered and laid them on the table. He opened the bill folder for Mohan's signature. Mohan put a hundred-rupee note in the folder as a tip. The bearer thanked him profusely and left with a deep bow. The room waiter was watching. He asked if sir would need anything. 'No,' replied Mohan.

Mohan had his evening quota of three large whiskeys and polished off the plate of canapés. He did not want to go down for dinner; he had had enough to eat. He rang for the room bearer. After the bearer had cleared the table, Mohan gave him a hundred-rupee note. The bearer was pleased and asked if he could be of any other service. This time, without thinking, Mohan replied, 'Can you get me a woman?'

'Sure, sir. How much?'

'Anything. Five hundred to a thousand. She must be young and attractive.'

A few minutes later the bearer came back leading a woman of about thirty. She had short, neat hair and was smartly dressed in a long grey skirt and a low cut yellow blouse. She did not look like a prostitute. The bearer left them together. Kumar asked the woman to sit down. She sat down on his bed and said, 'You pay first.'

'How much?'

'The bearer fixed a thousand for one time. You can pay me more if you like it.'

Kumar took a thousand rupees from his wallet and handed them to her. She counted all the notes and put them in her hand bag.

'Tell me when you are ready.'

'Take off your clothes and let me see what you look like.'

She obeyed: the blouse and the skirt came off first; then the bra and the panties. Mohan's member stiffened. He was delighted. In that one instant all the anxiety and frustration of the past several months was wiped out. He was his old self again. He pulled down his pants and showed her what he had. 'For that I should charge you double,' she said. 'Most women who see it want it for free,' replied Kumar with a leer.

There was no passion in her movements. When he tried to kiss her on the lips, she turned her face away. She let him kiss and suck her breasts. But her nipples did not harden. He went into her. She tried quick heaves to get him to come fast. He took his own good time; he had not had sex for months. When he came, she feigned a climax. It was all very mechanical but he was satisfied; relieved that he had not become impotent.

She cleaned herself in the bathroom and got back into her clothes. Kumar gave her another one hundred rupees. 'If you want me I can come again. Don't ask the room bearer or anyone else. He takes his cut, the pimp takes his commission, I get less than half of what I earn.'

'Come tomorrow evening, same time. What is your name?'

'No name,' she replied. 'I will come tomorrow through the main entrance. There will be another bearer on duty; he does not know me. Keep your door open.'

The woman with no name came the next evening as she had promised. This time dressed in a sari, a bindi on her forehead, sindoor in the parting of her hair, looking like any respectable middle-class housewife. As far as her pimp and the room bearer were concerned, it was her day off. The money she got from him would all be hers. She did not ask to be paid in advance. It made quite a difference to her performance. She was not the indifferent, get-on-with-it-and-finish-as-soon-as-you- can woman of the earlier evening. She was gentle, almost loving in her endearments. Her nipples responded to his kisses and nibbling and she was wet when he entered her. She was eager to prolong the intercourse and came when he came: no feigning. When Mohan gave her money— with an extra hundred added as a tip—she did not sit down to count it, but gave him a kiss on his lips.

'You use no effel?' she asked, using the old word for condom.

'I do sometimes. But I was not expecting sex in Bombay,' he replied.

'You should,' she advised, 'it is safer.'

'You won't tell me your name? What if I want you again when I come to Bombay?'

'No name. I am a married woman with children. I do this dhanda because my husband does not earn enough. You ask the same bearer to get you the same bai he got for you last time.'

She gave him another kiss and slipped out of the room.

Mohan Kumar returned to Delhi, reassured that he had not gone kaput.

*

Mohan recovered his zest for living. Sex had lost its old urgency but he was content with the knowledge that if the opportunity came he would not be found wanting. He was out wining and dining with his friends every other evening. Twice a week he had a party in his home—the best food and beverage in town. His friends noticed how high-spirited he had suddenly become after months of moodiness. 'What's happened?' asked the young wife of one of his friends at a party in his home. 'Have you won a lottery? Made another couple of millions? Or have you found a new sweetheart?'

'All those and more,' he replied and added cryptically, 'I have rediscovered my manhood.'

'Go on with you!' she quipped. 'You've always been the macho man of Delhi. A kind of "sarkari saandh"—a stud bull employed by the government to impregnate cows. If half of what I've heard about your prowess in bed is true, you've always been a favourite with women. So what's new? What's made you so bloody cheerful?'

He did not tell them. They had lots of fun and laughter at his expense. He did not mind it at all.

Seventeen
A Fatal Illness

It must have been more than six months after his return from Bombay that Mohan's health began to deteriorate. Till then he had not suffered a day's illness. Regular surya namaskars kept his bowels clean—constipation, he knew, was the mother of most diseases. He hardly ever caught a cold, and if he did, it lasted barely two days. He did not need glasses: his vision was perfect. So was his hearing. All thirty-two teeth were in perfect condition: he visited his dentist once every six months just to make sure he had no cavities and nothing was wrong with his gums. He had never suffered from the fevers that visit Delhi periodically: malaria, dengue, typhoid, cholera. No coughs, no breathing problems. Nothing. He had never been to a hospital as a patient, only to visit sick friends. His robust good health giving up on him disturbed him.

It started with an upset stomach. He thought it would go in a day or two. It persisted. He tried to control it by taking Isabgol which is said to both relieve constipation and control diarrhoea. This did not help him, so he took recourse to allopathy. The diarrhoea stopped, but only for a few days. Once again he had to rush to the loo six or seven times a day. He began losing weight rapidly. He thought he had eaten something which had disagreed with his stomach, or perhaps got some bug in his intestines. He persevered with allopathy, and after almost a fortnight, it seemed that he had got rid of whatever he had inside him; his evacuations became normal.

The relief was brief. The bout of diarrhoea was followed by fever. Because he had never had fever before, he did not even have a thermometer in the house to find out how high his temperature was. It was Vimla Sharma who remarked one morning in office: 'Mr Kumar, you don't look well. Your face is flushed.' She took the liberty of putting the palm of her hand on his forehead. 'It feels hot, you must have high fever. Shall I send for a doctor?' He shook his head, replied, 'No, send for a thermometer.' She went to a chemist in Nehru Place and got a thermometer. She washed it under a tap, shook it vigorously, examined the mercury level and inserted it in his mouth. She kept her eyes on her wristwatch and after two minutes plucked it out of his mouth. 'Hundred and two point five,' she pronounced gravely. 'You should be in bed and not in office. You should send for a doctor at once.'

He took her advice and went home. He took a couple of aspirins which he kept to get over hangovers, had two hot cups of tea and lay down in bed. He sweated profusely. The fever came down to normal. He took his quota of Scotch but did not like the taste. He had tomato soup and baked beans on toast. The food tasted flat. His servants looked worried: 'Sahib, you are not well,' said the cook. 'One of us will stay in the bungalow to be near you if you need us at night. We can't leave you alone in this state.' Mohan nodded his head.

He took two more aspirins before going to bed. He thought they would induce sound sleep and rid him of the fever. The fever went, a cough came on—a dry, racking cough which pained his abdomen. In the morning the fever was back. He took his own temperature. It was 100 and he knew it would probably go up as the day proceeded. It did.

The ever-caring, almost maternal Vimla Sharma turned up at eleven to see how he was doing. She put her hand on his forehead and declared: 'You still have high fever.' She took his temperature. 'Hundred and two point five. The same as yesterday. Mr Kumar, if you don't send for a doctor, I will,' she said in a tone of authority.

'I don't know any doctor. I've never needed one. How's work going at the office?'

'You get the office out of your mind, Mr Kumar. I can look after it, I only need to get your signatures on letters and salary cheques. If you don't know any doctor I suggest you send for Dr Malhotra. He's a young man who had a large practice in Washington. He's shifted to Delhi and set up a very fancy hospital, latest gadgets and a highly qualified staff of doctors. Try him. Your shouldn't put this off.'

'Get him on the phone.'

Vimla consulted the telephone directory and after a while got Malhotra on the line. Kumar asked him if he visited patients in their homes. 'Not normally,' he replied. 'I like to see them in my clinic where we can put them through different tests. But if you are too unwell to come, I'll certainly come over to see you. I can make it anytime after six this evening when I've finished my game of golf.'

'Are you a member of the Golf Club, then? So am I. I don't play much, but we must have seen each other in the bar.' Mohan thought this would establish his credentials, that he was no 'aira-ghaira' but belonged to the elite of Delhi society. Dr Malhotra agreed to drop in around half past six. Vimla asked him if she could be present. 'Sure! if you want to know all the dirty details of my insides.'

Vimla was back at six. Dr Malhotra arrived half-an-hour late and was escorted up by her. 'I'm Mr Kumar's secretary,' she introduced herself. 'Mrs Kumar is living with her parents, and he has no one to look after him except his two servants and his driver.'

The doctor was a dapper young man who spoke English with an American accent. To impress him further Kumar told him he was a Princetonian and had taught classes in Georgetown University. 'You must have been a baby then,' he said to compliment the doctor on his youthfulness.

'But you look younger than you are, if that is true,' replied the doctor, drawing up a chair beside Mohan's bed. 'Now let's see your medical history.'

'Blank,' said Mohan. 'Never been ill before in my life. Just last month I began to have loose motions, then this fever and now a dry cough.'

The doctor took Kumar's temperature, felt his pulse, went over his chest with his stethoscope. He tapped his abdomen and groin, examined his tongue and eyes. 'I think, Mr Kumar, I'd like to put you through a thorough check up in my clinic. It will take the best part of the morning. We'll get a complete picture of what's wrong with you. When can you come? If you like I can send my ambulance to fetch you.'

'I can still walk straight,' Mohan replied with a wan smile. 'I'll come in my own car. Tomorrow morning at nine.'

'Nine will be fine. I'll be waiting for you.'

As he put out his hand to say goodbye, Mohan asked, 'Doctor, what about your fees?'

'Don't worry about that. I'll send you a consolidated bill after I've done all the tests. See you tomorrow. Keep smiling.'

Vimla Sharma saw the doctor off in his car. She came back to say goodnight. Once more she put her palm on his forehead, then kissed it and said, 'Get well soon.' She turned to his two servants and Jiwan Ram. 'You look after the sahib. He's worth his weight in gold.'

Jiwan Ram replied on behalf of all three. 'He's our mai-baap (father and mother), memsahib, our anna-daata (provider). May God take years off our lives to prolong his!'

Kumar was very touched.

Next morning all his three servants accompanied him to Dr Malhotra's clinic-cum-hospital. They were told to stay outside. Kumar was taken over by the clinic doctors and the nursing staff. First, a long form to fill about his age, parentage, marital status, children and ailments he had suffered from in the past. In the last column he wrote, 'None till about two months ago.' They put him through a succession of tests carried out by specialists: his eyes, ears, nose and mouth were examined. His muscular responses were tested and noted down. Then they did a CAT scan of his skull followed by blood and urine tests, an electro-cardiogram, and a few other routine tests. The procedure took over two hours. Finally he had a cup of coffee with Dr Malhotra. 'So far we haven't found anything wrong with you. But we'll have to get results of the blood and urine tests before we can be certain. That may take a day or two. Meanwhile keep your fever under control—aspirins and sponging with ice-cold water.'

The doctor saw him off to his car. 'I'll get back to you in a day or two. Not to worry too much.'

Three days later the doctor rang him up. 'I'll come over in the evening to see you. Perhaps over a drink. I'd like to talk to you alone.'

He came after his evening round of golf. He had a sizeable dossier in his hand. He sat down in an armchair. Mohan was in his dressing gown. The fever had not left him. Nor the cough. In addition he felt a constant itch all over his body and scratched himself incessantly. The doctor poured a drink for himself and gave one to his patient. He came to the point at once. 'All the tests are clear, Mr Kumar, except the blood. I'll need to take another sample to make sure. You've had a busy sex life, haven't you?'

'Nothing to complain of,' Mohan replied, 'lots of girls in Princeton, married and unmarried. A few here.'

'Did you use condoms all the time?'

'No, most of them were on the pill. I did use them after I got married and had a son. I continued till we wanted a second child.'

'I gather your marriage broke down some years ago. Did you have affairs with other women?'

'A few,' replied Mohan honestly. 'Some on a quasi-permanent basis. If they were not on the pill, I used condoms. One had nasbandi, so I did not have to use anything.'

'Did you indulge in anal intercourse with any of them?'

'Never. It was always straight sex. I don't fancy buggery.'

'Any oral sex?'

'Only when I didn't get an erection and the woman wanted it a second time. I let her rouse me by taking it in her mouth for a minute or two. The idea of a blow job nauseates me. But why are you asking me all this—not that I mind talking about it.'

'It's important, Mr Kumar, that I know this. When did you last have sex?'

'More than six months ago in a Bombay hotel.'

'Did you know the woman? Did you use a condom?'

'I don't know who she was; she refused to tell me her name. The

room bearer brought her—through a pimp, no doubt. I had to pay
her handsomely. I didn't have any condoms because I wasn't expecting
sex till the urge overcame me. Anyway, she looked clean and healthy.
Doctor, what are you driving at? Have I contracted some venereal
disease, syphilis or gonorrhoea?'

'Both are easily curable these days. I'll be blunt, Mr Kumar. Your
blood test shows you are HIV positive. As I said, I'll take another
sample to make sure.'

Mohan's heart sank. 'There's no cure for HIV, I'm told. How long
do I have?'

The doctor patted Mohan's hand to reassure him. 'We can control
HIV and prevent it growing into full-blown AIDS for many years. You
don't have to worry about longevity. You can have a full span of life—
another ten or twenty years. But no more sex. You must not expose
others to the disease. And if you must, you should always use condoms.
Most of all, don't brood over it. Your fever will go, your itching will
subside. You'll regain natural health if you keep the virus under control.
I'll help you to do that.'

'Doctor, everyone will get to know I have AIDS. I'll be treated as
a pariah. How will I face the world! What will my children think of
me!'

'No one need know. So far only I know you are an HIV case—not
even my laboratory staff know in whose blood they've detected the
virus—and I'm under oath not to divulge the ailments of my patients.
As long as you don't open your mouth the secret will remain between
us. As I said, don't worry too much about it. You have to fight it with
cheerfulness and hope.'

The doctor left. A pall of gloom enveloped Mohan. There was no
one he could turn to for comfort. He had only himself to blame for
what had happened to him. But blaming oneself does no one any
good. And Mohan hated wallowing in self pity, which only made one
more miserable. But the shock was too great. He shut the sitting-
room door, fixed himself a Scotch and slumped into his armchair. He
undid his flies and pulled out his penis. Limp, it was like a baby
python blissfully asleep—silken smooth, without a blemish from

head to root. Suddenly Mohan burst out in a stream of expletives—
'You bastard, mother-fucker . . . you slimy sister-fucker . . . Look
what you've done to me, you son- of-a-whore!' The baby python
remained asleep and unblemished. Mohan looked at it awhile. He
was reminded of all the pleasure he had known in life, and knew that
he only had this little snake to thank for all of it. He felt stupid. He
buttoned his flies, poured himself another drink and told himself to
be reasonable. That evening he had more than his quota of three drinks,
ate little, and went to bed slightly drunk and disoriented.

As the doctor had predicted, the fever left Mohan. He stopped
coughing and scratching himself. The second blood test confirmed
he was infected with the HIV virus. He had to have regular treatment
to keep it under control. Outwardly he looked his normal self; but
his insides were being corroded. His servants, staff and friends
congratulated him for recovering his health. When they asked him
what had gone wrong, he was evasive. 'Some kind of viral fever. The
doctors don't know much about these fevers. They come and go.'

The prospect of dying a horribly painful death continued to haunt
him day and night. He kept awake at nights brooding over it. He told
Dr Malhotra. The doctor chided him: 'You're an intelligent man, Mr
Kumar—you know death comes to everyone. We doctors are there
to see that the passage from life to death is not painful. If sleep's the
problem, take a sleeping pill. One Calmpose when you go to bed. If
you wake up at night, take another. But not more than two.'

Mohan had never suffered from insomnia. Now he could not go
to sleep without the help of a sleeping pill. Sometimes he had to take
another at midnight, and felt groggy till mid-morning. He asked Dr
Malhotra if he should make a will: by now the doctor had become his
closest confidant because he was the only one privy to the secret that
Mohan had a time-bomb ticking away inside him. The doctor gave him
sane, no-nonsense advice: 'I think it's always wise for people in their
fifties to make a will if they have property over which there may be
disputes. Or if they wish to leave something to people they are
beholden to.'

Mohan made his last will and testament after consulting his lawyer over the legal terminology: The first charge on his estate was Rs 50,000 in cash to be given to the people who had served him faithfully—his cook, the bearer, the driver Jiwan Ram and Vimla Sharma. Then there was Ranjit Villa which he had promised to his son—he decided to give the house equally to his son and daughter. They could decide which portion they wanted to have, or they could sell it (it was worth over two crores of rupees) and share the proceeds of the sale. Likewise he left his company to the two children equally. The jewellery which his father had given Sonu was to go to Mohini. His car he left to Jiwan Ram who had served him longer than the other servants. His lawyer took him to the Registrar's court to have the will registered. A copy was given for safe custody to Dr Malhotra.

Mohan felt a little lighter. He had cleared his debts to everyone to whom he felt he owed something. If only Dr Malhotra could rid him of the dreadful disease he could die an honourable death and spare his children the stigma of having a parent succumb to a sexually related disease.

Eighteen
The Death of Mohan Kumar

For nearly two years after Dr Malhotra had pronounced the dreaded verdict, Mohan led a relatively healthy and outwardly normal life. He eschewed sex. It was difficult at first, but gradually he learnt to not let it torture him; he crowded his waking hours with work and harmless socializing with his old friends and at night he slept soundly, often after having taken a sleeping pill. he followed with great interest and greater hope the progress of doctors all over the world as they struggled to find a cure for AIDS. He was careful about his diet, exercised regularly and consulted Dr Malhotra constantly about treatments and medication.

Then, in October that year, the season changed, he caught a chill. It turned into a virulent cold. He could not shake it off. When Dr Malhotra examined him, he detected symptoms of TB in his lungs. He passed the death sentence on Mohan as gently as he could. 'I'm afraid you have AIDS. I can control its onset with your help but I can't cure it.'

Mohan tried to take the verdict manfully. For the next week he recited the Gayatri Mantra from sunrise to sunset. He started reading the Bhagavad Gita. He had his father's copy, which he had found at the ashram in Haridwar. Much of what he read in it made sense to him, but the passages on death confused him. 'There is no death,' Lord Krishna said. 'The eternal in man cannot die; it is only a passing from one form to another. Just as a person casts off worn out clothes and dons new ones, so man when he sheds his mortal coil is reborn in some other form.' The Lord was right in saying, 'For one that is born, death is certain,' but there was no proof that Mohan knew of to support Krishna saying, 'For one who dies, birth is certain.' Mohan knew it was an attractive idea for a dying man. But he did not understand it. He would soon die, but that he would soon be reborn he could not accept.

Mohan gave up taking sleeping pills and stored them for future use. If sleep did not come to him he recited the Gayatri mantra over and over again till he dozed off. One night he was shaken by a violent bout of coughing. The phlegm was choking him. He went to the bathroom and spat it into the basin. His phlegm was full of blood. That decided his fate. He went back to bed and lined thirty sleeping pills on his bedside table. For a moment he thought about the implications of his suicide. What would people say? What would they think? He didn't care, he thought, as long as they didn't connect his death with AIDS. And they could not, he decided, for only Dr Malhotra knew, and he wouldn't talk. He thought about his children. What would they make of it all? But perhaps they would be better off without him. Besides, hadn't he ceased to matter to them already? The image of his father, alone and content by the Ganga in Haridwar came to his mind, and he clung to it as a deep sadness overwhelmed him and tears slid down his face.

Then he resolutely composed himself and took the first Calmpose; as he gulped it down with a sip of water, he recited the Gayatri Mantra. He did the same with the second, and the third, till the last: thirty Gayatri Mantras with thirty pills. Then he put his head on the pillow and closed his eyes.